HAROLD'S DREAMS

Robert Denton Brownell

ISBN: 9780615616254

Cover art and design by Glenna Rummels
Third Edition © 2016

ISBN: 0615616259

For Bobby

REBIRTH

Near Fleville, France November 4, 1918

Acold, ghostly white mist settled softly into the shell holes and the maze of ruined trenches surrounding the gun emplacements as the German artillery fire lessened slightly, then finally lifted altogether. Other than the occasional distant rumbling from other guns up and down the front lines the night became strangely silent and ominous.

A large man, an American sergeant, stood and wiped his eyes with bloody, dirty hands which trembled slightly. He paused for a moment to light a cigarette before stepping gingerly among the dead looking for his men. Seeing one lying face down in the mud, he knelt and turned the body over. He carefully undid the buttons on the coat and shirt, removed the identification disc from the string around his neck and placed it in a small leather pouch he carried. Another man, a private and just a boy himself, wordlessly followed the sergeant with a larger cloth bag which he filled with the few possessions his dead friends had carried once he'd carefully tied them together and labeled each bloody bundle.

American medics and men from the rear areas moved about quietly carrying wounded men, both American and German, back to the makeshift aid station set back further from the gun emplacements along a road suddenly alive with military traffic.

Once the sergeant had taken identification discs from his men, they and the other dead American soldiers were carried back to a field on the side of the road and laid out on the ground until Graves Registration could come and pick them up. The dead Germans were dumped into a section of still-standing trench once their pockets and packs had been rifled by some of the less than scrupulous men from the burial detail. Once the huge artillery gun, *Dora*, and her equipment were removed from the position, a wooden marker would be pounded into the ground telling anyone who cared to examine it the number of Germans buried here.

Hearing a faint voice moaning the sergeant stopped, put a hand to his ear and listened carefully for a moment, then stepped forward picking his way along until he found the source. It was Private Brooks.

"You okay Brooks?" he asked squatting by the boy's side.

Harold groaned and slowly came back to consciousness. His head throbbed with pain. "Sergeant Miller?"

"Yeah."

"Am I alive?" he croaked.

"Looks like it to me."

"What happened? I don't remember…"

"The Huns nearly overran us. If those reserves hadn't shown up when they did we'd all have gone west."

Sergeant Miller coughed deeply and wetly. "Damn, that Phosgene is bad stuff. My eyes and lungs are burning like hell. Good thing the wind picked up and blew it out."

Harold struggled to raise himself up on an elbow but fell back. Reaching to his painful head he realized he was covered with a stickiness on his neck and face.

"Here," Sergeant Miller said. "Don't move, let me get a bandage on that."

"The Germans, they overran us."

"They did. Here, raise your head up."

Miller finished the makeshift bandage then sat back on his haunches.

"Smoke?"

Harold nodded and felt himself drift away for a moment into a twilight between sleep and consciousness wondering if this were some strange nightmare. Was he really in France in the war? And if so, was he so completely insane from this strange, horrible life there would be no way he could ever hope to escape it? He was so worn down, so sick with pneumonia and so exhausted that he couldn't really tell the difference anymore. He desperately wished he was at home with Bobby and Margaret. But then again, he was also glad to be here too, with his friends.

"You still with me Brooks?"

Harold slowly came back to consciousness at the sound of Miller's voice. "Yes, I think so."

"Here," Miller said putting a cigarette in Harold's mouth and lighting it. "Let's sit you up and get you out of here."

With the help of the sergeant and the young private, Harold sat up and began coughing painfully. His memory was slowly coming back to him and he shivered remembering the panic he had felt hearing the gas shells hissing and the sight of the Germans looking evil and ominous in their gas masks lurching out of the haze.

"Take a minute and don't try to breathe too deeply. Drink," Miller said putting his canteen to Harold's lips.

Harold drank deeply relishing in the warm putrid water as it seemed to help him come around.

"You know, you surprise me Brooks."

"Why's that Sergeant?"

"Hell, you were swinging your entrenching tool around and screaming like a madman when the Huns got all mixed up with us in here. I thought you'd lost it."

Harold took a drag on the cigarette and shook his lowered head. He suddenly remembered what he had done with the entrenching tool. The fear and the indignation of being beaten on much of his life by his heavy-handed father had exploded into an anger he'd never felt before when he saw the Germans killing his friends. His first instincts had been to run away but something held him back. "I was frightened."

"Shit, all of us are. If any man says he's not frightened he's nuts."

"You mean you feel the same way?" Harold asked with surprise.

"Yeah, all the time."

"But, you act as though you're invincible, as though nothing bothers you."

Sergeant Miller laughed. "Hell, Brooks, I'm a sergeant. I'm supposed to act that way. But I'll tell you this; every time we move to new positions with that damn gun I shake like the devil from fear wondering if it's going to be my turn. I get the shits something awful too.

"I didn't know. I thought I was the only one."

"No. Everybody feels that way. And everybody deals with it differently."

Harold stared at his sergeant with newfound admiration.

"Come, let's get you up the aid station."

Miller and Private Horman, who everyone called, The Kid, helped Harold struggle to his feet and shuffled over the bodies of dead men and out of the gun emplacement. *Dora*, now silent and stained with powder towered over them in the night sky, a sad reminder of what their lives were now.

Harold looked at her with remorse remembering how innocent he'd been not so long before truly believing himself incapable of taking another man's life. Now, surrounded by the bodies of the men he had killed, Harold knew that he would never be the innocent boy he had once been. He knew deep in his soul what he had done was wrong but he didn't regret killing the Germans. Strangely, he was proud of what he had done.

"Jesus," Harold said softly glancing back to the gun emplacement and trenches. "I remember."

The Germans had appeared like ghosts through the billowing fog of Phosgene gas and the steamy, fearful breath of men in the cold air. They had been close enough that he had seen their eyes, wide and white with fear charging into Harold and his friends before they had known what hit them. In an instant, they were through the supporting infantry and on top of them shooting, slashing, beating and killing. Harold fought back with a sense of pure animal survival. As long as he could go home and be warm again and feel safe again, he wanted to live and he would do anything to achieve that one goal. If the hazy world he had left so long ago still existed and wasn't just a dream, he wanted to go home to marry Margaret and he wanted go fishing in the river with Bobby again.

He began crying quietly to himself while Sergeant Miller and the Kid led him slowly along. After being in France for six months and seeing so much devastation every day he couldn't force his mind to accept what his life and the lives of his friends had become. Sometimes the gruesome reality of the war made it seem as though his family, Iowa, his life before the army were nothing more a fantasy world.

"You still with us?" Sergeant Miller asked.

"I don't know."

"Let's rest a minute."

Miller and the Kid carefully set Harold down on the ground and sat with him.

"How many...how many did we lose?"

Sergeant Miller removed the battered pie-tin helmet from his head and ran a hand through his dark greasy hair. "Don't know for sure. Several are wounded."

"How many dead?"

"Nine."

Harold wiped the tears from his eyes and looked down on the emplacement with sadness. He'd tried to save himself and silently wondered which of his friends may be dead because he hadn't done enough. He began crying again.

Hitting the first German soldier had surprised him. Despite his fear he trembled remembering how it made him feel. It was a terrifying yet exhilarating sensation.

The German soldiers swarmed over the sides of the gun emplacement leaving little room to move while some stood on the sandbags ringing *Dora* firing their rifles down into the crowd of men in the bottom. Artillery fire from both sides exploded on and near the men adding to the confusion and noise. Harold screamed but couldn't hear himself doing it. Around him men cried out in German and in English while trying to kill one another with their rifles, fists, canteens, and helmets, anything they could get their hands on.

Harold had been knocked into the mud at the bottom of the emplacement by a German who had attacked him with a rifle butt as he ran up the narrow path away from the battle. Sick with fear, Harold managed to stand, grab the man's arms and fight off his blows. They pushed and pulled, breathing hard, wrestling and screaming at one another until Harold, using all of the strength he could muster, swung himself around on top of the man and choked him to death. The German, a young man perhaps Harold's age gasped and choked writhing with panic until Harold felt his body shudder, then go limp.

A sharp blow to his back knocked Harold face first onto the man he'd just killed. He struggled and fought to get back up but the sharp tip of a bayonet plunged deep into his shoulder from behind. Harold screamed like a wild man, falling face-first back into the mud. He felt a heavy boot push down on his back as the man pulled the bayonet out of his body and Harold knew the next blow would be fatal. His mind screamed at him to get back up and fight. He had to live. Suddenly, his hands somehow wrapped themselves around an entrenching tool. With a deeper hatred than he'd ever known before growing within him he'd managed to stand and began swinging the weapon. He lashed out at the fearful faces behind the gas masks in the gray uniforms with all the frustration and anger he had experienced in his short eighteen years and smashed a man's face with one solid blast. The German's brains were knocked out of his skull splattering his, and Harold's friends alike and slid down the sides of the sandbags in the gun position. In the fading light of a flare he could see the blood and brain tissue steaming in the frosty air. The sight sickened him but his anger was nearing its explosive peak. Another German fired a shot at Harold grazing his head before burying itself in the stomach of Lieutenant Swanson. As the man tried to work the bolt to cycle another cartridge, Harold cleaved his head nearly off with a downward slash of the shovel. He turned, continued swinging and screaming until his voice gave out. Now, wide-eyed and covered in blood, he grabbed a German trying to escape and threw him to the ground and without thinking, savagely beat the man to death. A few surviving Germans tried to surrender while another few tried desperately to claw their way out of the hole but Harold and the other men cut them down. One of the Germans, a young boy stood shaking, his uniform and face streaked with blood. He held his rifle high in the air pleading with Harold, desperately trying to surrender. His eyes bulged with fear.

"*Kamerad! Kamerad!*" he cried. "*Töten Sie mich nicht, bitte! Bitte töten Sie mich nicht!*"

Remembering the .45 pistol in the holster on his belt, Harold drew it and took a step towards the boy who fell backwards onto dead and wounded men. Raising the pistol he paused for a moment and shot him in the face. Harold stared at his handiwork for a moment watching the blood pool beneath the shattered head.

He turned to look for any other Germans who were still alive. He intended to kill the rest of them. Then, all went suddenly and painfully white, then blackness.

"God help me," Harold thought to himself as the world went dark around him.

PART I

HOME

Sac City, Iowa March 27, 1918

Harold faded away from Miller and the Kid and found himself in a dream he hadn't had for as long as he could remember. He was home. The white clapboard house he had grown up in with his parents, sisters and baby brother canopied by the old swaying elm and surrounded by maple trees never changed. He could always see the house in his mind; the crooked front porch that sagged in no particular direction and the moss-covered shingles that lined the north facing shadows. The late, darkening afternoon sun of early spring turned the world a pale, rich yellow and the sidewalk was exactly twelve steps, if one was so inclined to count, from 12th Street to the first step at the front of the house.

Harold walked up the steps to the front door hearing the familiar creak of the third step as he stepped up to the porch. He paused before opening the door and brushed his coat off. The March winds rustled through the trees around the house stirring up small whirlwinds of the previous fall's brown and red leaves.

They smelled musty in the fresh cold air mingling with the comfortable smell of wood smoke and the lingering cold of winter almost past. Home.

Harold walked in and was enveloped by the heavy, musty smell of the old house. Taking off his cap and coat, he was careful to hang them up in their usual place. Pulling off his brown, mud encrusted boots he could hear laughter coming from the dining room. Hurriedly putting his boots, coat and sweater in their place, he was especially careful to take the shiny, brand new pocket watch and chain out of his pocket and hung it next to the sink. Just as he started the water his oldest sister Irene rushed in and smothered him with a hug and gave him a quick kiss on the cheek.

"They're all ready. Wash up and come in," she said happily.

"I'm hurrying. Am I late?"

"No, but father's getting impatient. You know how he is."

"Okay, I'll be right in."

Harold watched as she disappeared back into the brightly lit kitchen. "Feeding time for the old bear," he said quietly to himself.

Harold quickly washed his hands and face, careful not to get the lye soap in his eyes and toweled off. He then put on the fresh shirt his mother had left for him and checked his face in the mirror with a broad smile crossing his face. It had been a good day ever since he had awoken before dawn.

"Today is my birthday. Today is my eighteenth birthday."

His eyes wandered to the beautiful, shiny watch that ticked away softly next to the sink. Carefully gathering it up with his clean hands he put in back in his pocket and smiled to himself more broadly at his reflection in the tiny mirror above the sink. This had been a good day.

As he turned to walk into the kitchen he was surprised as his second-oldest sister Edith flung herself at him, squeezing him until he couldn't breathe. Harold let out a yelp.

"Edith! What are you doing here! You're supposed to be in New York!" he cried returning her hug as tightly as he could, doing his best to make her back crack.

"Hi little brother," she said grabbing Harold's head and planting a sloppy kiss on his cheek. "Surprise!"

"Eddy," he said staring at her as a smile crept across his face. "I can't believe you're here!"

"What? Do you want me to leave?"

"No, of course not!"

"Well then, aren't you happy to see me?"

"It's great to see you!"

Edith gripped Harold's ears tightly. "It's great to see you too you weak little puppy! Come on then, let's go sit down."

The two strode into the dining room together where the rest of the family sat waiting.

"Sir, your chair," Edith said holding Harold's chair out with flourish.

"Madame," he replied bowing.

Harold slid into his normal seat next to his father who was scowling with impatience and hunger while he tapped his heavy gold Masonic ring on the table with displeasure. Sitting at the side of the table his other, younger sister, Mary, was at his right, and little brother Bobby was seated across the table smiling and chattering to everyone as usual. Next to Bobby was their four-year old niece Helen, perched on a wooden box to bring her up to eye level with the table. She was busily sucking her thumb doing her best to ignore Bobby's babble and his constant poking. Her father, William Molsberry, wearing the fine suit that identified him as a local business man sat next to Helen. Irene, Helen's mother and the true beauty in the family, bustled in and out of the kitchen with their mother carrying endless porcelain bowls to the table. Harold inhaled deeply through his nose; the smells of home were the best.

Cooking food, the sweet scent of his sister's perfume filled the air and of course, the rich smoky scent of his father's fat cigars which had permeated everything in the house. It created for Harold a cozy, hazy feeling that signified safety and warmth.

"I think we're ready," Irene said falling into the chair next to William. Frank held up a hand signifying silence.

"Bless us, oh Lord, and these thy gifts which we are about to receive from thy bounty, through Christ, our Lord. Amen."

Frank raised his hands again. The family immediately stopped talking. "Since its Harold's birthday he gets to go first. Nina, fix his plate."

Harold smiled. "Thanks dad. It looks and smells wonderful."

"Well, I traded old G.W. Schectenberg some good lumber for it. One of his yearling cows, nice and tender," Frank said, rubbing his sizeable belly.

Everything on the table was Harold's favorite: Corn and string beans from the garden, potatoes fried in butter with thick slices of onion, and fat slabs of his mother's sourdough bread and the entire meal rounded out with a pitcher of fresh, cold milk. The family visited happily between mouthfuls about their day.

Will looked over at Harold with a smile and a wink. "Well, since you're going to be out of school soon, what do you think you'll be doing? You're a man now."

Harold glanced nervously at his father who was busily working his way through his plate. He'd hoped this wouldn't come up for some time.

"I don't know exactly, Will. I think I'd like to be a mechanic. With all of these new cars and machines there should be a lot of call for people to work on them," he said shrugging. "Or I could join the Army and travel the world. I'd like that too."

Frank looked up from his plate and pointed his fork menacingly at Harold. "No, you're going to college in Ames to study business. We've talked about that."

Harold picked at his food. He was carefully choosing his words. "I was thinking, maybe I could serve in the military first and save money to pay my way through school. I could learn to work on engines there. When I come back we could have a mechanic shop at the lumber yard. It would be good for extra business."

Frank stopped eating and looked down over the top of his glasses at Harold. "We're not discussing it. Besides, the way things are going we're going to be in on the war in Europe before long. The worst thing for you would be going over there to fight for the Europeans. Let them kill each other off."

"But dad, everyone in New York is talking about how we don't have many options left. President Wilson..." Edith began.

Frank slammed his fist down on the table. "No more!" he yelled. "We don't discuss politics at this table, especially the politics of that half-wit professor in the White House. Harold knows what his responsibility is to this family and he will do what's expected of him!"

Will steered the conversation towards the problems he was having with his suppliers, something he and Frank had in common while the rest of the family ate in silence. After nearly an hour of feasting the family leaned back in their chairs contented and full. Frank pushed back from the table belching contentedly, his suspenders hanging from his side and rubbed his thick moustache with pleasure.

"Another fantastic meal Nina. I don't think I can eat another bite," he said lazily pushing his plate away. Harold and his siblings all smiled and young Bobby stifled a laugh. Looking at his father he exclaimed,

"Dad, you can always eat more. After we go to bed you'll be back in the ice box looking for leftovers!"

"Only if I beat you to it young man. I have to eat a lot to keep up this strength of mine," he said flexing an arm.

Bobby and everyone else laughed.

"Yeah, and when you're done you'll be asleep in your chair," Bobby said flexing his arms imitating his father.

"Not me!" Frank protested. "It's just, well, I work so hard and I need a lot to eat and a lot of sleep."

A former gold prospector, homesteader, and general jack of all trades, Frank was short but barrel-chested and incredibly strong for a man of fifty-two years. He could unload a freight car of lumber by himself at the train station faster than the four or five men who were usually sent along to do the job. He took great pride in himself and was often showing off. He wanted people to remember him as an important man.

"Tell us dad, you worked out in the gold fields in Wyoming was it?" Harold asked. He and Bobby loved to hear their father's old stories. Frank smiled, relishing in this family tradition.

"Well as you know, the rumor around Sac City is true. I was eighteen and working out in a Wyoming mining town. Didn't have a penny to my name and everything I owned I carried on my back. My father had loaned me fifty-dollars when I left home on the condition I pay him back once I found some gold. There were thousands of men in the camps all lured there by gold. Some were good Christian men such as myself, but there were a great many sinners there too. Awful men who indulged in drink and flesh, men who gambled and swore. Men who worked on the Sabbath. Some even killed their brothers and friends for a speck of gold. No, not the sort of people I'd want any of you around."

"And one them stole from you isn't that correct, dad?" Bobby asked with wide eyes.

"Yes, one night I got the sense that something was wrong. I just knew it. Could feel it in my bones. Well, I peeked outside of my tent and there was a funny little man, drunk, who was trying to steal my goods. The goods I'd bought on loan from my father. I confronted him and said, "What's all this then? Stealing from me?" This little man had the audacity to swing a shovel at me. My shovel!"

"What did you do?" Harold asked.

"I did what any man would do. I took the shovel away from this little man and beat him senseless with it."

"Didn't he die?"

"Yes, but not because of anything I'd done. He fell down and hit his head on a rock and died right there."

"After you beat him."

"Yes, after I beat him. I certainly didn't kill him though."

"But, you beat him with your shovel and he fell down. On the rock."

"Enough!" Frank shouted. "It was God's will the drunken fool fell on the rock and split his head wide open!"

Harold coughed and covered his mouth trying to suppress the urge the laugh out loud. Across the table Will squirmed in his seat trying his best not to laugh either.

"Okay dad, I believe you."

Frank sat back in his chair and rubbed his mustache obviously proud of himself. The rumor gave him an aura of old western gunfighter toughness, something which he did nothing to dispel. According to some, he had buried the man with the same shovel taking great pains to clean the blood and dirt off before it rusted. Frank certainly new the value of a one-dollar shovel.

"Well boy, should we have some cake? I'm starving for some of your mother's sweets!"

"Yes sir," replied Harold. He had looked forward to this part of his birthday supper for days knowing that vanilla cake with chocolate icing was one of his mother's special treats for her children.

"We even have ice cream," Frank said with wide eyes.

"I made the ice cream!" Bobby cried. "I cranked it all afternoon!"

Their mother looked sourly at him: "You cranked for about half an hour, all told. That was all I could get you to do before you ran off to the river again to look for critters and your treasures."

Edith reached out to ruffle her littlest brother's hair. "If Harold had been around, he would have kept you on the job."

Bobby was Harold's responsibility—and had been since the boy's birth.

Harold laughed: "Even if I'd been here, I would have had a hard time keeping up with him, let alone keeping him busy on the ice cream. Maybe we ought to make frog-catching or reassembling some of the junk in the shed part of his chores. If he sees them as work, it'll be easier to keep him from chasing the wildlife or taking apart things around the house."

"Such as my washer tub?" Nina asked slyly pointing a finger at Bobby who blushed deeply and giggled.

"But mom, you kept saying it was broken. I wanted to fix it," The family shook their heads and laughed in unison and the child's feeble attempt at explaining why he'd torn the machine apart. The broken washer tub now sat in the shed with other bits and pieces of machinery that the child tinkered with.

"Yeah! Yeah! I'm ready too! For some cake!! And, and, for some of the ice cream I made!" he said slapping his hands together gleefully. "Whoo whoo!" Bobby chanted. "I'm the ice cream man! Whoo whoo!"

Frank leaned over casually and swatted at the child hitting him on top of the head. Bobby went flying out of his chair crashing to the floor. "Shut up boy! Where are your some manners? This isn't a roadhouse eatery full of trash! It's your brother's birthday and you will sit there and be quiet!"

Bobby slunk back into seat fighting back tears. "Yes sir."

Harold could feel his face burning with anger. It was his birthday, and birthdays in the family were supposed to be special for everyone. "Come on dad, he's just excited that's all."

"What?"

"You heard me. He's excited. That's no reason to hit him."

"Don't you talk that way to me! You might be eighteen but you don't raise your voice to me ever!"

"I didn't raise my voice," Harold said calmly. "I'm just saying Bobby's excited and I don't think that warrants a punishment."

Before Harold could get the last words out of his mouth Frank swung his heavy hand across the table hitting Harold in the mouth and knocking him to the floor. The family sat frozen with fear.

Gathering himself up, Harold slowly stood and put a hand to his mouth. When he pulled it away he noticed he was bleeding.

"Sit down and shut that mouth of yours!" Frank shouted half-standing.

Harold glared at his father with burning hatred for a moment then sat down.

WAR

April 6, 1917

"Gosh dang it," Harold grunted throwing an armload of 2x4's into the wooden bin he was filling in his father's lumber yard after school. "Look at that Stan, this splinter's six inches long!"

Stan, who had worked for Frank in each one of his business's for many years smiled at Harold who held out his hand to show the old man the splinter jammed into the side of his index finger. "You poor thing. Want me to pull it out for you?" he asked.

"Nah, I can manage," Harold replied pulling it out slowly with great interest. "Look, it's bleeding."

"Better wrap that up. If your old man sees blood all over his lumber he'll thump on you."

Harold laughed and wiped several drops of blood from several boards which had crashed into a jumble at his feet. "I know. Heaven forbid if I bleed on Frank's precious wood."

"Or the raccoons doing their business all over them."

"Stupid 'coons," Harold answered. One of his jobs each day was to go around and scoop up the piles raccoon feces which seemed to be everywhere in the cluster of wooden buildings which made up Brooks Brothers Lumber and Hardware Inc. "Bobby and I have trapped seven of them just this month. You'd think we'd have gotten all of them by now."

"They're breeders, that's for sure."

After wiping his bloody finger on his pants and sticking it in his mouth to suck the remaining blood off, Harold sighed and got back to work. Outside a growing swell of voices began to rise in the street and became louder as more and more townspeople flooded out to see what was going on. Some were shouting, others were singing drunkenly while many more were cheering and carrying on. Clearly, something important was going on.

Stan stopped his labor and wiped his face with a filthy handkerchief. "Wonder what all the hubbub's 'bout?" he said casually spitting a stream of brown tobacco juice into the dust.

"Don't know,' replied Harold. "I'll go take a look."

After peeking out to see whether or not Frank was out in the yard Harold quickly bolted out to the street. Frank hated anyone who didn't work when they were being paid and Harold knew if the old man caught him there would be the devil to pay. Besides, his father didn't pay him to work in the lumber yard anyway. It was his so called, "duty" to help out in the family business.

"What's going on?" Harold asked his uncle Alfred who was part owner of the lumber yard with Frank. He was clearly amused by some of the adult men in town cheering and dancing like schoolboys in the street. One was frantically waving an American flag in the air chanting, "Kill Kaiser Bill! Kill Kaiser Bill!

"War's been declared. We're at war with Germany. Just came over the wire," Alfred announced solemnly. "Was a matter of time. Now that damned Wilson has his war. The one he said we'd never fight in."

"What? It can't be, can it?"

"I'm afraid so, Harold."

Harold felt a shiver go down his back. "Thank God."

"What's that?"

"Um, nothing, just talking to myself."

Alfred shook his head, turned and walked back into the office while the excited throng of people gathering downtown grew as news spread around town. Some joined in the revelry while others stood and watched, not sure what to think. Harold grinned feeling excitement thumping away in his chest. He'd been following the war in Europe since its beginning in 1914 and eagerly devoured the *Des Moines Register* every day for news of the far off battles in France. During the insufferably long days at school he had wondered when the United States would finally be in it hoping it wouldn't end before he might have the chance to go and fight. The papers had been full of President Wilson's warnings to Germany and he seemed determined to go to war despite saying and campaigning to the contrary. This was big news.

Harold did a little jig while watching the celebrations as he thought about going off to fight. If he were a big famous war hero he could live the life of his choosing and not the one his father had in mind for him. War heroes don't stack lumber and pick up raccoon shit, they have beautiful women chasing them and men patting them on the back, buying them drinks and offering them cigars. What would Frank think of him then? He would be forced to respect Harold then but would he? He paused for a moment and then quickly ran back to the lumber sheds before his father saw him.

"Well, what is it?" asked Stan.

"War," Harold replied breathlessly. "We're at war with Germany."

Stan grimaced and shook his head, the flabby gray skin of his jowls shaking as he did so. "I 'spose it was a matter of time before we got into it. The way it looks in the papers there's gonna be lots of boys dying over in France for nothin'."

"What do you mean for nothing?" asked Harold with surprise. "The Germans have been sinking our ships and killing Americans. Besides, we'll be fighting against all those things they did in Belgium."

"Ha!" spat Stan. "That goddamn war's about finished. We're just jumpin' in to get the spoils and a little power in Europe now that the old country's there are in ruins. All that talk about right 'n wrong is horseshit. Just plain goddamn horseshit."

Harold leaned back against the wall to prevent his father from seeing him through the open door. Stan was known to be very opinionated when he was sober.

"I'll tell you what war is boy. It's murder. Plain and simple. Ain't no other way to see it and it sure as hell ain't glory and all that flag wavin' either. You know, I've seen it."

Harold nodded in agreement. He knew Stan had been a cavalry soldier during the Indian Wars out West and had heard some stories from him on a few occasions but he normally didn't talk about it much. Harold loved reading the dime novels about the brave white men fighting the savage Indians and settling scores for all of the innocent whites the Indians had butchered and scalped.

Stan pulled himself to his feet and began throwing lumber into the bins. "Damned government," he mumbled to himself throwing a board. "Damned killin,'" as another board flew haphazardly.

Harold watched Stan, fascinated by his outburst because he'd never seen him like this before. He thought about retreating out the door to another part of the lumber yard to escape this strange outburst but his curiosity got the better of him. Stan was clearly upset about something which was unusual for the old man who was usually cheerful and talkative, especially after a few drinks throughout the day.

"Tell me Stan," Harold asked, "What's it like? I mean, what did you do when you were in the Army?"

Stan stopped throwing lumber. Facing the wall he pulled the soaked handkerchief out of his pocket and wiped his face again. Harold could hear his labored breathing and noticed his shoulders had slumped. Without turning around, he asked, "You ever hear of Wounded Knee?"

Harold nodded excitedly. He'd read about the battle of Wounded Knee in his history class at school but the book had only briefly mentioned it. Before Harold was born, when Frank had been trying to earn a living as a homesteader in western South Dakota, Frank, Nina and Irene had lived near the battlefield but they never mentioned it. All Harold knew was that the Army had wiped out a band of renegade Indians who, as he had read, left the giant government reservations in the Badlands and were killing white people. Savages, murderers, that's what Harold thought about them.

"Um, yeah, I've heard of it," answered Harold. "Don't know much about it though."

Stan had walked to the other side of the shed and was prying up a loose floorboard, carefully watching Harold and the open door. With the board loose he lay almost flat on his belly as he reached in underneath and into a small secret opening. He felt around carefully and stopped.

"Where's your old man?" he asked. With a quick two steps towards the door, Harold peeked around the corner and seeing no sign of his father turned back to Stan. "I don't see him around. He must still be in the office."

Stan pulled a dusty half-full jar of Alton Senior's finest week-old moonshine out of the hole. Sitting back on the dusty floor, he removed the metal lid. "Praise the Lord," he said holding the jar up to the sky. He then swallowed with obvious pleasure.

"Let me tell you something about Wounded Knee," he began slowly wiping his mouth. "Those Indians weren't murderers and renegades like all the papers and books say they was." He drank again, this time more deeply. "They was living there because the government had put them there. Women, kids, old people and only a handful of young men. The *government*," Stan spat this word out as though it were poison, "had killed off all the rest of their men and warriors."

Harold sat on a stack of sweet smelling pine boards captivated by Stan's story.

"We was told what people think it's about now. That they was a band of murderin' Indians. Our officers told us they'd killed homesteaders...mostly kids and women. So, we attacked them at dawn when they was all sleepin'."

Stan stared off into the distance gripping his jar tightly and trembled from old, hidden memories. Harold stuck his head out of the shed door looking for his father and not seeing him, ducked back inside the dark interior of the shed and nodded to Stan to continue.

"Can you tell me more?" he asked. "I mean, I don't want to upset you.

Stan continued looking away as if he had been transported back to that cold snowy morning so long before. "We got into the village right at dawn and there were a few Indians up and about getting ready for the day. Our men, I...we opened fire on them with our rifles. My horse, her name was Buttercup, was charging hard and we rode hard into them. When they was all good and awake they started coming out of their lodges and we kept shooting them down. The officers were hacking them down with their swords and shootin' them with their pistols. I kept shootin' and killin' 'em too. Then, I realized that none of 'em was shootin' back. I looked down at a couple I'd killed..." Stan looked away and caught his breath.

"They was little kids, little Indian boys who couldn't have been more than ten or twelve and they was bleedin' out red all over the white snow. They was trying to defend themselves and was fighting back with sticks, their bare hands and a few bows and arrows but none of 'em had guns. We killed 'em all too. The women, the old people, the kids. Hell, we even killed their dogs. We killed 'em all. Wasn't a damned warrior among'em."

Harold stared at Stan in disbelief. He'd never heard that side of the story and it unnerved him to think the United States government would do such a thing. Why would they massacre innocent women and children in their sleep? Why would Stan tell him that? Outside the shed in the yard Harold could hear his father coming, his boots crunching heavily on the rock driveway as he visited with a customer.

"Up and at 'em Stan. Dad's coming," Harold hissed. Stan put his jar back in one easy, well-practiced motion and leapt to his feet.

Frank appeared in the doorway with his customer in tow. Looking curiously at Harold and Stan who were busily stacking lumber he said, "Boys, give Mr. Hope some help loading his order. Here's what he bought and he'll bring his horse and wagon around."

"Yes sir," Stan replied taking the list as Frank and Mr. Hope walked back to the front of the yard.

Stan looked at Harold in the dark shed. "You don't believe me do you?" he asked, his eyes red rimmed with tears. "Seems like no one ever did. Most folks don't want to believe we're nothing more than brutal murderers like we said the Indians was. Now they're all sayin' the Germans are the murderers and bad folk that need to be hunted down and killed."

With that, Stan walked out into the bright sunshine to fill Mr. Hope's order.

FAITH

April 15, 1917

"You make sure you and your brother are seated with your mother and are quiet before the service starts this time," Frank said sternly as the family climbed the steps to the enormous Sac City United Methodist Church. "If either of you two are late or have mud on your trousers, both of you go to the woodshed when we get home. Understood?"

"Yes sir," Harold replied with a yawn. Turning to Bobby he grabbed the boys arm gently when Frank disappeared inside. "You hear that? No running around after Sunday School today."

"I don't want to go to church," Bobby complained quietly. "I'm tired."

"Well, I'm tired too. Just stay inside the building. I don't feel like getting it from him today."

"Okay."

"What are you going to do? Tell me."

Bobby sighed and threw his arms down to his side in disgust. "Wait for you outside Mrs. Vander Wahl's room."

"That's right. If I have to come find you it's all over," Harold said with a smirk as he drew a finger across his neck.

Bobby laughed as Harold held the door open for him.

Every Sunday Harold and his family would troop to church either in the heavy heat of summer or the bone chilling Iowa cold. Frank would have it no other way as he saw himself as a virtuous Christian who had the good fortune of serving as a Deacon of the church. The entire family except for Frank liked and respected Reverend Nicholson, a huge man who took his duties as minister of the Sac City Methodist Church seriously. He had a playful side however and enjoyed more than just the occasional drink and sharing off-color jokes with some of the local men. Frank despised him for both. During the rising intensity of his sermons he would begin to sweat until he was literally soaked with perspiration, something Harold and Bobby looked forward to with glee.

"How sweaty do you think Reverend Nicholson will be today?" Bobby asked as the boys climbed the steps to their Sunday school rooms.

"Hard to tell. It can't be any worse than the time last summer."

"Yeah," Bobby snickered remembering the Reverend slipping on his own perspiration and falling down the steps of the sanctuary. "He flopped around like a fish trying to get back up."

Harold laughed as the boys reached Bobby's classroom on the third floor. "Be good in there and remember, wait for me and don't go outside."

"Bye! Have fun with all of those girls in your class," Bobby said plunging into the mass of children.

Harold shook his head with a smile walking down the hall to his classroom where ten girls and four boys his age waited for the Reverend's wife, their Sunday school teacher, to arrive.

No one in town could understand why the Reverend had married his wife, a timid, pale and unhappy looking woman who never smiled. The couple had three daughters, the older two from her previous marriage to an alcoholic former industrialist who had left her for a much younger, happier woman. The oldest girls, Lily and Judith shared their mother's grim resignation and unfortunate looks but the youngest girl, Margaret who was the Reverend's and Harold's age, had obviously gotten her looks and attitude on life from her father's side. She was a pretty, soft-spoken girl who had a beautiful singing voice and used it well in the church choir.

The Reverend, Harold knew, had served briefly in the Union Army towards the end of the Civil War and had experienced war only once at Petersburg in Virginia, a battle notable for its maze of trenches, mud, and slaughter. His sermons were peppered throughout with lessons on the evils of corruption, war, murder and all other forms of insanity he had experienced as a fifteen-year-old private in Lincoln's Army of the Potomac. He claimed to have had a vision of Jesus on the horrific battlefield, during which Christ spoke to him and convinced him to become a man of God, something he constantly reminded his flock of. Harold loved the story and often pressed Reverend Nicholson for more stories about his wartime service.

The Reverend's occasional fire and brimstone sermons based mostly on The Book of Revelations were Harold's particular favorites. The chaos, the fire, the war between the minions of Satan and the Angels of God all aroused excitement in Harold's young imagination. The Bible was full of strife, conflict, wars and murder and the Reverend had a wonderful way of telling the stories while at the same time using them to teach his flock about sin and salvation. With the Great War raging in Europe the Reverend had only to read the newspapers to find fodder for some of his more fiery sermons.

"It would appear," he said quietly from the pulpit later the same Sunday, "that we're seeing the great conflict between good and evil happening now in Europe."

Harold, who had begun to nod off during the sermon was interested in anything having to do with the military and had been following the war news since 1914. He sat up listening intently.

Reverend Nicholson continued. "Imperial Germany," he said raising his voice then pausing for effect, "Is perhaps the most insidious, most evil empire to exist in modern memory. German troops rape and kill innocent women and children in every town they occupy. They plunder and loot. They burn cities and towns to the ground in the name of their Kaiser. They destroy the land and enslave their enemies!"

Harold sat transfixed hanging on every word. Bobby fell forward with a crash into the back of the pew in front of him. He had been sound asleep on Harold's arm. Frank looked at his sons and scowled. Bobby gathered himself and sheepishly buried his bright red embarrassed face in Harold's side.

"This is from Revelation 12:9 and it fits perfectly with what we see happening now," the Reverend said pausing to wipe his now heavily perspiring face. "And the great dragon was thrown down, that ancient serpent, who is called the devil and Satan, the deceiver of the whole world—he was thrown down to the earth, and his angels were thrown down with him."

The congregation was completely silent. There were great divisions among Americans as to which side was right and which was wrong and the Reverend had made it clear where he stood. Harold heard some muffled grunts and looked over his shoulder to see several people walking out.

"The forces of good in the world consist of the *Entente* led by France, Great Britain and Russia. But how long can they hold out against the legions of darkness? The United States, a pious and God-fearing nation, must take her rightful place in the kingdom of God and save Europe and the rest of the world. If we do not raise an army soon the sky will be filled with fire and Satan will rule mankind! It is God's work that we now send our young men to Europe for the greatest Crusade!" Reverend Nicholson was spitting as he roared these final words out.

Harold wanted to jump up and shout. Looking over at his parents, he realized they weren't as enthusiastic about the sermon. Nina's mouth was shut tightly in a frown. Frank had the large crease on his forehead signifying that he was not pleased. They liked their sermons to be traditional ones; lessons for everyday living taken straight from more gentle sections of the Bible. Certainly not from Revelation.

Bobby giggled at Harold's side. "Look at dad's head," he whispered. "It's going to pop like a balloon."

Harold looked at his father and suppressed a smirk. Frank's bald head had indeed turned a remarkable shade of red.

"Boom!" Bobby whispered while throwing his hands out. Harold almost laughed out loud but snorted loudly when he tried to keep it in.

"Pay attention!" Frank hissed tapping Harold on the chest with the back of his hand.

The Reverend continued on for several more minutes before nodding to Miss Pew, the ancient spinster who played the organ. She began to play and the congregation took its cue to stand and sing the final hymn of the morning. Bobby giggled even louder now.

"Shh!" Harold hissed. "Don't get him any madder."

As the congregation began singing the first verse of *Am I a Soldier of the Cross* Frank slapped his hymnal shut and stood tapping his Masonic ring on the pew in front of him. Harold and Bobby acted as though they were singing but Harold couldn't stop thinking about the sermon. He liked the idea that America would save the world. He secretly hoped he might someday be able to go to war and do just that.

MARGARET

Harold, Bobby and the rest of the family shuffled along the tables piled high with a huge assortment of steaming hot, homemade food occasionally stopping to balance more on their already overflowing plates. The Sac City Methodist church had a family potluck dinner every fourth Sunday of the month and it was something Harold always looked forward to. He anxiously scanned the table ahead hoping some of Mrs. Cochrane's locally famous chocolate cream pies were left. Everyone in the congregation always saved a little extra room for her pies and when they would begin to run low at the monthly dinners, competition for the last slice could become heated. Frank, who usually ate his dessert first never missed out on his piece. He always went through the line backwards, starting at the dessert tables. He loved his sweets.

"Harold, I just wanna sit down. I'm hungry," Bobby whined wide-eyed. "And I don't want any of THAT either," he said pointing to a bowl of some mysterious looking food.

Bobby was picky and stuck with what he knew best: Meat, mashed potatoes, green beans and three or four slices of pie if he could get away with it. Harold made his way along alternately filling his plate and Bobby's. This was one of Harold's tougher chores, to watch the boy at the potlucks and make sure that he had more than just pie on his plate. Mary, who couldn't stand meat, followed along sticking her nose in every dish and bowl on the table to smell it first. Nina, who was working behind the table with the other women hissed under her breath to the girl to stop before she got a beating later on. Mary exhaled loudly and rolled her eyes continued down the line with barely a thing on her plate. Frank, who had already devoured his rather large slice of pie, was back in line, this time to fill his plate with everything else. He enjoyed the Sunday dinners at the church and spent the time visiting with the other men.

"Do you want some of this?" Harold asked Bobby. "It's potato salad. Looks good."

Bobby glanced at the heaping bowl and shook his head vigorously from side to side. "No. I wanna sit down."

"You have to eat something."

"I just want some pie."

"No, you have to have some meat and potatoes first."

Harold helped himself to a generous spoonful carefully balancing his plate as he plopped it on.

"I'm not hungry."

"I don't care," Harold said putting some food on Bobby's plate. "This comes first."

"Harold..."

"Go find us a table then. I'll get your drink," Harold said with exasperation while he scanned the remaining dishes and bowls for more goodies.

Bobby happily skipped off through the visiting crowd carelessly hanging onto his plate. Harold hoped he would find a table with

Will, Irene and Helen. He didn't want to sit with the aged Beasley sisters again like they had the previous month. They smelled musty and had talked incessantly about their father who had been dead for forty-two years. One was missing most of her teeth and couldn't keep food in her mouth. She made Harold and Frank sick to their stomachs with her open-mouthed chewing while Bobby and Mary snickered at her. Bobby had trouble keeping food in his mouth too.

Satisfied that his plate now weighed enough, Harold strode quickly over to the desserts table. He looked over the cakes, pies, cookies and other sweets lining the table trying to find Mrs. Cochrane's thick pies. They were huge and stood out above everything else rather like Mrs. Cochrane herself, Harold laughed to himself. The woman was absolutely enormous but her husband Ollie was a tiny little man who weighed maybe as much as one of her legs. He was certainly no bigger than one of them. Frank had made a guarded comment one time years before that she would be lucky if her backside would fit into a railway car which Harold still laughed about each time he saw her. Her pies however, were indeed special. Walking around the table once more, he realized there wasn't any left.

"Darn it," he muttered under his breath. "No pie again." Disgusted, he turned to find Bobby.

"Harold, are you looking for some of Mrs. Cochrane's pie?" asked a sweet feminine voice.

Harold turned and came face to face with Margaret Nicholson who stood smiling broadly.

Margaret's bright blue eyes shone at Harold from beneath the long blonde curls that streamed over her forehead and shoulders nearly to her waist. She was a little shorter than him and her very feminine hourglass figure made his eyes wander for an instant. Her skin was a beautiful ivory color and she practically glowed in

26

the pale light of the Church basement. She smelled wonderful too. Like lilacs.

"Um," he began. "Uh, yes, I was. It looks like I got beaten to it again," he answered glancing at the still smiling Margaret. Without taking her eyes off him she took a small step closer.

"I knew that you fancied her pies so I saved a couple of pieces. Just for you," she said holding a plate with two huge slices of chocolate cream pie.

Harold smiled back at her. "You didn't have to do that," he replied. "That's, um, very nice of you."

Margaret beamed. "Come on," she said. "Let's find out where your family's sitting and I'll carry this for you."

Harold walked carefully through the crowd looking for Bobby and finally caught sight of him sitting next to Will and Irene. *Good boy,* he thought to himself. Arriving at the table, Harold set his plate down and turned to Margaret who hadn't stopped smiling.

"Here you go," she said holding the plate of pie out for Harold. "I hope you like it."

"You know I will."

As Harold took the plate from her, their hands touched gently. It was as though lightning had shot through his hands and up his arms.

"Thanks Margaret," he said looking down at her. "You're very sweet," He blushed deeply. Margaret's cheeks also flushed red against her ivory skin.

"You're welcome. Can I get you anything else?" she asked earnestly.

Bobby looked up with a mouth full of food. "You can get me a drink," he mumbled spitting mashed potato on the table.

"Be quiet Bobby!" Harold grumbled but Margaret laughed at the boy.

"Sure," she replied. "Harold, would you like some milk or water?"

"Yes, um, water please. That is, if it's not too much trouble."

"No trouble at all," Margaret replied happily. "I'll be right back with some!"

As she disappeared into the crowd Harold fumbled with his chair and almost fell as he sat down. Seated and ready to dive in, he suddenly felt uncomfortable. Looking up, he saw Will and Irene staring at him from across the table both grinning with obvious amusement.

"Well, well my boy," Will began. "I do believe a certain young woman has it on for young Harold."

Harold blushed again. "Naw," he said casually taking a bite of roast beef. "She was just helping me out. You know."

"Oh, I think I know," Irene said leaning low across the table. "I think she likes you. Quite a bit, from the looks of it."

Harold continued chewing while trying his best not to meet the interested looks from Irene and Will. Bobby stopped his noisy chewing and looked up at the three wide-eyed. "Who likes Harold?"

"Nobody, Bobby. Just eat!" Harold said crossly.

Irene persisted. So did Will. "I've seen how she always watches you and goes out of her way to talk to you," Irene said still smirking. "I'm a woman remember. It's fairly clear to me."

Will leaned forward. "If she saved not one, but two slices of that pie for you she's definitely got it good for you. She's sending you an invitation. Now don't mess it up! Besides," he went on, "Old Frank will love it. You, courting a minister's daughter. You're in my boy. *In.*"

Harold blushed again. "Leave me alone," he muttered. Will and Irene burst into laughter.

Margaret suddenly reappeared holding a glass of milk and one of water. "I'm back," she beamed. Her eyes were focused only on him, no one else. Will began to say something but was cut short by a loud slap on his leg under the table from Irene. Harold met her gaze and both stared at one another for a moment.

"Well," she said. "Here's some water for you and some milk for Bobby." When she leaned over between Bobby and Harold to set the glasses down her shiny blonde hair fell partially into Harold's face. He suddenly felt another jolt of lightning surge through his body again.

"Thanks Margaret," he said. Glancing carefully at Will and Irene who were trying to act as though they weren't paying attention, he whispered to her. "Could I um, talk to you later, when we're done?"

"Yes," Margaret replied quietly. "I'll have a little time before we have to do the dishes. How about outside by the west door?"

"Um, sure. Okay," Harold said smiling feebly.

As Margaret walked away she gently, and discreetly ran her hand across Harold's back. He almost shivered from the tingling sensation it gave him. Looking back across the table at a visibly amused Will and Irene, Harold pointed his fork at them.

"Not a word. Not a single word."

"What's going on here?" said Frank pulling out a chair. "You're all grinning like conspirators."

"Not a thing," Will answered. Just having a little fun with Harold here."

"Yeah," Bobby mumbled, now spitting roast beef out of his stuffed mouth. "Harold likes Margaret. She likes Harold too."

Harold flushed with anger and embarrassment. "Bobby!"

Frank looked over his glasses at Harold genuinely surprised. "Well," he said leaning heavily into the old wooden chair which groaned and creaked, "She's a good girl and has a good family." He pointed his fork at Harold menacingly. "Don't act like a knave or a fool with that girl, boy," he threatened. "You act like a gentleman at all times. Understand?"

"Yes sir," a surprised Harold answered.

Across the table Will squirmed in his seat trying his hardest not to laugh out loud while Irene winked at him. Bobby continued to chew noisily.

THE MEETING

April 22, 1917

Harold nervously paced back and forth just outside the west door of the church sucking his teeth and continually running a sweaty hand through his thick autumn dark hair. He wanted to look his best when Margaret came out to visit with him. Taking a few steps to the back of the building, he peeked around the corner to watch Bobby playing with the other children in the expansive backyard. The boy ran and shrieked with delight as he and his friends played their favorite version of tag which meant tackle the next boy.

"Mom's going to be angry if you tear those trousers," Harold muttered grinning to himself as Bobby gleefully jumped onto the pile of laughing little boys also busy dirtying and tearing up their Sunday best. Behind him, he heard the enormous heavy west door creak open. As he spun around he instinctively brushed his shirt off and ran his hand through his hair again.

"Hello Margaret," he said smiling.

"Hi Harold," Margaret answered smiling broadly as she held her long dress up a few inches while she walked up the ten steps from the basement door. Harold reached out to help her up the steps holding her hand gently as she walked. Reaching the top, she stopped directly in front Harold until they were almost touching and looked up at him. Harold smiled feebly not knowing what to say. The afternoon sun made Margaret's hair glisten and her eyes seemed to sparkle more than he'd noticed before.

"How was your lunch?" she asked. "Was the pie good?"

"It was very good. Especially the pie. Thank you again for saving me some."

"You're welcome," she replied. "I'm glad I did. From the look you had on your face you might have exploded."

Harold blushed and looked away. "Was it that obvious?"

"Yes," Margaret giggled.

The two stood and continued looking at each other. Harold shifted his feet and squirmed in his Sunday clothes which were becoming unusually warm. He didn't know what to say. Margaret finally broke the silence.

"Come," she said taking Harold's arm. "Let's go for a little walk."

"Um, okay," Harold answered. Both looked at one another and smiled before setting out to slowly walk the church grounds.

"Do you remember when you saved my sisters and me from Tommy Sanborn and Richard Millhouse after we first moved here?" Margaret asked.

Harold smiled at the memory. "Yes. The three of you were covered with mud."

"That was the first time we met."

"Was it?"

"Yes. We had just moved here from Pennsylvania. It was the second or third day of school if I remember correctly. Tommy and Richard were calling us cows and splattering mud on us."

"Oh yeah!" Harold replied snapping his fingers. "Tommy called me a chicken because I wouldn't do it too."

"And," Margaret said clutching Harold's arm, "You knocked him down right into the puddle. Richard too."

Harold laughed and nodded at the memory. "We haven't been friends since then either. They're both bullies."

"You know, they never bothered my sisters or me after that. Not once."

"I know."

"So, why did you help us?"

"I don't know. It wasn't right. Besides, my sisters would have thumped me if they'd have known I'd stood by and done nothing."

Margaret looked up at Harold with a modest smile. "You're very nice."

"Really?" Harold asked with surprise.

"Yes, I think so!"

After several minutes Harold's nervousness finally began to go away. The couple walked slowly and comfortably discussing anything that came to mind. Bobby came running by being chased by a gang of little boys.

"Can't catch me!" he shouted. "Can't catch me!"

Harold and Margaret laughed as the noisy herd flowed around and past them.

"I've watched how you are with Bobby for a long time," Margaret said. "He's lucky to have you."

"Well, someone has to take care of him and keep him away from our father," Harold replied. "And besides, I like having him around. He's a good boy most of the time."

"I've heard your father has a temper. Is that true?" Margaret asked.

"Oh yes," Harold laughed. "You've surely seen some of the bruises on my face before?"

"Your father does that? I thought you just liked to fight and wrestle with the other boys in the park after school," Margaret asked with surprise. "Oh my Harold, I'm sorry!"

"It's okay, really. No, I don't like to fight. I get enough of that nonsense at home. But, that's why I want to get out of here someday. I don't want to work in his lumber yard for the rest of my life. You can bet on that."

Harold saw something move out of the corner of his eye. "I think someone's following us."

"Oh, it's Judith," Margaret said turning her head to see her sister quickly dodge behind a tree. "I told my mother I was coming out to talk to you so I'm sure she sent Judith out to spy. Anyway, it must be time for me to go back in and help with the dishes."

"So soon?"

"Yes, I'm afraid so."

"I've certainly enjoyed our little walk," Harold said with a big grin. "Would it be okay if we talk again? Or go for another walk? I'd um, really like to see you again."

"Yes. I'd like that very much."

"How about later this afternoon then?" Harold asked.

Margaret laughed and was about to speak until Judith interrupted. "Margaret," she said sternly. "It's time to go in. Mother is waiting."

Margaret waved her hand at Judith and nodded.

"You know Harold, I've had a crush on you for quite some time."

"You have? I mean, really? How come you never told me?"

"Yes you silly. I suppose I was always afraid to tell you. I guess, well, I don't know...I was afraid you wouldn't like me."

Harold laughed out loud catching Margaret by surprise. "Margaret, I like you too. You're very nice and I think you're um, well, very pretty."

"Thank you. That makes me very happy," Margaret answered with a smile. Her eyes sparkled even more as she gazed at Harold. Behind them, Judith coughed loudly.

"I'll see you later then," Margaret said squeezing Harold's arm as she turned to leave.

"Okay. If not this afternoon then I'll see you in the morning. Can I walk you to school?"

"Of course. I'll wait for you in front of the church. Haven't you ever noticed I wait for you and Bobby to walk by every morning? Now I won't have to hide," she said wagging a finger.

Harold hadn't thought about it much until now, but Margaret always did seem to leave for school at the exact time he and Bobby walked by her house every day. And, she always left school at the same time too. She often walked right along with them visiting about the day and the things going on in each other's lives but Harold was completely oblivious to the fact that she adored him until now. He shook his head and smiled to himself as Margaret skipped away to the door of the church. Half-way to the door she turned her gaze back, smiled and waved. Behind her Harold could see pale-faced Judith scowling at him while she held the door open for Margaret. With a laugh sounding more like a bark he waved his hand enthusiastically in the air.

"Good day to you Judith!" he called out. "I hope you have a wonderful day!"

Margaret stuck her head out of the door nearly knocking Judith down as she did so.

"Goodbye!" she cried.

"Goodbye!" Harold answered.

"Church steps at seven-thirty?" she asked giggling hysterically.

"Seven-thirty it is!" Harold replied still waving like an insane man.

FISHING

June 10, 1917

The cork bobbed gently in the clear gurgling water while the slow current pulled it against the string. Harold laid back in the shade of the riverbank holding the smooth, well-worn bamboo pole loosely in his hands. The air rustling through the trees were full of the droning song of cicadas and the chirping of robins, sparrows, and barn swallows all looking for an afternoon meal. Further down in the deeper shade of the river bank the frogs croaked noisily at one another. Rubbing his bare feet in the cool weeds, he let out a deep sigh of contentment. Sunday afternoon fishing in the warmer months of Iowa was as relaxing and comforting as it was possible to imagine. In the tall, green weeds ten feet away, Harold could hear his father snoring deeply. The warm day and the large Sunday meal settling in Frank's stomach had made him heavy with sleep. He had been in a good mood that day. Earlier in Church, Reverend Nicholson had delivered a fine sermon on the finer points of the Ten Commandments which was very pleasing to Frank and Nina, much more so than the sermon on Revelation and the War he'd given two weeks before.

Still further down the bank Harold knew Bobby would be serious about his fishing. The boy was only eight years old, but he was already a great fisherman and had snagged several nice catfish and a handful of bluegills already. At least supper wouldn't depend on Harold and Frank and never did when they fished together. They could always count on Bobby for a basket full of big fresh fish every time. The best part was, Bobby usually cleaned the fish and even helped his mother prepare them in the kitchen. Harold smiled knowing if Bobby put as much effort into his chores at home as he did with his fishing and his constant tinkering with anything mechanical he'd never be in trouble. But he didn't and that's what made Bobby who he was.

Harold looked at the white clouds barely visible through the canopy of green leaves above and tried to create pictures out of the shimmering green, white, and blue splash of color. He loved trying to imagine what the world would look like from up in the sky. He had always envied birds and their freedom as they sang and flew wherever they wanted. No rules, no masters, nothing but pure independence from the chaos of the human world. What would it be like to take off and fly with the wind in your face, Harold imagined going to different corners of the world to see the things he'd only read about in the dusty stacks of National Geographic magazines in the Sac City library. What did mountains look like? What was the ocean like? How did the Eskimos in the Arctic live? What was the world outside of Sac City like? There were so many things to do and to see. Harold often daydreamed about doing dramatic, even dangerous things to prove his manhood to himself and to Frank. All offered more excitement than his current life in the remote northwest corner of Iowa.

Further down the bank Harold could hear Bobby talking excitedly to himself. Slowly sitting up to see what his brother was up to, he could see the boy pulling yet another catfish out of a dark hole on the bottom that seemed to be full of them.

"Whoo hoo!" Bobby cried with excitement pulling the wiggling catfish onto the bank. "That's three!"

As he began unhooking the fish he called to Harold and their father who was sound asleep. "How you both doing?" He puffed his chest out while he held the catfish out for Harold to see "I must be the best fisherman ever! I'm the greatest ever!"

"Yes you are."

"How many have you caught Harold?"

Harold just smiled. "Nothing yet, Bobby. But I'm getting some great bites over here. You should try my spot for me."

Bobby laughed. "Yeah, I bet you have some bites. Dad scared 'em all downstream to me with his snoring."

Harold laughed and turned to look at Frank who stirred in the grass then rolled over onto his side and began snoring even louder. Bobby carefully ran a long piece rope through the catfish's mouth and gill, tied the loose end back onto the stick at the edge of the water with the other fish he'd caught and placed it back into the cool shallows. He bounded through the tall grass silently, like a wild animal and was at Harold's side in an instant.

"Is he still asleep?" Bobby asked peering over the long grass at his prostrate father.

"Looks like it," Harold answered. "Why? What are you going to do now?" He eyed his brother with a half-smirk knowing he loved to play practical jokes on people.

"Watch," Bobby said doing his best to walk Indian-style through the grass to Frank's side. Harold stifled a laugh watching him crouch lowly taking each step slowly and deliberately. He looked like a little monkey pictured in National Geographic Harold thought to himself. The boy had also painted two stripes on each cheek with mud from the riverbank and looked like a modern day savage out hunting his prey. Harold sat up on his knees intently watching his brother creep closer to their father.

Bobby got to within a couple of feet of his father who still snored deeply and pulled a long blade of grass out of the ground. He was well hidden, lying flat on his belly just to the left of Frank in the tall, lush grass and weeds. With the long blade in his left hand, he carefully extended his arm out and gently tickled Frank's nose with it. Frank grunted and waved his hand around his face. Both boys snorted trying to keep their laughter in. With a grin towards Harold, Bobby reached out again and tickled his father's nose with the blade of grass. Again, Frank grunted loudly and waved his hand at the mysterious nuisance. This game went on for a couple of minutes and each time Bobby tickled him, the louder his father's grunts and the more animated his waving became. Bobby decided to go all the way and jammed the blade of grass fully into Frank's nose causing him to sit up with a start.

"Oh my!" he grunted "What in the world..." Frank waved frantically at his face trying to figure out what was going on. Harold fell over onto his side with laughter and Bobby, who was still well hidden in the grass began laughing hysterically.

Frank stood up with a grimace and looked over at Harold who was still roaring with laughter. "I see!" he bellowed. "Playing tricks on your old father again huh!" Frank reached down into the grass and pulled Bobby out by both arms.

"We weren't doing anything dad," Bobby said through his laughter. "Honest. You had a bee buzzing around your nose.

"I don't believe a word of it," Frank said hoisting Bobby over his shoulder. He was smiling now too. Retribution was always swift with Frank. "In that case we'll have to tell your mother that you somehow fell into the river!"

Bobby shrieked and was wiggling away trying his best to get out of his father's grip and off his shoulders. Frank took three giant steps to the edge of the river and threw his youngest son in with flourish.

He stood on the bank with his hands on his hips proud of his work. Bobby shot to the surface in the shallow water gasping for air through his laughter.

"Damn son," Frank said with a wide smile. "Why'd you fall in the river? Your mother won't be happy about that."

Harold rolled in the grass laughing so hard that his sides hurt. Frank turned to Harold.

"And you! What's so funny?"

Harold looked up at Frank still laughing. "What? I didn't do anything!"

Frank was on Harold now. They playfully wrestled around in the grass trying to get the upper hand on one another. Frank couldn't pick Harold up any longer as he had Bobby.

"Looks to me like you both fell in today for some reason." Frank said through grunts trying to manhandle Harold.

"Not me," Harold replied. "I think you fell in trying to save Bobby." The two continued grappling and trying to get a good hold on the other. Bobby stood out in the shallow water cheering them on with glee.

"You...can't get the best of me," Frank grunted.

Harold and Frank had locked arms together and were now trying to unbalance the other. Frank was breathing heavily doing his best to throw Harold. He had underestimated the strength of his oldest son. Harold pushed on his father who stepped on an old washed up log losing his balance for an instant. Taking advantage of the situation, Harold did his best to throw Frank into the water but the old man held on tightly. Both fell splashing into the river in an enormous geyser of water.

Coming to the surface they laughed together. Bobby swam over to them and began splashing water. Frank stood up in the knee deep water and pulled his gold pocket watch out of his pocket. Clicking it open, water ran out. With a shrug, he shook it and put it to his ear. "Well boys, we better head home. Mother's not going to be happy!"

With that the three waded out of the water, gathered their fishing poles, the fish on the line and began the long, wet, walk home.

EDITH

August 3, 1917

The old cast iron scale leaned uneasily to one side when Harold reached into the brass bin hanging on the right end of the scale to remove a small handful of nails. The scale tried to right itself then slowly clanked back down on the heavy side. Throwing the handful of nails back into the well-worn wooden bin labeled #6 to his left, Harold reached into the brass bin to remove just a few more nails in order to right the scale and have it level off with an even two pounds. The pale lined face of the old farmer grimaced as he always did.

"That look good enough," he said. "I take that amount." He looked at Harold with piercing blue eyes that told everyone he expected to get his way once again.

Harold sighed and continued to take a few nails out of the bin knowing he had to get the weight just right. The old farmer grimaced when he took a few more out until the scale clanked back to the middle level signifying an exact two pounds. Finished, Harold slid the nails into a paper bag and handed it to the old man who was clearly upset now.

"Here you go Wilhelm. Exactly two pounds like you asked. Not a nail more," Harold said with a smirk. He knew how to make the old man angry and relished in each and every chance he could to goad him.

The man spat at Harold's feet. "I told you that amount before. Not zis," he said waving the bag in Harold's face. "You screw me again like your *vater.*" Old Wilhelm shuffled away with his bag of nails to pay Frank at the front door and complain about his mistreatment.

Wiping his oily hands off on his trousers, Harold could hear him complaining in broken English and German to Frank about his latest mistreatment. When Wilhelm got angry he spoke German in a high pitched, tinny voice which seemed to reach higher and higher the angrier he got.

"I told you," Frank boomed from the front room of the office, "10 cents like always for two pounds of number six! If you can't pay it then leave the nails!"

Wilhelm grumbled loudly to himself in German while digging through his pockets for ten cents. He always made a show out of counting out his money and would audibly count out each cent just to be sure he, and everyone else within earshot heard him parting with his money.

"*Eins, zwei,*" he dug deeper looking carefully and each penny as it came out of his pocket. "*Neun* and *zehn,*" he said loudly slapping the pennies on the counter. It was difficult for him to part with them.

Frank beamed and said as nicely as he could, "Thank you Wilhelm. Please come again."

The old man snatched the bag from the counter and strode out the door making sure to slam it behind him. The tiny bell atop the door rang strongly as it always did each time he left the lumber yard.

Harold peeked around the corner catching Frank's eye when he did so. Both suddenly burst into laughter. Walking to the back room, Frank patted his son on the shoulder.

"Did you give him EXACTLY two pounds?" he asked with a gleam in his eyes.

"Yes sir," Harold replied. "Not a nail more. He kept trying to take some out and slip them in his pocket whenever I turned around. He kept complaining that the scale was off. Again!"

Frank laughed loudly pulling at his suspenders. "That old miser has the tightest backside I've ever seen," he laughed. "It's going to take a hundred men to carry his casket to the graveyard with all of the money he's taking with him to the here-after! No wonder the Kaiser kicked him out! Damned old Prussian!"

The tiny bell rang much quieter as someone entered the store. Frank turned to Harold smiling. "If you're about done tell Stan to close up the back. It's close to five and I'm getting hungry."

"Yes sir," Harold replied.

Frank disappeared to the front of the store to greet his last customer for the day. His father was in one of his good moods that day and had been ever since Harold had arrived to work after school at three. With a laugh to himself he wondered if his father had gotten the best of old Vince Boylan again, something Frank looked for every opportunity to do. The two had had a long-running feud going for years and both men would go out of their way to torment the other if an opportunity presented itself. Perhaps the clean-cut bastard had slipped and fallen in the horse shit in the street again like he had one day the previous summer. Harold, Frank and Stan had been walking back to the lumber yard after lunch and had seen old Vince fall backside first in the steamy fresh mess soiling his fine suit in the process. Harold had never seen his father laugh so hard.

"Hey Vince," he remembered his father yelling. "You look better somehow! I think you've found your calling!"

Vince glared at Frank not saying a word while the rest of downtown Sac City had a good laugh at the sight of their local banker and Mayor who had just proven he was just as human as the rest. The year before, Frank lost a close mayoral race to Vince which only fueled their personal war against one another. To make matters worse, Vince had also been elected as Master of Occidental Lodge three years before that while Frank stewed in the second-elected chair as Senior Warden.

Opening the back door of the store Harold called out. "Hey, Stan! You still back here?"

Stan emerged slowly from one of the back sheds. "Yeah boy," he answered through a yawn. It had been a slow day and he had been sleeping in one of the back sheds again.

"Dad said to shut her up for the night. I'll see you tomorrow. So long!" he said to his father's oldest companion.

Stan half-heartedly brushed himself off and waved nonchalantly at Harold who wrestled to close the creaky old door, lifting hard on the doorknob and shoving it in with his shoulder making sure to lock it as he pushed. Just as he made his way to the front of the office to leave he heard his Father's voice explode with displeasure.

"Goddamn son-of-a-bitch!" he yelled from his tiny corner office.

Harold froze and peeked around the corner to see the telegraph man, Amos disappear out the door in a flash. He'd left so quickly the bell had barely rung.

Harold waited not really wanting to walk to the front door to get out of the office and out of the line of fire. But after barring the back door there was no choice but have to walk by the office. For a moment he considered scurrying to the door on his hands and knees but quickly dismissed the idea knowing Frank would see him anyway. Harold chewed on his lip trying to work up the courage knowing when Frank was angry about something it didn't matter who had done anything. Usually, the first unfortunate to cross his path got it good. Oftentimes, that was Harold when he didn't get his homework or household chores done to his father's satisfaction. Moving quietly to the back door, Harold unlatched it and leaned out to see Stan shuffling his way towards the building looking forward to a much deserved weekend of drunkenness.

"Stan," Harold hissed. "Dad's in a mood again. Don't breathe too heavily on him."

"Got it son," Stan replied grimacing. He knew the drill; tread carefully around Frank when he was irritated especially when he knew Stan had a few drinks to get himself through the day which with him, was all day every day. Frank despised drink and knew about Stan's problem but he rarely ever said anything to him about it. The other drinkers in town weren't so lucky even in Frank's best of moods. He would purposely cross the street to avoid walking by, or having to greet any man he knew to be a drinker.

Normally Stan would have slipped out over the back fence of the lumber yard into the back alley but it was Friday and it was payday. He was running low on his stashes of moonshine and the weekend offered a chance for a good, uninterrupted two-day binge.

Harold and Stan returned to the office to see Uncle Alfred standing by the front door sipping his never empty cup of coffee while staring absently out the window. He was used to his brother's temper and had one himself. Looking over the glasses always perched just at the end of his nose he motioned to Harold and Stan to come to the front of the office. As they approached the counter he saw his father holding his now bright red face in his left hand a sure sign that he was badly upset. The telegram was crumpled into a ball in his other huge hand.

"Dad," Harold said softly. "Stan and I are going if that's okay. It's after five."

"That's fine," Frank said without looking up. "Your pay is on the counter. Have a good weekend."

"Yes sir," Stan replied snatching the white envelope containing his weekly wages from the well-worn counter. "See you Monday, Frank."

With that, Stan was out the door in an instant walking double-time to get out to Alton Moore's. Harold hesitated for a moment not sure what to do. If he were going to get it he knew it would be coming shortly. Frank looked up his face still bright red with anger.

"Go on home son. Tell your mother I'll be along shortly."

"Yes sir," replied a relieved Harold. Saying good night to Alfred he quickly left the jingling door behind him taking care not to slam it shut.

Stepping out into the bright late June sunshine Harold sighed deeply with relief and considered himself lucky…for now. He didn't know what was wrong and was curious about the telegram he had received. Maybe it was one of his lumber suppliers telling him his weekly shipment would be late. Or, perhaps it was Harold's other Uncle Richard, over in Lytton needing another loan to keep his farm going. It was hard to tell. Frank had no patience for untrustworthy suppliers and he had absolutely no time for people wanting money, even his own brother. Harold didn't want to be around to find out what it was but he knew the entire family would hear about it sooner or later. With a sigh of relief for the time being, he turned and started towards home trudging up the long hill along Main Street as the afternoon heat trapped in the sidewalk burned through his old leather shoes.

Harold walked the six blocks to the top of the hill quickly, enjoying the cool canopy of shade the ancient elms and oaks provided. Every few steps he looked back over his shoulder to make sure Frank wasn't stomping along behind him. Finally reaching the top of the hill where the enormous Methodist church sat, he ran around to the north side where the parsonage house sat and slid in behind a bush. Peeking through the thick leaves, he was able to get a glimpse of a flash of blonde hair in the backyard in between the clean white sheets that billowed on the long line in the warm breeze. Smiling, he made his way to the corner of the yard watching for Margaret's parents and two older sisters. Not seeing them he made a quick dash to the clothesline and hugged Margaret from behind who let out a shriek.

"Hands up," Harold snarled. "This is a stick-up!"

Margaret turned around with a laugh to give him a hug. "You scared the daylights out of me, mister," she said happily before giving Harold a quick kiss on the cheek. "What are you doing?"

"Just going home," he replied. "I didn't see your folks around so I thought I'd come over and say hi."

"You're sweet," Margaret replied. "Where's your father? He usually walks home with you."

Harold stood on his tip-toes and glanced over the top of the clothes line. He wasn't allowed here except for the stuffy Sunday afternoons he spent with Margaret in the Nicholson family parlor with her family supervising his visits. Margaret sat on one side of the room between her sisters and Harold sat on the other side of the room perched on an uncomfortable wooden chair by himself choking in a tightly buttoned shirt with its itchy collar, a tie and jacket. The Reverend Nicholson and his wife always positioned themselves to watch both Harold and Margaret. It was horrible but that's what Harold did to see her. Officially anyway. Sometimes his mother accompanied him too which made it worse. She would sit with the Reverend's family and discuss the Bible at length while he and Margaret carefully gazed at one another.

"Still at work and in another mood. Thought I'd get out while I could," he said with a shrug. "Do you think we could see each other tonight?"

"We can try. Come over about ten. That is, if my parents don't catch me coming out," she said nodding towards the small wooden garden shed that sat well behind the house in the huge backyard.

"Or, your lovely sister," Harold answered with a smirk. Judith was by most standards the homeliest woman in Sac City. At age twenty-four she still lived at home with her parents and had no prospects for marriage or anything else for that matter.

"Judith," Margaret muttered shaking her head. "She's jealous of me because I have you, a real live man. All she does is read the Bible all day and look for ways to get me into trouble. I'd like to punch her in the eye."

Harold covered his mouth with his hand to try to stop the yelp of laughter escaping his mouth. Just as he did both heard the creaking back door of the house open.

"Margaret!" her mother called. "Why aren't you done with those sheets yet?"

Margaret turned quickly back to her work as Harold scurried on his hands and knees through the yard behind the clothesline and into the bushes.

Walking, skipping and whistling, Harold made his way through back yards until he reached home. Turning the corner of the house to the back yard he ran into Bobby who was sitting on the bench by the back door busily carving a long stick with the treasured pocket knife Will had given him for his birthday. Long strips of greenish white wood littered the ground at his feet as he intently worked on the stick. The boy loved to whittle and kept a large collection of interesting looking sticks piled behind the dog shed. Mary busied herself skipping rope around the yard and singing Hymns loudly and well out of tune.

Sliding onto the bench he nudged his brother. "What's doing Bobby?"

"Nothing much. I found this stick today after school. See?" he said holding the c-shaped maple stick up for Harold to see. "I'm going to make a bow out of it and shoot the rabbits in the garden."

"Sounds great," Harold answered with a smile. "What are you going to make the string out of?"

Bobby stopped his carving and thought for a moment, his forehead creased with concentration. "I dunno, maybe you can give me some old string from the lumber yard. Do you think you could get me some?"

"Sure, just make sure you can put it on there tight just like the Indians did. It's got to twang when you pull it. Cut a notch here, and here," Harold said pointing to the ends of the stick. "If you do that, you'll have a good place to put your string and it won't slide off."

The back door opened and Nina stuck her head out. The smells of supper came wafting out and Harold's mouth watered. He was hungry. "Where's your father?" she asked. "He's not working late again is he?'

Harold stood and walked over to his mother. "He got a telegram today and isn't too happy about whatever it said. Told me to come home first," he said quietly so Bobby and Mary wouldn't hear.

Nina closed her eyes tightly and shook her head. "That means he's sitting down there stewing about it then and he'll really be worked up when he gets home. God be with us all."

Turning to go back in, she looked back at Harold. "You make sure that all of the chores are done. Bobby's too. You know how he can be."

"Yes, mom, I will," Harold answered as the door shut.

At that moment he heard his father's heavy steps on the front porch as he returned home. The front door opened and slammed shut. Harold quietly slipped in the back door being careful not to be heard. Taking small steps, he crept up to the threshold just four steps down from the kitchen door which his mother had left slightly open and waited hearing Frank stomp heavily into the kitchen.

"I got a telegram today," he rumbled, "from the military police at Camp Green in North Carolina."

The silence was piercing. Harold knew his father was really getting angry and he was building up to the next part of the story.

49

"It seems," he said with labored breath, "That Edith is being held in the camp stockade." Frank slammed the wadded telegram on the counter.

"What?" asked Nina in amazement. "She's in college in New York! How, why is she in a stockade in North Carolina?"

"I don't know!" Frank yelled. "But I'm going to find out why!

The next few days went by uneventfully but the entire family made extra sure to tip-toe around Frank and to do nothing to aggravate him as he was furious from morning 'till night. Harold made sure to help Bobby and Mary with their chores and did his with greater effort. Luckily Uncle Alfred sent him out to work with their building crew putting up a new house on the west side of town and Bobby tagged along as usual to help and to look for more interesting pieces of wood to haul home.

On Saturday morning Harold's made his way downtown to Wills store to pick up a few things for his mother, one of more enjoyable chores he had at home. Entering the dimly lit store he walked to the back counter where Will sat engrossed in the order sheet he was filling out.

"Hi Will. What's new today?"

"Harold, my boy. Another list from your mother? Where's Bobby?"

"Yes, a short one this time thankfully. Bobby was running around this morning so he didn't come along."

"Well, let's have it," Will said putting down his clipboard.

As Will walked around the shop filling a box with Nina's order the two visited about the latest news and gossip around town. "So, tell me, have your parents told you anything about Edith yet?" Will asked with a smirk on his face.

"No, nothing. Why, what have you heard?"

"Well, maybe I shouldn't say."

"Dammit Will," Harold growled leaning in close to his brother-in-law. "You know something. Tell me."

"Your father told Irene and me this yesterday...he and Edith have sent telegrams sent back and forth. Old Frank got one from the military authorities in North Carolina."

"And?" Harold asked leaning in closer. Will was speaking quietly so the few other customers in the store couldn't hear. "You'll like this. Edith was arrested and put in the Camp Green stockade; she cut off her long hair, disguised herself as a man and enlisted in the army as a private."

"What?" Harold almost shouted. "You're pulling my leg Will, that's nonsense!"

"No. It's true, I swear," Will removed his glasses to wipe his eyes and began laughing. "Evidently she did a good job of hiding herself as a man. She lived and trained for nearly a month with the men before being discovered one day while her training company was bathing in a river. Evidently she went further upstream to bathe away from the men and the sergeant saw her out of uniform. The game was up."

Harold stared at Will for a moment open-mouthed. "I can't believe it. Edith really did that?"

Will laughed much harder now turning red-faced. "She really did that. Edith has a lot of guts. Your father is beside himself but don't let on that you know."

Harold stood dumbfounded while Will continued to laugh. That explained why Frank had slapped Harold the previous night for no apparent reason.

"Don't worry Will, I won't say anything.

Later that night after supper, Harold's parents sent Bobby and Mary to bed earlier than usual. While Frank told Harold about Edith's little adventure Harold found it hard not to laugh out loud or act as though he knew anything. Frank and Nina were shocked and embarrassed.

"If anyone in Sac City finds out about this the family will be laughing stocks," Frank said as he angrily tapped his ring on the table. "Something I will not allow. Bobby and Mary won't be told."

"Yes sir. I understand," Harold answered fighting back the urge to laugh in his father's face. Only strong-willed Edith would have had the guts to try and pull something like that off. It surprised them all because like Irene, Edith was a very pretty woman with very definite feminine features but was naturally stronger than most men. She also had her father's temper and had inherited his incredible drive to succeed her way.

"I've sent her a number of telegrams admonishing her and telling her to come home. She has refused," Frank continued. "The army has found a job for her in the medical corps as an army nurse. I hope it's a punishment but she claims it was her choice."

Edith, Harold knew, was incredibly bull-headed and very confident in herself. She was staying and Frank could do nothing about it. He admired his sister.

All of this made Harold envious too. Since the U.S. had declared war on Germany several months before many men from Sac City had enlisted in the Army, the Navy and some in the Marines while he continued to exist in his boring, pre-destined life in tiny, isolated Sac City. He didn't want to go to college and come back to sell lumber and nails, he wanted to join up and fight the Germans before the war was over. His biggest fear was that he'd miss his only chance at doing what he felt would be something worthwhile in his life.

MOONSHINE

September 23, 1917

Harold took two giant steps forward in the pungent green hay and raised the .22 rifle to his shoulder. The pigeon fluttered excitedly and banged into the glass windows at the top of the mow then turned back and landed on the enormous wooden beam running the entire length of the structure.

"There you go Harold, shoot it!" his friend Alton Moore Jr. cried.

Harold lined up the front sight post with the rear sight, exhaled slightly and gently squeezed the trigger. The gun fired with a loud crack in the enclosed space. The pigeon fell fluttering and shaking into the hay below.

"Whoo-hoo!" another one!" Alton yelled clapping his hands. "Roasted pigeon for supper tonight!"

"I never thought that one would hold still. What was that? The fourth shot?" Harold asked.

"At least the fourth. That one you fired into the roof is going to leak the next time it rains." Alton Jr. said with a laugh. "And my old man is probably going to tan my hide for it too!"

Harold shuffled forward through the thick hay towards where he thought the pigeon had landed when he suddenly stepped on something hard and turned his ankle causing him to fall with a whoosh into the hay.

"What was that?" he asked rubbing his ankle. Reaching down, he pulled out a mason jar filled with what looked like water and held it up for Alton Jr. to see. "Look what I stepped on."

Alton Jr. placed the dead pigeon into the cloth bag he carried with the other birds he and Harold had shot and bounded over to his friend's side. "That's some of the old man's hooch," he said with a sly grin. "Must have forgotten about it up here. He used to hide it in here until the sheriff got wise last year. C'mon, you want to drink some of it?"

"I don't know if I should. I'm not supposed to be out here anyway," Harold said uneasily. "I have to be home soon to finish my chores."

"Aw, come on Harold. Just a few sips. All real men drink you know."

"Not my father," Harold said. "He'd beat me senseless if he even knew I was even out here."

"Well, that's your father's problem," Alton Jr. said. "He doesn't drink and that makes him uptight and mean. It's all of that religious stuff you know. Seems like all of them have their shorts in a bind about something all the time."

Harold sat in the hay and considered it for a moment. In his mind the easy-going Moore family was fun to be around, certainly more so than his religiously strict parents. He was forbidden to have anything to do with any of them but he and Alton had been friends since first grade and they'd spent many years playing, fishing, hunting squirrels and running around together. Alton's father, Alton sr. was the local moonshiner and Frank and Nina abhorred anyone who even possessed alcohol let alone take a drink now and then. Defying Frank was a dangerous thing to do but the older Harold got the more he seemed to enjoy doing what he wanted to do.

"Oh, come on. We'll take just a drink or two to see what happens then we'll hide the jar for another time," Alton said convincingly.

Harold sighed in resignation. "Well, okay. Just a couple of sips. No more."

"Great! Let's go down to the woods where the old man won't see us!"

The two boys took off for the privacy of the woods and the little creek they often fished and swam in on hot days. Harold had never been drunk before and the first couple of drinks made him feel good and strangely, wanting more. The liquor burned his throat and stomach. After four big drinks he was dizzy and giggling with Alton Jr. and before he knew what was happening he passed out. When he awoke it was dark outside and Alton was nowhere to be seen. The empty Mason jar lay in the dirt with the previous year's dead, dry leaves.

"Oh no, I missed supper and my chores didn't get done," he mumbled to himself as he tried to pull himself up off the ground. "Oh, my head…"

After twenty minutes of half walking, half running through the back yards and alleys and vomiting three times, he cautiously walked up the sidewalk to the front porch of his house. He recoiled in fear when Frank appeared out of the darkness.

"Where in the hell have you been?" he boomed.

Before Harold could answer, Frank had him by the throat.

"Holy Jesus! What's that I smell? Are you drunk?"

Harold choked for breath and clawed at his father's hands as began to squeeze his throat.

"My God boy! Drunk! I can't believe it!" Frank shouted, his huge fists slashing quickly out of the darkness blinding him with their fury. "You know how I feel about that!"

Harold went limp with each shattering hit. The first few hurt then he felt nothing but a numb, dull ache. Frank continued beating him with a fury only known in the Bible. With his survival instincts kicking in, Harold curled himself into a tight ball until Frank finally quit. For several minutes which seemed like hours in a daze, he painfully shuffled his way to the front door only to discover it was locked and the house was dark. The back door too, was locked. With little else to do, he inched his way over to the rusty water pump and pushing the squeaking handle up and down. Cool water gushed out into the bucket hanging from the spout in which Harold washed his rapidly swelling face. Taking a long drink from his cupped hands he realized that he was missing a tooth. Shivering, he cursed under his breath,

"I hope your hands are all cut up you old bastard. Try explaining that to all of your damn righteous friends," he wept.

Even though it was summer the air was chilly and a stiff breeze rustled through the branches of the ancient maple trees surrounding the house. Pulling himself up from the water pump Harold crawled to the old shed in the back corner of the yard. A low growl greeted him out of the shadows.

"It's okay pup. Just me," he called. The old yellow dog immediately trotted quietly over to Harold with his tail excitedly fanning the cool, humid night air.

"Want some company tonight Teddy?" he asked the dog scratching his ears. Harold crawled through the old broken shed door and plopped down into the musty straw. The dog, glad for some company rubbed closely to Harold with his nose working furiously. Smelling the blood on Harold's face, he licked cautiously and gently.

"Yeah I know," he muttered while he choked with tears. "He got me again."

Teddy's big brown eyes peered at Harold's battered face in the darkness of the shed. With another careful lick he curled up next to him and sighed deeply. The dog knew all too well the extent of Frank's fury. He'd also been thumped many times before usually for getting into the trash in search of a rancid meal or two. Harold softly cried himself to sleep with Teddy's big head resting comfortably on his chest.

Throughout the rest of the night his sleep was restless and broken. Even though his father had beaten him his entire life for trivial things this one had been worst yet. Harold felt empty and alone and the fear of facing his father again made him want to retch. To calm himself he imagined he was one of the red winged blackbirds that fluttered about carelessly and gracefully in the fields and woods. They were free and they could go where they wanted. He dreamed he was standing in the yard watching his father beat Bobby with his huge hands but for some reason he was frozen in place.

The next morning, the creaky door of the shed flew open, the sunlight blinding Harold.

"Get up boy. Clean yourself up and get ready for church."

Harold groaned and tried to get up. He was sore all over and his head was pounding from the moonshine. The dog was gone on his daily search of the neighborhood's garbage bins. Evidently he'd heard Frank coming and decided to make a break for it.

"Get up!" Frank shouted.

With every inch of his body screaming in pain Harold finally managed to pull himself up to lean on the rickety doorway. Frank grunted and strode quickly back to the house slamming the door behind him shaking the walls. Harold knew that this was only the beginning of his punishment and could look forward to several more weeks of endless chores, abuse and living in fear. Frank never let anything go without weeks and sometimes months of reminders and off-handed comments.

As he approached the Harold could hear his mother and father arguing. *Mom must be in fine form today* he thought to himself.

Normally she didn't argue or even dare talk back. Pausing below the kitchen window he could tell that they were talking about him. Clearly, his mother was furious.

"Don't tell me about your excuses Frank! I saw what you did to him last night. You could have killed him! And all over a little moonshine!" she shouted.

Franks hand slammed down fiercely on the wooden cupboard shaking the glassware inside. "Dammit, Nina, he was drunk. *Drunk!* I can't have *my* son acting like that. What will people think of me? I'm a church deacon and a Mason! Besides that, I have a business to run in this town and I'll be damned if I lose customers because he's a lush! It doesn't look good for any of us!"

Nina had a wooden rolling pin in her hand. Pointing it in Frank's face she yelled back. "Who cares what people think of you? I don't like drinking and sin any more than you do. What, are you afraid that someone might think less of you for what all boys will do? Why don't you tell about what you did in your younger days? You were just like him! Just look at Harold's face! Now everyone in town will know exactly what you are! It takes quite a man to do that to a defenseless child!"

Harold watched in amazement as she began poking Frank in the chest with the rolling pin but she wasn't backing down. Mary and Bobby sat motionless at the dining room table, clearly frightened, their breakfasts cold and forgotten about in their fear of what might happen next. To everyone' surprise Frank turned and stormed out of the house without a word. The rickety screen door fell off of its hinges as he slammed it.

FINALITY

November 4, 1917

Dim light from street lights outside the tiny shed cast a faint haze over Margaret as she ran her hands over Harold's face as she kissed him. His bruises had slowly healed in the weeks since he and Alton had gotten drunk together but deep inside himself, he hadn't. He knew he had to get out of Sac City. After seventeen years of beating his son Frank had finally broken him.

"What did he hit you for this time?" she asked softly.

"I don't know," Harold replied looking away trying not to cry. "Bobby didn't go straight home after school like I told him to do. After I left the lumber yard it took me until dark to find him down on the river bottom and we were late for supper. On top of that, he hadn't done his chores either. I got it good but dad just sent Bobby to bed without supper."

The cool fall breeze whistled through the cracks of the old potting shed where the couple often met in secret.

"I think you know what you should do. It's time," Margaret finally whispered to Harold.

Harold nodded and took a deep breath. "I just want you to know that I don't want to leave you but I don't feel like I have any choice now."

Margaret flushed. "You can't stay here. As much as your father beats you...I'd like to hit him over the head with a board for what he does to you."

Harold smiled at the thought of Margaret knocking big Frank down. He had learned one thing during the past few months of their courtship; Margaret was completely devoted to him and she would do anything to protect him which was something Harold had never experienced before. It felt good.

Harold ran his tongue into the empty spot where his upper-left molar had once been. That too had finally healed allowing him to eat without so much pain. He was glad Frank hadn't knocked out one of his front teeth otherwise he'd look like Stan or worse, his grandmother Culp. "If his recent temper tantrums keep up I won't have any teeth left."

"What did your father say about it all?" he asked Margaret.

"He wasn't happy," she replied with a frown. "And he told me that the devil takes on many different forms. I know it's not much but he's been praying for you and for Bobby."

Harold laughed. He'd never imagined his father as the devil. But as he'd grown, he *had* realized Frank wasn't quite the great man whom he had seen him as during his youth. Frank had worn Harold down with years of beatings, goading him to the decision he was now sharing with Margaret.

"You promise you'll look after Bobby while I'm gone? If it's going to be too much for you I won't go." Harold pulled Margaret tightly to him. He had to know that his younger brother would have someone looking out for him. But it tore Harold up inside too. The thought of leaving Bobby to the devil was unsettling and it hovered over his every waking moment.

"I don't know what to feel, part of me says to go but still, I feel like I'll be abandoning him if I do," he continued, his voice wavering. "I can't live Bobby's life for him. I do his chores, I dress him every day, I…I keep him out of trouble with mom and dad. I do everything for him and…"

Margaret's eyes welled up. She knew Harold had to leave town because it would be the only way he would ever be able to break free of his father and the life that he had laid out for his oldest son. She also agreed with him about Bobby. Harold was responsible for his brother to the point that it seemed that he was more the child's father than his brother.

"I know how you feel," Margaret replied. "You've seen Judith. She's hopelessly attached to mother. I doubt she could even think for herself or even take care of herself any longer. She'll never leave home."

Harold shook his head as he thought of Margaret's pathetic sister Judith who spent her days helping with housework, reading the Bible and fawning over her mother incessantly.

"I don't like telling you this but Bobby could turn out just like her. You have to let him go and let him find his own way in life."

"I know…"

Although Harold would never admit it, he had become somewhat resentful of having to give up everything in his life to raise Bobby. Harold was only seventeen; he wanted to live his own life and he wanted to travel and find adventure with Margaret at his side. Thinking about it tore him apart. What would happen to Bobby if he left? What if he, Harold were killed in the war? Who would take care of him then?

"I wish God would give me an answer, a miracle or a vision," Harold said wiping his eyes. "Then it would be easier."

Margaret ran her fingers through his hair and looked deeply into his eyes. "You know I'll do my best for him and if I start seeing bruises on his face like you've had then I'll have my father do something. Maybe we could take him in. Besides, if my father gets involved your parents will probably sing for joy when we come to take Bobby away from them. You've told me how much they don't want him. This might be their chance."

Harold stared at the cracked glass in the shed window. "You're right," he said. "But what if they send him somewhere else after I'm gone? Somewhere we don't know about? Like the orphanage in Fort Dodge? Like my mom's sister Aunt Nell? She's a mean old witch who smells like sweat and cats. Bobby always laughs at her when she comes to visit. Last year he kept pinching his nose shut. When Mary asked him what he was doing he told her Aunt Nell's smells were hell."

Harold and Margaret laughed. Bobby had a sharp sense of humor and he told it like it was. Frank had knocked Bobby to the floor for that comment.

"What we've been trying has been working out well, just trust in it all," Margaret said.

When Harold had inched closer to his decision to leave Sac City, he had started sending Bobby along with Margaret on different occasions; walking him home from school some days, taking the boy to her house to help her father work around the church on other days. They wanted him to get used to being around someone other than Harold. At first he had fought them but Harold was amazed by the patience and kindness Margaret had shown in return. Bobby, like Harold, thrived when treated with love and compassion, something that was a rare in their family.

The couple held each other in silence inside the dark dusty shed as the moon crept across the night sky each lost in thoughts of an uncertain, frightening future.

"I hope I'm doing the right thing. If I go that is," Harold said after several minutes. "It's time he learned to care for himself and how to get around dad. Still, I'm worried."

Margaret took Harold's face in her hands and looked into his eyes. "You have to do this for both of you. You've known that for a long time so do what we've talked about."

Harold stifled a sob and prayed that he was doing the right thing.

THE RING

December 4, 1917

After the last school bell of the day rang Harold waded through the throng of students and managed to stop Mary outside the doors of the imposing limestone school building. "I'm heading down to the lumber yard to see if dad and Stan need a hand today. Could you take Bobby along with you?" he asked.

"I suppose," Mary replied shrugging her shoulders. "But there's no taking him along. He's already gone. See?"

Harold's eyes followed her outstretched finger to see Bobby already racing across the yards to beat her home.

"Bobby! Wait for Mary!" he shouted to the boy who stopped and stood grinning at his brother.

"Thanks, Mary. Make sure he gets a start on his chores. I shouldn't be too late. And do yours too."

Mary huffed and took off after Bobby.

"Can't catch me!" the boy shrieked. "Scary Mary! Can't catch me!"

Harold shook his head and laughed at the boy.

"Are you going to the lumber yard today?" Margaret asked approaching Harold to discretely touch his arm.

"Um, yes. I need to keep in dad's good graces for now. I don't want him to suspect anything."

"But I didn't think he was very busy these days."

Harold shifted uncomfortably on his feet trying to keep a straight face. "Oh, he's not but maybe I can sweep the office or make a pot of coffee or something."

Margaret eyed him suspiciously and gave him a sly grin. "Well, okay. Walk me home?"

"Of course."

The two joined in with the last smattering of children leaving the schoolyard and began the walk towards Margaret's house. Harold hoped she'd bought his feeble attempt at telling a little white lie but he was sure she hadn't. He made it a point to never lie to her but what he had in mind was a surprise.

Margaret was correct however knowing Harold rarely had to work in the lumber yard anymore. Even though the United States had only been in the war for eight months, business had fallen off significantly because of the war and rationing. The government had requisitioned most of the existing supplies of building materials in the U.S. to construct huge military camps to deal with the influx of thousands upon thousands of new soldiers.

"Here we are my dear," Harold said smiling down at Margaret. "Can um, I have a kiss?"

Margaret's eyes quickly scanned the house and church before pulling Harold behind a wide old maple tree. "Yes," she murmured before planting a wet kiss on his puckered mouth. "I'll see you tomorrow. Stay out of trouble, okay?"

"Yes, I'll do my best. I wish I could see you later."

"So do I," Margaret replied giving him another quick kiss. "Off you go."

Harold left her and ran down the long Main street hill to Will's market. Stepping inside the dimly lit store, he stomped the light snow off his boots and began scanning the shelves for just the right item. The narrow store was piled high with all sorts of everyday goods; canned food, clothing, jewelry, light bulbs, dinner ware, silverware – a little bit of everything a person needed to have a comfortable household. It smelled heavily from years of tobacco and wood smoke from the stove.

"Can I help you?" came a voice from the back.

"Hi Will," Harold said in greeting to his bespectacled brother-in-law who emerged wearing his customary white apron over one of his nice suits. His eyeglasses shone in the sunlight cascading in from the street.

"So, what are you doing today?" Will asked leaning over the counter. "Want another look at the postcards?" he asked with a sly grin. Will had a wicked sense of humor and would often share his hidden collection of French postcards with Harold when the store was empty. They both agreed that one model had a remarkable resemblance to Miss Tarrant, the English teacher at the school.

"Nah," said Harold. "I'm looking for something special. For, um...a girl. But don't tell anyone!"

"I see, I see," Will laughed. "And who would the fine young lady be if I may ask?"

Harold shifted uncomfortably and looked around the store. Only a couple of men were sitting at the back of the store by the stove drinking coffee and telling tales. He leaned in closer to Will. "Margaret," he said. "But don't tell anyone."

"Margaret Nicholson?" Will exclaimed loudly with a grin. "You've finally come around! Good for you my boy. Good for you. Now, what date have you chosen for the wedding?" he exclaimed smoothing his hair back with both hands. He loved to tease Harold.

"I mean it Will. Today's her birthday and I want to buy her something nice," Harold replied.

"Aahh, the wooing of a woman," Will replied holding his hands to his heart and gazing away. "If you want miracles we don't sell them here. But, I do have a couple of things you might be interested in."

Will walked behind the counter and pulled a few drawers out, shuffled through them, and shut them again.

"No, that won't do. Hmm," he said to himself. "That neither."

With his hands on his hips he looked up to one of the higher shelves. "I've got it!" he said excitedly grabbing the ladder on rollers and briskly sliding it down the row. Reaching into a shelf high above the floor he pulled out a box and peeked inside.

"Ah, perfect!"

Bringing it down, he handed it to Harold. "What do you think of this?" he asked handing the box over.

Harold opened it and saw a beautiful porcelain doll complete with an odd looking faux silk dress and matching umbrella. "That's, um, nice. What's so special about it?"

"Well, it's oriental. Came from Japan or China or somewhere like that. We've had two of them here for years and never did even set them out. Got'em in a shipment of other things once. Never even paid for them."

Harold knew what he wanted to buy Margaret but was afraid to tell Will. He placed the doll back on the counter. "It's nice and all but…I want to buy her a ring."

"What?" Will shouted wide-eyed. "How long have you known her? A ring?"

"Yes, a ring," Harold replied trying to avoid Will's bulging eyes. "I've known her long enough to know that I love her. I don't want to buy a diamond, just something nice."

Will shook his head and coughed with laughter. "Okay, okay," he muttered turning to pull out another drawer to dig through small boxes containing jewelry and shiny things.

"How about one of these? These are very nice and will last a long time. Made of gold," he said opening a small box with a beautiful gold ring in it. The ring was intricately carved with a nice swirling design. It seemed to glow.

Harold touched the ring and smiled. "I'll take it. How much?"

Will did his best salesman act. Standing upright, arms crossed, he rubbed his chin thoughtfully. "Well, since you're a man obviously in need of a good gift I'll let you have it for say, two dollars. It's actually a four dollar item."

"Sold!" Harold replied slamming a handful of coins down on the counter. He enjoyed dickering with Will. Before taking his hand off the coins he looked at Will facetiously. "Can you gift wrap it for me too?"

"What? That'll be another dollar!"

"I won't buy it if you don't gift wrap it for free."

"Good lord, you're starting to sound like your father. Oh well, come on, I'll wrap it up nice for you."

Will busied himself wrapping the ring. "You know," he said, "It didn't take me a lot of work to land your sister. I think she's the one who had to do all the wooing."

Harold smirked remembering how much Irene had actively pursued Will. Even though she was only sixteen she, like Harold, knew she had to get out of Frank and Nina's strict household and Will gave her the opportunity to do so. Will was nineteen at the time and already in business with his father which to Irene was an attractive and practical solution. At first Will had dismissed her attentions as nothing more than a child with a serious crush but Irene persisted and got Will down the aisle six months later. Six months after that, their first child, James Franklin, had been stillborn. Despite a rough, and often-gossiped about start to their married life, they had been happily wed for seven years. Little Helen was their angel and they spoiled her at every opportunity. She never lacked for toys, nice dresses and the attention of her aunts.

Handing the package to Harold, Will smiled. "Good luck my boy. Let me know how it goes."

With another quick look around the store Harold had something else he had to share but finding the courage to say it made him sweat.

"What's the matter? Having second thoughts?" Will teased.

Harold shifted uncomfortably on his feet. "I have to tell you something and um, you have to promise me that you won't tell anyone, especially mom and dad."

Will leaned on the counter bringing his face closer to Harold's. His brow creased with concern. "Oh my, what did you do? You didn't get that Nicholson girl in trouble did you?"

Harold flushed. "No, but this is serious. I um…I'm…I've made a decision about my future. I'm going to join the Army. Please don't tell anyone!" he pleaded.

Will stood and crossed his arms and began pacing back and forth. "When? You're not old enough, you know that. They're only taking men who are twenty or twenty-one and…" Then it dawned on him. "You're going to run away and join up just like Edith did."

Harold nodded apprehensively.

Will rubbed his forehead and exhaled slowly. "You're right, you shouldn't let anyone else know. When do you plan on doing this?"

Harold's eyes scanned the store nervously. "I'm not sure yet. Maybe when the Tuesday and Thursday midnight trains come through town. One of those nights. Alton Moore wants to go with me. Margaret knows all about it and she supports me. I have to go Will, you should understand that. You saw the bruises he left on me back in September. He hits hard enough now to knock teeth out. See?" Harold said pulling his lips back to show the empty place.

"Holy Hell Harold," Will replied still rubbing his forehead. "I know you're right but Frank won't like this one bit especially after Edith's adventure. He'll probably beat you to death if he catches you."

"Yes," Harold replied in a whisper. "I'm sure. I have to get out of here. If I'm in the Army dad can't get me out. Especially if I'm in France. Besides, if I stay here you're right, he'll kill me."

Will gazed at Harold with shock. "What if you get killed in France? Ever thought of that? What about Bobby? Jesus Harold!"

"Well," Harold began, "I was hoping that I could count on you to help look after him. Margaret's promised to help too. I know it's probably wrong to leave him but I have to go."

Will took off his glasses and rubbed his eyes. "Are you absolutely damn sure you want to do this? I'll do what I can for you. You know that. Besides," he said with a smile. "I never could picture you staying around here and wasting your life in that lumber yard. You have too much wanderlust in you. Just like Edith. Besides, Irene and I have been married long enough for me to see how your father treats you. I'd leave too if I were in your shoes."

Harold felt a huge sense of relief come over him. He'd told his secret but strange new doubts began to weigh heavily on his chest. Will was right: what he was doing could at the very worst get him killed or if caught, beaten so badly he'd want to die anyway. He had two choices: follow through with his plan and hope that it succeeded somehow or stay put and live out his days in Sac City at the lumber yard. Harold couldn't fathom the thought of staying any longer because over the years the beatings gradually became worse the older and bigger Harold got and he knew Frank would indeed eventually kill him.

He looked at Will who was staring out of the wide windows at the front of the store. "So, you'll keep my secret?"

Will turned to Harold and extended his right hand. "Yes, of course. You know I will and I'll do what I can to help you."

With relief washing through his body Harold took Will's outstretched hand and squeezed it tightly. Suddenly, Will wrapped his arms around Harold and hugged him tightly. "I've always loved you like you were my own brother," he said sincerely. "You do what you have to do but promise me you'll come back. Do you hear me? Don't try to be a hero over there. Just be safe."

"I will," Harold replied. "I love you too."

THE BUILD UP

December 28, 1917

"You stand there and listen to me boy!" Frank shouted at Harold who shifted uncomfortably from one foot to the other. There was little else he could do except stand and take the abuse. Frank paused a moment before continuing and from the look on his face, Harold knew he was just warming up. "There will be no more sneaking around behind my back. You seem to believe that you can do whatever in the hell your heart desires! No more!"

Before he knew what was happening Frank slapped him hard enough to knock him to the floor.

Wiping his mouth and seeing blood on his lip, Harold looked up at his father with hatred in his eyes. In a show of defiance he began to stand when Frank took a large step and kicked him back to the floor.

Instead of kicking again, Frank pulled him up and drew his face in close to Harold's.

"So tell me boy. How long have you been sneaking out in the middle of the night to see that Nicholson girl? I can only imagine what you're doing to her. What would her parents think?"

"Don't know"

"Well I sure as hell can imagine! You, sneaking out of your bedroom window to defile the daughter of a minister!"

"I'm not defiling her!"

"Don't you talk back to me!

Harold knew he was in for it no matter what he said or did. For several weeks he'd been sneaking out of the house in the middle of the night to visit with Margaret in their secret meeting place in the shed behind her parent's house. Other times they would see each other at the city park which was three blocks from each other's houses. It was the only way they could ever be alone and Harold had always been careful not to leave if he knew either of his parents, Bobby or Mary were up. Sometimes Frank spent half the night reading and half-dozing in his chair downstairs leaving him no choice but to stay in. But, after sneaking in and out of the house many times and not being caught he'd become careless and hadn't waited long enough to make sure everyone was asleep. Well after midnight Bobby watched him climb out of their bedroom window, jump down on the tree limbs outside and disappear into the night. He couldn't blame the boy for going to wake his parents; he thought it strange to see his brother leaving the house in such a fashion at midnight and it had scared him. When Harold returned two hours later Frank was sitting on the chair in the boy's bedroom in the dark waiting for him.

Harold continued to glare at his father with a hatred which he found surprising. "I love Margaret and if I want to see her then I'll see her. What I do with her is none of your damn business!"

"What?" Frank cried, his eyes nearly bursting from their sockets from rage before swiftly delivering another blow to Harold's already red and swelling face which knocked him back to the floor. This time he decided he'd had about enough and jumped to his feet with raised his fists.

"You bastard!" he screamed "No more!"

Frank took a giant step forward when Harold suddenly hit him in the mouth with all of his strength. His father went sprawling backwards smashing his head on the corner of the stone fireplace. Harold stood for a moment breathing heavily, his fists clenched tightly as he stared down at his prostrate father who held the back of his head. A trickle of blood seeped between his fingers and ran down to pool on the floor. Hearing a loud gasp behind him, Harold turned to see his mother clad only in her nightgown staring with horror at the scene in front of her.

"What did you do?" she demanded rushing to Harold to grab him by the arms. Seeing her son's battered face she gently placed her hands on his cheeks and scowled with anger.

"Grab some ice out of the ice-box and get out of here" she said pointing "Get yourself over to Will and Irene's and stay there. Don't you dare go back to Margaret's. Do you understand me? I'll deal with him."

Harold's eyes welled up with tears. "Yes mom," he croaked. Forgetting the ice, he ran into the cold night crying and choking. After two blocks he stopped to duck behind an enormous old maple tree trying to catch his breath. For one frightening moment he thought he saw Frank's shadow coming after him in the pale light of the streetlights flickering in the wind. He continued running dragging his feet in the snow, watching the entire time until he realized that his eyes were playing tricks on him, his good eye anyway. The left one had by now swollen completely shut.

Harold took one more careful look and dashed through the snow-covered backyards and alleys until he was across town at Will and Irene's. Since it was nearly three o'clock in the morning the house was dark and silent. The wind picked up considerably and whooshed noisily through the trees and cast dead leaves and small sticks down in the yard.

After making his way carefully around to the back of the house Harold noticed a faint light on in the kitchen. He approached the back door and peeked in and to his relief Irene was sitting at the table rubbing her tired eyes. Harold tapped lightly on the door causing Irene to jump. She immediately got up looked out of the window before opening it slightly. "Harold? Is that you out there?"

"Yes, it's me." he replied. "Can I come in?"

"Go to the door."

Harold did as he was told and went to the back door.

"What's going on?" she asked. "Mom just called on the telephone and said you were coming over. She didn't sound well."

Harold took off his boots and coat and sat down at the table. "Dad got me again," he began pointing to his swollen eye. "And before he could hit me again I knocked him down. He hit his head on the fireplace mantle when he went down."

Irene gasped and covered her mouth. "You did what?"

"Yeah," Harold said, his shoulders slumping, "I knocked him down and hurt him for a change. I don't know what happened. I just…snapped."

Irene looked at him with barely concealed shock. Finally, she shook her head and reached in the ice box to break off a chunk of ice. After wrapping it tightly in a towel she gently pressed it to his face. "Here," she said. "Hold that on there."

"Oh my Harold." Irene said sitting down on the opposite side of the table. "I can't believe you did that. No one's ever stood up to him like that. No one's ever knocked him down before!"

"I know," Harold said wincing from the ice and the pain in his face. "I guess I'm tired of being treated like a punching bag. I'll fight back again, you can count on that."

Irene stood and hugged Harold tightly. "You better not go home for a while. You just stay here with us."

"Thanks, Irene." He knew she and Will would protect him but he also knew he couldn't hide from Frank at their house forever either. Since the beating he'd gotten in August, Harold had begun saving money and working on a plan to leave Sac City. He and Margaret had even discussed it again tonight. Frank hadn't touched Harold during the weeks before Christmas and had even somewhat kind, but the after what had just happened he now knew for certain that the sooner he left the better. There was no way his father would ever forgive him now.

DECISION DAY

Harold stomped down the sidewalk in the freezing morning air holding his school books in his left hand while he blew on his cold right hand. He was on his way to meet Bobby and walk him to school and hopefully catch a glimpse of Margaret.

"Damn cold weather. Stupid parents. I'm never coming back to this backwater of a town ever again. I hate this place," he muttered. It seemed as though everything were suddenly unraveling and no matter how hard he tried to think of a way to fix it all, nothing made sense. The conversation he'd had with Margaret two days before at school still haunted him as did the image of her tear streaked face.

"My mother and father told me that I'm not allowed to see you anymore. Your father stopped at our house the other day after you two had had your fight and told them we've been meeting in secret at night. They know everything Harold. My father whipped me with his belt."

Even though it had been a couple of days Harold was still furious but Margaret managed to remain calm throughout it all. Before leaving the school grounds later that afternoon they both agreed that they would still be able to see each other at school and possibly at Will's market downtown when or if she was sent on errands by her mother. But they had to be careful. Both agreed it wouldn't be a good idea to sneak out for quite a while until things had cooled off but they would write letters to one another daily to and exchange them with one another at school. Harold wanted to walk her home as had been their routine before and after school but said no, Judith was charged with walking along with her now to make sure Harold wasn't around her.

"Stupid old hag Judith," he spat.

For nearly a week, Harold stayed at Will and Irene's while the entire family waited to see what Frank would do. He continued going to school and would meet Bobby a block from home in the mornings to walk with him and to also find out what was going on at home. From what little Harold was able to get out of the child it seemed as though nothing had happened. About the only thing that made Harold smile was when the child mentioned was large bandage on Frank's head that no one was supposed to talk about.

"Dad said he hit his head at the lumber yard but I know better," Bobby said to Harold as they trudged along. "He looks like a Hindu or whatever you call those people in India."

"Oh yeah?" Harold asked with a smirk. "What do you know Bobby?"

"You hit him that night you crawled out the window. I saw you."

"You did?" Harold asked eying the boy.

"Yeah, after he threw you down the stairs I sat up there and watched until mom sent me back to bed. Are you going to hurt dad again? If he hurts you again I'm going to hit him the next time," Bobby said confidently.

Harold stopped and stooped down, forcefully grabbing Bobby by the shoulders causing him to drop his books in the snow.

"You listen to me Bobby. Don't you ever even think about hitting dad. You stay away from him. You have to. If you ever hit him he could really hurt you badly and I don't want that to happen. If he ever hits you, run away. Promise me! Just run away!" Harold said shaking Bobby who squirmed and tried to pull away.

"Dammit! Promise me Bobby!" Harold shouted.

Bobby's eyes welled up with tears. "I promise." he said weakly.

Suddenly what he was doing dawned on Harold and he released his grip. He'd never scolded Bobby before and he looked away. "Oh, Bobby, I'm sorry," Harold said pulling Bobby close and hugging him. "Come on. Let's pick these books up. We need to get to school."

Bobby sniffled while Harold picked up the books. The two walked in silence until they reached the door of the school, which was odd because the boy usually chattered constantly.

"I'll see you later. Have a good day okay?" Harold said handing the books to him. Instead of saying goodbye, Bobby ran into the building without saying a word.

"Oh hell," he muttered feeling a lump in his throat. "It just keeps getting worse. I can't win."

The day crept agonizingly along. Harold sat in his math class gazing out of the window at the bare trees swaying in the cold wind trying to look as though he were paying attention but he was more focused on the letter he was writing to Margaret which was hidden under his math book. Geometry and school meant little to him now. As stuffy old Mr. Deem demonstrated a geometry problem on the blackboard Harold quickly wrote a few more lines. He was trying to convince her to run away with him and find a place where they could start a new life together. The letter was a plea from his heart but he knew Margaret wasn't the type to run away from home and leave her family. She insisted that Harold go and find his way in life whatever that was going to be before coming back for her.

Staying at Will and Irene's wasn't an option either and Harold knew for certain Frank would exact his revenge upon Harold and probably hurt him badly if he did go back home. In their short meetings after lunch at school and in the letters they were secretly exchanging Margaret was increasingly pushing Harold to speed up his decision and get out of Sac City before he was forced to face his father again. She also knew what would happen next and it terrified her.

While Mr. Deem continue to drone on the class heard a knock at the door. Mr. Deem, who hated being interrupted flushed deeply. Harold sat chewing the end of his pencil when suddenly he heard his name being called.

"Harold. Harold Brooks. Grab up your things and go to the office with Mrs. Sanderson."

Harold looked up from his letter not sure of what he'd heard. Everyone in the classroom was staring at him.

"Now Mr. Brooks!" Deem yelled.

"Yes sir," Harold muttered quickly gathering up his book, pencils and letter which he jammed in his pants pocket. *What now?* he wondered. Getting called to Mr. Caldwell's office was never good for anyone as he knew all too well. As he hurried towards the door Harold stumbled over his own feet and nearly fell to the floor causing the geometry class to snicker at him. Mrs. Sanderson, the high school secretary held the door as he passed and then quickly turned down the hallway.

"Come with me," she said flatly.

"Did I do something wrong Mrs. Sanderson?" Harold asked smiling feebly.

She ignored the question and walked quickly down the hall with heavy footsteps in her enormous old shoes echoing loudly off the walls. Like many of the older high school teachers and staff Mrs. Sanderson was an aging, straight-laced Victorian disciplinarian who didn't seem to ever smile and certainly didn't engage the students on a personal level. She took her duties as the assistant to the principle, the fearsome Mr. Caldwell with his huge hands seriously. Harold and most of the other boys at school thought of her as the gatekeeper to Hell.

Reaching the office she opened the door and held it open. "Go on into Mr. Caldwell's office immediately but make sure you knock first," she said curtly.

"Yes ma'am."

Taking five shaky steps to the inner door, Harold stopped and knocked three times.

"Enter," A deep voice rumbled from within.

Harold wiped his sweaty hands on his pants and opened the door. To his horror, Frank was seated in front of Mr. Caldwell and his huge oak desk.

"Come in Mr. Brooks," Mr. Caldwell said. "Stand here in front of your father and me."

"Yes sir," Harold croaked. His shaking legs didn't seem to want to cooperate but somehow he managed to slink to where Caldwell was pointing.

"Your father and I have had a very nice visit about you and some of the problems you've been having," Caldwell began. "And I don't like seeing any of my young people going down the wrong path, certainly one that involves lying to one's parents and one that defies the word of God. That just won't do Mr. Brooks. It won't do at all."

Harold stood silently with his eyes down.

Caldwell leaned forward placing his enormous hands flat on the desk. "Furthermore, when one of my young men finds himself filled with lust and sin and then has the audacity to attempt to ruin a fine young lady while defying his parents I see that I've failed and that fills me with a tremendous amount of regret. I can fully understand your father's duress."

His dark eyes pierced through Harold's soul. "Look at me, Mr. Brooks."

Harold slowly raised his eyes to look at the fearsome principle.

"Your father and I have agreed that he will take care of this and we've come up with a good solution to end your troubles. You'll be leaving with him immediately to go home. Is that understood?"

Harold looked at Frank and back to Mr. Caldwell. "Yes sir."

Mr. Caldwell stood and extended his right hand to Harold.

"Good luck young man. Come and see me once you've gotten things in order."

Frank didn't say a word during the walk home and stared straight ahead with no expression on his face either. Harold had a hard time keeping up with him and half-ran as they made their way the six blocks home. With each step closer to home, the fear rising in his chest made it harder and harder for him to breathe. No matter what the outcome was going to be Harold did know one thing for certain: If he were going to get beaten again he would fight back just as he had before even if it killed him.

The two continued walking in silence. It was a cold, still and sunny day but everything appeared to be abnormal and out of place: the winter sunlight cast an unearthly glare on the world. Harold looked at the sun-soaked houses, yards and trees though the eyes of someone who knows something bad is about to happen

Once they reached the house Frank held the door open. "Go in and sit at the dining room table," He ordered in a low voice.

Harold paused for a moment sure that Frank would hit him as soon as he walked past. Strangely, his father hadn't made eye contact with him since he'd seen him at the school.

"Yes sir."

Walking in and removing his coat, Harold saw his mother jump up from where she'd been sitting at the table. In her left hand she clutched a handkerchief tightly and from the looks of her she had been crying for some time. Harold took a deep breath which calmed him slightly. He knew from years and years of experience that Frank wouldn't beat him too badly in front of his mother so maybe it wouldn't be too bad.

After sitting down Nina reached over and squeezed his hand before sobbing into her handkerchief. Other than this, the silence was overwhelming.

Frank didn't bother sitting down but instead pulled a large envelope out of his pocket and slapped it down on the table. He then stood with his chest puffed out and put his hands on his hips, something he did when he was about to say something important. "Your mother and I have decided along with Mr. Caldwell to send you away to a new school for the rest of the year."

Harold froze and felt his stomach churn into a knot.

"After the other night I realized that I've raised a selfish, mentally troubled young man who can't control himself or his sinful urges. That hurts me son. I've always had high hopes for you and I thought that I'd done better. It seems that I haven't and I will not allow you to defy me."

Harold looked across the table at his mother who had been watching him intently. She burst into tears.

Frank continued on in a monotonous rumble. "Since you've decided to turn away from your family and your faith I don't have any other choice. You're going to St. John's Military School in Minnesota on Friday. That's in three days. In that time you will pack your suitcase and you will not leave the house. If I need to, I'll have the constable lock you up downtown. He owes me a favor and believe me, I've considered it."

Harold stared at him with horror etched on his face. Everyone in the northwest part of Iowa had heard of St. John's. Tommy Rowe, a friend of Harold's at school had a brother named Ralph who was there. It was a prison where the boys were routinely beaten for minor offenses and the doors and windows were barred and locked. No one was allowed to leave the grounds without their parents and most boys were locked in the grounds for several years at a time until they graduated. Harold thumbed through the literature Frank had thrown on the table in front of him and felt his insides crawl. It claimed they provided young men with military discipline in a strictly Christian environment which would make honest, morally upstanding citizens out of troubled young men. It sounded as though the school was a great place but he knew better. Ralph, he remembered, had been a real troublemaker and was notorious in Sac City for breaking into houses and stealing everything he could carry away. There were also rumors that he'd held a local girl down and forced himself upon her after beating her senseless. Ralph wasn't a nice person and if he were in St. John's that told Harold what kind of place it really was.

"Is there anything you'd like to say?" Frank asked, his eyes burning into Harold.

"No sir," Harold replied. "Not a word."

Frank's face flushed a deep red. "I see."

After the initial shock, Harold suddenly realized that this could work to his advantage. After all, once he was on the train heading north for Minnesota and the hell of St. John's all he'd have to do is simply jump off and go where he wished. A tiny smile crept into the corners of his mouth. Frank however, was one step ahead of him.

"It's probably best if you didn't. You and I will be leaving on the morning train Friday. It usually comes through town about nine o'clock." He turned to Nina. "I'll need at least two or three days' worth of clothes and possibly one of my suits," he ordered. "And, the boy and I will need some sandwiches and food to get us there."

Harold wanted to scream. He knew that if his father were riding along to deliver him to the school he'd never let the boy out of his sight so his plan to jump off the train somewhere was impossible.

Nina stood up and walked over to hug and kiss Harold. She was still crying. "It wasn't my idea," she whispered in his ear.

Harold found he couldn't breathe because of the pounding in his chest. What was he going to do now and how was he going to get in touch with Margaret if he was going to be locked in the house until Friday?

Frank looked on with a smile. He hadn't moved since beginning his lecture and Harold could see that he was quite pleased with himself. "Go on up to your room and start packing your things. The list is right there in the packet they sent me and I expect you to take exactly what they've listed. Understand?"

Harold decided to play along with his father for now in the hopes that he'd find the opening he needed. "Yes sir." Harold replied. "I'm sorry for what I've done, I really am. How long will I have to be there?"

Frank rubbed his chin thoughtfully. "Well, at least until May when the term is over. If I get good reports from the Colonel we might have you come back in the summer. If you cause problems you'll stay there until you graduate. That's over a year, boy, so you better straighten up."

Frank's tone of voice had changed dramatically from authoritative into a more normal, calm voice. Harold could tell that he thought he'd gotten the best of his son. *You'll find out otherwise old man,* he thought to himself.

Harold trudged slowly up to his room while his mind raced with ideas about how he would get out of Sac City before Friday morning. Reaching his room, Harold noticed one of his parent's old suitcases sitting in the middle of the floor. Throwing the St. John's literature onto his desk, he looked out the window to the tree he'd climbed on as he came and went to his secret meetings with Margaret. With his hands on the window sill Harold could feel that the wooden frame had been slightly dented and dinged and the window seemed to be racked. Running his fingers along the top he could see and feel the reason for the window's distress. His father had nailed it shut with number eights, nice long heavy nails that wouldn't come out easily.

"Son of a bitch!" Harold almost yelled.

"What was that son?" his father asked.

Harold spun around to see Frank standing in the doorway still wearing the amused smirk on his face.

"Nothing. Just, looking out the window," he answered letting the curtain fall back.

Frank didn't move from the door. "You better start packing. Once you're done I'll inspect the suitcase to make sure you don't foul that up. You'll need to make a good first impression on your new schoolmates."

Frank turned to leave but suddenly turned back. "Don't get ideas about sneaking out either. I told you that you're to stay in this house until we leave on Friday. If I catch you outside I'll skin you then it's straight down to the city jail. Understand?"

"Yes sir."

"And no more with that Nicholson girl either. You've done enough to shame her and her family."

Frank stomped away leaving Harold alone.

MIDNIGHT FLIGHT

January 11, 1918

B obby sat on the edge of the bed watching Harold pack his things. He sniffled and wiped his nose on the dirty sleeve of his nightshirt. Harold reached over and ruffled the boy's hair. Bobby had cried when their mother had told him that Harold was leaving.

"I wish you could stay home Harold," he said. "I won't have anybody to play with when you're gone. Why do you have to go away?"

Harold stopped folding the pants he had been packing in the suitcase and sat on the bed next to Bobby. "I told you. Dad wants me to go to a new school for a few months so that he and I don't get into tussles anymore. Like the one we had last week. It's going to be okay Bobby. I swear it will be."

Sighing deeply, Harold turned to retrieve more clothes out of his dresser. His biggest worries had always been about Bobby and keeping him safe from their father. There was no way around it now. During their walks to and from school he kept working with the boy teaching him how to avoid their father and what to do if he came after him. Harold's advice was simple: run, either to Will and Irene's or to the Nicholson's.

Bobby fell back on the bed gently bouncing himself up and down. Harold reached into the dresser and grabbed some underclothes while carefully watching him out of the corner of his eye. The boy was lost in thought so Harold stepped to the closet and knelt down to put the socks and underwear into the small canvas duffel bag he had carefully hidden amongst the old clothes and toys filling the closet.

With the suitcase for St. John's packed and the duffel hidden away, Harold flopped onto the bed and turned to watch Bobby who by now was almost asleep. Reaching over, he stroked the boy's hair gently.

"It's going to be okay. Whenever I come back you'll come and live with me and we can go anywhere we want. Margaret will be with us too."

Bobby barely opened his eyes and rolled over to Harold who held him tightly in his arms. "Alright," he mumbled before drifting off to sleep.

Harold continued to hold him until he too fell asleep.

The next morning he awoke with a start and sat up in the darkness in a cold sweat. His sleep had been restless and broken and the night was filled with terrible dreams in which he was being dragged back home, bloody and beaten by his enraged father. Rubbing his tired eyes, Harold realized that today was the day he finally put his plans to work.

After doing his daily morning chores of stoking the furnace with coal, Harold disappeared upstairs to bathe in order to avoid a silent, uncomfortable breakfast with Frank. Despite the steaming hot water he shivered at the thought of what the day would bring. After several months of planning and discussing it all with Margaret he was fairly sure he could pull it all off. The unknown and unexpected however gnawed at him.

Toweled off and dressed, Harold walked into his room to help Bobby get ready for school. The child was puffy-eyed from sleep and his blonde hair shot out in several directions. Yawning deeply, he tried to button his shirt but couldn't manage to get the button through the hole so. Harold sat down on the edge of the bed to help him. He was trying not to cry.

"Okay Bobby. You're set."

"Yeah," Bobby replied yawning again. "I don't want to go to school today. I want to stay home with you."

Harold's eyes welled up. "Sorry. You have to go to school. But, I'll see you later."

Harold looked back at the door and reached into his pocket to pull out a nickel and a folded, sealed envelope. He held them up in front of Bobby. "I have a secret job for you to do today. You can't tell anyone about it, not ever. Understand?"

Bobby nodded.

"When you go to school today you make sure you give this to Margaret but don't let anyone see you do it, especially Mary."

He handed the envelope to Bobby who shoved it deep into his pocket and continued. "Since this is a top-secret job that's very, very important I'm giving you a nickel. Remember. Don't tell anyone."

Bobby looked at Harold and nodded again. His eyes went from the nickel back to his brother. "Okay Harold. I won't tell."

"Good boy," Harold said patting him on the shoulder. "It's our secret."

Downstairs they could hear their mother calling up to Bobby to come down to leave for school. It was time for him to go.

Harold reached out and pulled Bobby in close hugging him tightly. Tears began streaming out of his tightly clenched eyes. "You take care of yourself today, okay little brother?"

Bobby hugged Harold back. "I will."

"When I'm gone I'll write you. You make sure you write me back and tell me everything that's going on. And you be good for

Mom and Dad and don't get in trouble. Can you do that for me? I want you to be a man now."

"I will Harold. I promise. I don't want you to go."

Bobby began to cry too and it tore Harold apart.

Nina stepped into the bedroom and watched her two sons for a moment. "Bobby, you need to get going to school so you're not late," she said softly. "Mary's already left."

Bobby looked at his mother and back at Harold.

"Go on. I'll see you soon, little brother. I love you," Harold said reassuringly.

"I love you too, Harold."

With that, the boy bounded out of the room and down the steps slamming the door on his way out. Harold stood at the window watching Bobby run down the sidewalk to school. He sighed deeply wondering to himself when, or if he'd ever see him again. Harold turned to speak to his mother but she too was gone, walking laboriously down the steps.

The next few hours were a torture. Harold alternately paced the floor, laid on his bed and worked on two letters one for Margaret and one for Bobby. Finally, at noon his mother called up to him to come downstairs for lunch. He had heard his father arrive home a few moments before and dreaded another silent meal with the man. Entering the dining room he could see that Frank had already devoured his pie and had turned his attention towards the chicken and biscuits on his plate. Harold's stomach was churning with fear and anticipation but he forced himself to eat knowing that he might not get much in the next few days. The three ate in silence until Frank spoke up, the first words he had spoken to Harold in nearly two days.

"Are you packed and ready to go?" he asked pointing his fork at Harold.

"Yes sir. I got it done last night. I used the checklist St. John's sent so I should have everything."

"Good," Frank answered before diving into his plate. "You don't need much. They'll give you uniforms and whatever else you need. Son-of-a-bitches are expensive enough."

Twenty-minutes later Frank pushed his plate away, stretched and wiped his mouth. "Well time for my nap and time for you to get back upstairs."

As Nina cleared the table Frank went into the living room and laid down on the sofa for his daily lunch-hour nap. Harold quickly went to the living room book case, retrieved a book and hustled back upstairs to his room. Closing the door behind him he opened the book and pulled out the map of Iowa that he'd hidden inside it the day before. It went into the hidden duffel bag with the rest of his belongings. This done, Harold sat down at his desk and gazed out the window and watched snow gently falling from the dark, overcast sky. The small clock on his desk slowly ticked away drawing him closer to the destiny that had pulled at him for so long. Finally, after nearly an hour of agonizing waiting in a trance-like condition he was overjoyed to hear his father's voice rumbling downstairs.

"Come on old man." Harold whispered to himself. "Get the hell out of here."

A thump indicated that Frank was finally on his way back to the lumber yard. Harold slid over to peek through the crack in the curtains to see Frank turn to walk the six blocks back to the lumber yard. While he watched he could hear his mother climbing the steps. In one swift move, he vaulted from the window to his bed, climbed under the covers pretending to be asleep. Nina gently knocked, then entered his room. Harold kept his eyes closed and felt his mother sit on the edge of the bed. She ran her hand gently over Harold's head and stopped for a moment as if she were lost in thought. Finally, wordlessly, she gently kissed him, stood and made her way back down the steps. Harold waited, wondering what she was doing. After a moment he heard the familiar thump of the front door and leapt from the bed back to the window. Below, he could see his mother all bundled up walking to the front sidewalk where she turned and began the walk downtown. She paused a moment and turned to look up at the window Harold was peeking out of and continued on her way.

"Where in the world is she going?" he said out loud. Normally, Nina did her shopping on Mondays and besides, Frank had told her not to leave the house as long as Harold was locked away upstairs. Without bothering to think about this sudden bit of good fortune any longer Harold jumped into action and ran to his closet throwing out the duffel bag and the old ratty coat that had once been his father's. With them in hand, he ran down the steps nearly falling in the process. Once in the kitchen he threw the bag and coat at the back door and yanked the door open on the icebox and grabbed several items of food including the leftover chicken and biscuits from lunch. These went into a smaller cloth bag that Harold had snatched from the kitchen earlier in the morning after doing his coal chores. Next, he took the empty milk bottle his mother had rinsed out after lunch. Running clumsily to the back door, Harold put on his boots and tied them with shaking hands, threw on the coat and a hat, grabbed the duffel bag and shot out the door. The cold wind slapped him in the face sending a chill through his body as he ran to the back of the shed and finished tying his shoes.

Pulling the cap down low over his eyes he strode out to the street and looked to his right. Several blocks down was his mother still walking away from the house. Luckily, he thought, no one else was in sight so he turned and headed towards the edge of town and the river.

Harold walked slowly and deliberately as though he didn't have a care in the world. He didn't want anyone in town to see him running along like a madman. That would arouse suspicion and Frank might find out if someone recognized him. Finally reaching the end of Tenth Street and the wooded ground, Harold carefully looked behind himself and ducked into the timber. After taking a few steps in the crunchy dead leaves and undergrowth he stopped behind tree and gathered himself with a smile: He'd made it out of the house, now he had to keep moving.

For the next two hours Harold made his way through the thick timber and undergrowth that lined the brown, half-frozen Raccoon River stopping occasionally to hide behind a tree and warm himself. Snow continued falling in light, airy wisps adding to the silence and solitude along the riverbank. He was thankful the snow wasn't sticking to the ground; otherwise he would leave tracks for his father to follow. The thought of Frank tracking him down in a rage made him shiver, and urged him onward. In the distance the bells in the courthouse rang out four times indicating it was four o'clock. That meant school was out for the day and hopefully Bobby had delivered the letter to Margaret. Sneaking along the riverbank was taking longer than he'd expected but Harold knew his way well here since he'd spent most of his life with Bobby and his friends exploring, fishing and hunting this long stretch of wilderness.

The north end of Sac City was at a curve in the river and ran around to the east before curving back to the south through the lower end of town. Harold knew if he followed it far enough he would reach the southern outskirts of Sac City and the cannery which was idle and empty this time of year. Beyond that another half a mile was Alton Moore's farm and his destination for the time being. However, he had to pass underneath the east-west road bridge and pass the pond, an area which offered little cover. He hoped the old torn up coat of his father's would convince anyone seeing him that he was one of the hobo's who sometimes passed through town.

The snow began coming down heavier as Harold reached the bridge. Pausing down close to the edge of the water behind an old washed-up log he watched and waited. A horse drawn wagon clattered across and was soon followed by a meandering, sputtering delivery truck. Harold watched both drivers as they crossed above him. Neither was looking around and saw only the road in front of them. Waiting and watching, Harold couldn't see any more traffic or people out walking and quickly left his cover to sprint the twenty yards of bare ground between the bridge and overflow pond to the south. Ducking back into the heavy timber, Harold exhaled with relief, turned back to look one more time and continued on. Thankfully the snow was now coming down in sheets and provided him with a little camouflage.

After another hour of pushing himself he finally reached the deserted cannery building which loomed out of the darkness and heavily falling snow.

"God, I pray Bobby gave Margaret the letter. Please…" He muttered to himself watching the vacant building. Just then his eyes caught a sudden bit of movement made him stop. It moved again and through the falling snow and rapidly fading daylight Harold could barely make out a lone figure standing behind the building. His heart nearly leapt out of his chest when he was able to get a glimpse of Margaret.

Harold carefully left the timber and ran directly to her.

"You made it. Thank God. You made it," he said breathlessly.

"Of course I did. I can't let you leave without saying goodbye," Margaret said squeezing him with a hug.

"I would have done anything to see you."

"I just can't believe your father was going to send you to St. John's? That's horrible."

"Oh, yes. You should have seen him gloating and feeling good about punishing me with that. He could barely contain himself," Harold answered with a laugh.

"At least I won't have to think about you being there. Are you sure of what you're doing though? Is this what you want?"

Harold paused for a moment before answering her. "I'm sure. This is what I have to do, that is unless you want to come with me. We can go anywhere we want. Boston, San Francisco, New York. Anywhere."

Margaret shook her head. "You know I can't. Not right now. You have to go and do what you've planned. I've prayed about it and God tells me that this is your destiny."

"I wish I was as sure about this as you are," Harold answered. "It just seems all so strange, like this is all a crazy dream of some sort."

"Posh," Margaret replied. "You've talked about this for a long time and you know it's what you have to do. I've told you all along, I'll be here waiting for you when you come back. You know that."

"I know but I feel like I'm abandoning you."

"You're not. You have to believe me, okay?"

The light of the day began to fade rapidly into darkness causing the temperature to drop several degrees.

"So, what's your plan?" Margaret asked through trembling lips.

"First, let's go inside out of the cold," Harold said gesturing to the back door. "We can get into the manager's office and warm up. There's a stove in there."

"Isn't the building locked?"

"Well, it's supposed to be. Alton's father hides moonshine out here when the cannery is shut down for the winter. The key should be hidden...right here," Harold exclaimed digging a small metal box out from behind a pile of empty crates.

Margaret giggled and followed Harold into the dark interior of the building. The overpowering smell of cooked vegetables filled their noses. "My goodness, it smells odd in here," she said.

"It sure does. You should smell it when they're up and running in the fall," Harold replied. "It will definitely put a person off green beans, beets and corn. Here, here's the manager's office."

Harold led Margaret into the small office and lit a lantern which Alton Jr. had left on the desk for him which bathed the space in flickering yellow light. Now that he could see what he was doing he went directly to the cast iron stove in the corner and started inside its belly with some firewood in a box next to it.

"There, it should warm up in here now. I brought a blanket along. Care to sit with me over here?"

"Yes, I'm freezing," Margaret replied through chattering teeth.

The couple sat together in the corner and wrapped the blanket tightly around one another. Harold sighed contentedly.

"I wish we could stay like this forever."

Margaret leaned in close and kissed him softly on the lips. "I do too."

Harold smiled and gently stroked her hair. Suddenly, a thought came to him which made his stomach cringe with worry. "Say, aren't you going to be in a lot of trouble for seeing me? You're not at home."

Margaret grinned excitedly. "Yes, I'm probably in a lot of trouble," she replied. "But, I just had to see you before you leave and thankfully you sent me the letter through Bobby. I'll have to deal with the punishment when I get home."

"But what if your father whips you with his belt again?" Harold asked angrily. "I can't stand the thought of that at all."

"Oh, it's okay. He never hits me that hard and besides," she said with a giggle, "I just put on extra undergarments under my dresses so I don't even feel a thing. I cry as though it hurts and then he stops."

Harold threw back his head and barked with laughter. "You're still going to be in a lot of trouble!"

Margaret reached her head up and kissed him again. "I'd do anything to be with you and I'll face my parents without any regrets," she said softly. "Now, what's your plan?"

"Well okay, I'm meeting Alton Moore here at midnight if he shows up. His parent's don't know he's running away with me and I don't know if he's still going to go through with our plan. If he does show up, we'll wait a day or two until things cool off in town, then we're headed south to Lake Mills or Auburn to jump the train."

"That's a good plan, Harold, but don't you think you should get out of here as soon as possible? The longer you're in the area the more likely the chances are your father will find you."

Harold thought for several moments before answering her. He knew his father was probably already in a rage and more than likely had convinced the local police to form a posse to search for him. Even though the cannery was three miles outside of town they'd surely search it at some point.

"I think you should wait for Alton and if he doesn't show up then go on your own. Head towards Odeboldt and catch one of the trains there," Margaret said, her eyes shining in the light of the fire as a plan began to take shape in her mind. "Besides, if I slip back home tomorrow morning we both know your father will start with me. And if I suddenly appear tomorrow he'll think you're long gone. Maybe I can throw him off for you."

"Are you sure you want to do that? I mean, he'll be fit to be tied."

"He wouldn't dare lay a finger on me nor would my father allow him to as much as raise his voice to me. I'm his little girl and your father is, well, a brute."

Harold nodded with a smile on his face.

"I think you forget how much my father dislikes your father," she continued. "Even though he's a minister I believe he'd thump on Frank's head with vengeance of biblical proportions if need be."

"Very true my dear, very true," Harold cackled. He paused a moment and reached a hand inside the heavy coat to gently stroke the small box he'd brought along. Despite the cold a bead of sweat ran down his face as he tried trying to work up the courage to pull it out.

"What is it?" she asked as he reached down to grip her hand tightly.

"I bought you something for your birthday a couple months ago but I decided to hang on to for a special occasion. This is just such an occasion."

Harold pulled out a small black box with a piece of pink ribbon tied around it. "For you."

Margaret took it from him and smiled. "You don't have to buy me anything. You need your money."

"I had to buy you this. I want you to know how much I love you."

Margaret undid the ribbon and slowly opened it. Inside was the gold ring he'd bought from Will. "Oh my..." she gasped. "Oh my goodness, it's...it's beautiful!"

Harold removed the ring from the box and gently slid it onto her ring finger. "There. Does it fit?"

Margaret's eyes glittered as she admired her ring. "Yes. I love it. Thank you!"

She began to cry while Harold held her close and stroked her hair. Without speaking, they looked at one another and smiled. They kissed and Harold gently, tentatively, touched her breasts causing her to gasp again and pull him closer. Her hands touched his chest. Before each knew what was happening they sought out the warmth with each other, their bodies not yet familiar but intimate. Neither had ever done this before but they felt comfortable in their deep and total affection for one another as they slowly made love, their body heat rising in small wisps.

An hour later the couple slowly stirred hearing a noise outside the office door.

"Oh, no," Harold whispered jumping to douse the lantern but before he could get to it Alton Jr. slipped inside and stood grinning from ear to ear as his eyes adjusted to the low light.

"My, my, Harold. You ain't got no clothes on!"

Harold blushed and instinctively looked down. He was indeed naked as the day he was born except for the wool socks on his feet.

"What you doin'?"

"Nothing!"

Margaret came back around and shrieked when she saw Alton Jr. standing in the room. "Get out!" she cried pulling the blanket over her body.

"Hell, she ain't got no clothes on either!"

"Alton! Give us a minute?" Harold exclaimed pointing to the door. "Now!"

Alton Jr. laughed and shook his head as he walked out. Harold and Margaret scrambled around throwing their clothes on.

"He saw me," Margaret said angrily. "Naked."

Harold couldn't help but laugh while pulling his trousers up. "If it makes you feel any better he saw me too."

"Harold!"

Once he finished dressing he turned his back and waited for Margaret.

"Okay, I'm dressed," she said breathlessly.

Harold opened the door suddenly and peered out into the dark interior of the cannery.

"Junior? We're dressed, come on back."

Alton Jr. appeared like a ghost from around the corner and entered the tiny office smelling of cold air, sweat and cooked vegetables. His face was still plastered with a smirk.

"Not a word!" Harold hissed.

"Oh, I won't," he replied setting the burlap bag containing his possessions down on the floor before going to the stove to warm his hands. "Uh, sorry I saw you naked Margaret."

Margaret glared at him with a fury in her eyes Harold had never seen before.

"So, what are we going to do?"

Harold walked over to put his arm around Margaret and also to shield Alton Jr. from her. "I think a change of plans: I don't want my father catching us so we leave right now. We'll head west to Odebolt on foot and jump the train for Des Moines there. Margaret's idea."

Alton Jr. nodded and looked at Margaret with the toothy smile he had. "Good idea. I'm ready when you are. I'll uh, wait for you outside."

"Good," Harold answered.

"Ready?' he asked Margaret. Her lips trembled as she nodded, her face screwing itself up while she tied a scarf under her chin. "I think so," she said feebly.

Harold led her to the door and led her outside into the darkness of the cold night which was still and silent. A dog yipped in the distance, its voice echoing sharply through the brittle air. The snow had eased but still fell in white floating wisps.

Margaret reached over and brushed snow from Harold's coat and smiled despite her tear soaked face. "Take care of yourself."

Harold enveloped her in a hug. "I'll write to you as soon as I can. I promise. Don't ever forget, I love you more than anything."

A choking sob escaped her mouth before she could speak. "I love you too. You better write me, you silly. I'll pray for you until you come home to me."

The couple continued to hold one another tightly and kissed again.

"Go," she finally said in a barely audible voice. "Go live your adventure."

"Well Harold," Alton Jr. asked quietly from the shadows. "Are you ready?"

"Yeah," he replied wiping his wet eyes and nose on his coat sleeve. "Let's go."

With that, the two boys swung their bags over their shoulders and set off walking west down the dark, lonely country road the twenty or so miles towards Odebolt and the train that would take them to Des Moines and hopefully, on to France.

CAMP DODGE, IOWA

January 16, 1918

Camp Dodge smelled of sweat, mud, horse shit, and fear. An unusual heat wave bringing high temperatures warmed the early winter afternoon and cast a dusty, depressing pall over a rickety, stinking building filled with young men about to enter the Army. Some who had come to enlist were swelling up boasting about their future acts of bravery, while those men who had been drafted mostly kept to themselves. Harold stood nervously waiting for something, anything to happen. When he, Alton and other Iowa farm, city and town boys stood in line at the recruiter's office in Carroll, Iowa he'd been afraid that the fat sergeant behind the desk wouldn't believe he was eighteen. Actually, he was only seventeen and only just that.

Despite their fears, he and Alton were fed a stale sandwich and packed on train full of boys who were barely old enough to be called men to be sent to Camp Dodge for their Army physicals and basic training. After a torturous two day trip to Des Moines, their fifth overall since leaving Sac City, they finally entered the sprawling Camp. A herd of scurrying, profane Corporals directed them off the platform with with shouts and kicks.

"You new men!" one shouted at Harold's group as they stumbled out of the stinking railcar into the strangely warm, humid air. "Line up right here and no fucking smoking and no fucking talking! We're marching your dumb asses over to Building C for your physicals. To your left. Move out!"

"Here we go," Harold exclaimed barely able to conceal his excitement.

"No fucking talking!" the corporal screamed with his mouth on Harold's ear.

"Think they'll let us have a bath once we're done?" Alton whispered. "I think I got some critters on me from that last boxcar we rode in."

Harold smiled at his friend and watched the corporal run down the line of men to scream at someone else behind them. "I hope so. We both smell like cows. I could eat too."

"Oh, brother, steak..." Alton Jr. said wide-eyed.

The Corporal reached the front of the building and stood with his hands on his hips. Some of the other men joked and laughed to see just how far they could push the corporal. Instead of screaming and slapping the offenders he only glared at this new batch of recruits with disdain.

"Line up here! Once the line starts moving inside you will enter the building and proceed through the designated lines. And you will all keep your filthy fucking mouths shut! I ain't tellin' none of you that again!"

Several men laughed while others looked away trying to avoid the probing red eyes of the corporal. While they waited for the line to start moving Harold noticed a few men walking back towards the front gates of the Camp from the end of the row of buildings where his group stood waiting. Many danced and sang like drunken men after being rejected because of flat feet, stomach ulcers or other physical ailments the Army disqualified men for. They were obviously draftees who had no wish to be forced into the service. Harold however, knew he had to get in and if for some reason he got rejected he'd try the Navy and then the Merchant Marine. From what he'd heard they were desperate for sailors to man the U.S. Merchant ships running war supplies to Europe and would take almost any man with a pulse. The thought of drowning in a dark ship in the freezing waters of the North Atlantic didn't sit well with him but even it had to be better than going home. If he had to die, he knew he'd rather it be as a real man, in battle against the Germans. For a time he'd also considered crossing the border into Canada and enlisting in their army before he'd left home but the newspapers said Canadians weren't accepting Americans into their armed forces anymore. That was a pity, a gambit like that would really have thrown his father off. An older boy Harold knew from Sac City had done that in 1914 and was killed a year later at some place called Ypres. His family never knew where, or if, he'd been buried. His mother openly cried in church every Sunday because she was afraid he hadn't been given a good Christian burial service.

"Next! Move up the goddamn steps!" A sallow little man with a tinny, high pitched voice shrieked at Harold and Alton Jr. His eyes were nothing more than small slits.

"Excuse me, what?" Harold asked innocently. The man's liver-spotted hands suddenly grabbed Harold by the throat.

"Move your fucking ass up the steps boy! Keep a-movin'!"

With a shove and a quick kick in the backside he threw Harold up the steps where he fell into a group of men who had just met the corporal. One had the imprint of a red hand swelling up on the side of his face. He was crying.

"That man struck me!" the boy cried. "You all saw it didn't you?"

The men around him muttered and moved away up the stairs. Harold looked around wiping stale, slimy sweat from his face and grimaced at the cowering figure at his feet. No one seemed to be willing to help him partly out of fear for more corporals further on up the line. Finally, another young man stepped forward to help the boy. Grabbing his arms he and Harold lifted him up despite the rancid sweat under his arms and the tears sliding down his face.

The other man was tall and blonde, muscular with broad shoulders and didn't seem to be bothered by the chaos going on around him in the least. With a broad, toothy smile he brushed the boy's stained shirt and wiped the tears from his sad eyes.

"Heavens, brother. What's all this about? Just need to keep moving along. I'm sure the corporal doesn't mean a bit of it, even if he is a rat-faced little monkey," he said loudly and with authority. Clearly, he didn't care if the corporal heard him or not. Judging from the size of this boy, Harold figured the corporal didn't stand a chance either.

"The little bastard might want to try me! Hell, I'll challenge him to a wrestling match. Right here, and maybe he can smell my backside while I'm at it too!"

The tiny corporal marched over in a fury and sized the large boy up with his squinty eyes and turned to disappear down the steps looking for a new victim to bully.

"I'm sure momma wouldn't like my unfavorable reference to one of God's creatures but he does remind me of a large steamy pile of cow shit," the young man said to no one in particular.

The corporal marched down the stairs to accost two men who'd decided to sit down while they waited for the line to move. "Now, just what in the fuck are you two doing? Get up! Goddamn, we're gonna lose the war for sure with this bunch of Iowa pig shit!"

Harold looked at the boy who had been crying. His face was bright red and his eyes didn't seem to register with what was going on around him. The big farm boy stood on the steps humming hymns to himself, oblivious to the sweltering chaos going on around him. He turned to look at the boy with a big smile.

"Doin' alright?" He asked.

The boy swayed and Harold struggled to keep him on his feet.

"I think," he answered weakly. "Sure am thirsty though."

With a sly look, the farm boy pulled a bottle out of his small cardboard case.

"Here," he said. "Take a drink but don't let anyone else see."

The boy drank deeply, relishing the warm, stale water. He sighed and with a blessing from the bigger man, passed the bottle to Harold who also drank eagerly.

"Good huh?" the bigger man asked.

"Like mother's milk," the boy answered.

"Yeah," replied Harold extending his hand. "Good. I'm Harold Brooks by the way."

The bigger man laughed deeply, carefully hiding his now half-full water bottle from the other thirsty eyes around them.

"I'm Merle. Merle Hamilton's the name!"

After nearly two hours of standing in line with other nervous, smelly men, Harold finally reached the first tables manned by corporals and sergeants where they were instructed to fill out a series of forms being handed out. Harold took his and moved to the next set of tables where other men sat and filled in their name, birth date, education level and more personal information. Some busily wrote while a few other men sat staring at the forms. Harold, the crying young man and the Merle quickly slid into chairs vacated by some previous men and began. After taking a minute to read through every word he started with his new birthday, March 27, 1897. That would make him twenty and he knew had to remember that from now on.

As he filled his forms out, he glanced up to see a young man across from him scratching his head and mumbling to himself. He had a nervous look on his face and kept licking his chapped, red lips. He hadn't written a thing down.

"What's the matter?" Harold asked gesturing to the man's papers with his pencil.

He looked over his shoulders and leaned in close to Harold with a shrug.

"Um, I can't read n' write so good. In fact, I can't read a thing. Don't know what to do with these papers."

The man went continued. "I got to join up. Got me a wife and two kids at home and another on the way. There ain't no jobs where I'm from neither. This way I can get away from the wife and make money to feed 'em all."

"Where you from?" Harold asked partly out of habit and mostly out of curiosity.

"Down southern Iowa." the man replied. "A little place called Davis City. I live out in the country on my daddy's farm but he's dead. So's my momma. I can't keep the place goin' and feed the wife and younguns so I'm joinin' up."

Harold looked over at his new companions, the crying boy and Merle. They both nodded to Harold. Merle spoke up.

"Help him out brother. The judge's son and I will wait until you're done with his and yours and we'll watch for those darned corporals. Come on now, help the man up like a good Christian."

The man smiled and Harold smiled back at him. Harold extended his hand and introduced himself. "Harold Brooks from Sac City."

"My name's Earl Noah Pugh. My momma liked Noah in the Bible so that's what she named me," he said with a wide gap-toothed grin as he shook Harold's hand. Harold introduced him to Merle and the crying boy whose name was T.C. Moore.

Taking Earl's forms, Harold began asking him the questions while he wrote his answers down. It went quickly. Earl had no education and wasn't sure of his birthday or his actual address either so the three made up a convincing life for him. Once he was finished the four men were kicked out by yet another screaming corporal to stand in line with the other recruits. On his way out, Harold saw Alton Jr. and waved. Alton Jr. waved back with a big grin on his face.

Harold and his new companions turned in their forms while a new batch of sergeants and some very old Lieutenants read through them, questioning each man.

The Lieutenant in charge of Harold's papers kept reading and glancing up at him. Harold knew he must look nervous. He did his best to act mature and to follow Merle's example, answering each question with confidence.

"You're twenty huh?" asked the Lieutenant.

"Yes sir," he replied shifting uncomfortably on his feet.

"Really? Have any proof of your birth? A birth certificate, letter from your parents, pastor, anything like that?" he asked watching carefully to see his reaction.

"No sir," Harold replied feeling what felt like a bucket of sweat run down his back. "I was born out west on my father's homestead in South Dakota which was about thirty miles from the nearest town. They sent me back to Iowa to live with my sister so I could go to school and I decided to stay." He'd rehearsed all of this on his trip to Des Moines and knew had to get it right.

"What have you been doing since you finished school?" asked the visibly tired Lieutenant rubbing his forehead.

"Building houses, sir. But I really want to join the Army and do my bit."

The Lieutenant looked Harold up and down again. "Hmm, is that right? If you're really a carpenter like you say, the Engineers could use you."

"I'll be happy wherever I can be used sir although I'd much rather be in the infantry."

The Lieutenant thumbed through a pile of folders at his side. Finding the one he wanted, he pulled it out and studied it for a moment. "Everyone wants to be in the infantry. Hell, all you boys think you'll all be big heroes'," said the Lieutenant stamping Harold's papers. "No one can get to the front lines if there aren't men there to build roads for them. Congrats, you're an Engineer if you pass the physical. They need all the men they can find who know anything. Next! Next man here!" he shouted. The interview was over.

"Goddammit," Harold muttered shaking his head disgustedly as he shuffled out of the line. He'd hoped to be in the front lines where all the action was, not building roads or digging latrines in the rear where nothing ever happened. He suddenly wished he'd joined the Marines instead. For a moment he considered walking out and doing just that but he hadn't seen anyone leave all day. Perhaps, he thought, it was already too late to change his mind.

Next came more lines and more waiting. Finally, the physical in which Harold was declared fit for duty as were Merle, T.C. and Earl who barely passed. Each man was given a folder containing all of their newly processed documents and sent down the steps of the building and out into the warm, still air of the parade ground. Men lolled about on the hard-packed ground waiting to be told what to do. Some smoked while others sat on the ground, some talking and laughing with friends, others standing with crossed arms and scowls on their faces staring at nothing.

After an hour of waiting, the hated corporals and sergeants came streaming out of the doors of the barracks yelling their usual profanities while slapping and kicking the men up into some semblance of order.

"Come to attention! Come to attention now!" yelled a sergeant striding through the mass of packed men. He stopped and grabbed Earl who was lagging behind in getting himself facing front and at attention. "Face this way you dumb fuck. And stand up straight!" he growled shoving Earl into place.

A Captain pushed through the crowd and climbed some steps up to a flag-draped platform to their front and began yelling through a hand-held speaking-trumpet to be heard.

"You men," he began. "Are about to undertake a noble mission in the service of your country. Raise your right hands and repeat after me."

Despite still being upset over his assignment to the engineers, Harold and the rest of the men filling the parade ground raised their right hands. Earl and a few others raised their left only to be pounced upon by the corporals. He knew he'd come too far now to back out and the faster the Captain administered the oath the slim chance that Frank would show up and drag him away evaporated.

"All right, engineers it is," Harold muttered to himself. "Maybe I can still figure out a way to get to the front once I'm in France."

With every man ready, the Captain continued: "I, state your name," he began. "I hereby declare, on oath, that I absolutely and entirely renounce and abjure all allegiance and fidelity to any foreign prince, potentate, state, or sovereignty of whom or which I have heretofore been a subject or citizen; that I will support and defend the Constitution and laws of the United States of America against all enemies, foreign and domestic; that I will bear true faith and allegiance to the same; that I will bear arms on behalf of the United States when required by the law; that I will perform noncombatant service in the Armed Forces of the United States when required by the law; that I will perform work of national importance under civilian direction when required by the law; and that I take this obligation freely without any mental reservation or purpose of evasion; so help me God."

The Captain looked out upon the mass of newly sworn-in recruits.

"Congratulations men," he shouted. "You are all now soldiers in the United States Army. Your training will commence immediately."

SIX WEEKS LATER

February 22, 1918

Freezing rain slapped noisily against the tar paper covered barracks, the wind finding cracks and then sweeping across the now well-worn wooden floor. Harold sat busily shining his good boots while smoking a Lucky Strike. He'd never smoked before joining the Army as it was one of the things his strict parents abhorred along with alcohol and after choking down the first few his second day in the army, he discovered he liked it.

Around him other men shined boots and smoked on this rare and cherished day off. Some were getting their bunks and gear folded and squared away, others cleaned their rifles while still more men whiled away the time playing cards, reading, writing letters home or sleeping. Sunday was the only day the men in the training company had any free time and they took advantage of it the best they could. Gazing into his distorted reflection in his boots, Harold thought about home, Margaret and Bobby. He had been at Camp Dodge for nearly two months and his father hadn't shown up yet. A good thing indeed.

"Hey Harold," a sleepy voice from above asked.

"Yeah?"

"Bum a smoke?"

Harold wordlessly handed the pack up to Alton Jr. and continued working on his boots.

"If only your old man could see you now," Alton Jr. said with a laugh handing the pack back. "Smoking and swearing like a sailor."

Harold exhaled smoke and held his boot out to look at the mirror shine. "He told me once that only pimps and bad women smoke cigarettes."

"So, which are you?" Alton Jr. jumped down and ruffled Harold's hair before picking up his matches to light the cigarette. "Any word from home?"

"Oh, a few letters from Margaret and a couple from Will since he's taking care of sending the one's she writes to me and then giving her the one's I write back. We can't write directly. You?"

"Naw, my ma and pa don't read or write so well but I've sent them a few. My brother's read to them."

"They doing okay?" Harold asked sliding the boots under his bed where they'd hopefully stay clean for the time being.

"My brother wrote me a couple weeks ago. Sounds like the folks weren't too upset about me leavin'."

"Oh yeah?"

"Yeah, one less mouth to feed I guess. The sheriff's been watching him a lot lately so the "business" ain't doin' as well as he'd like."

Harold flopped back on his bed and pulled the blanket over himself. "Sorry, Junior. I didn't mean to…"

"Aww, it's okay, Harold! Your old man…did he go insane? About you takin' off that is?"

"At first. Margaret said she'd never seen anyone so angry. He stomped around town for two days trying to find out where I went. Remember when I said he'd try to get a posse together to look for me?"

"He did?"

"Well, he tried but no one would help him except for Stan and I'm pretty sure he was forced into it. Not even his friends down at the lodge would help."

Alton Jr. threw back his head and roared with laughter until he began hacking. "I'll bet that was a sight to see, old Frank on the hunt like a coon dog!"

Harold laughed with his friend trying to imagine his father bug-eyed and red-faced walking all over town getting angrier by the minute. "Margaret said the first place he went was her house too. Evidently, he and the reverend had quite a row on his front porch when he wouldn't let Frank in to see her."

"Boy that would've been a sight wouldn't it? I'm off to the latrine," Alton Jr. said picking up his shaving kit. "What do you think the mess hall's going to have today?"

With a sigh, Harold rolled over and stubbed his cigarette out in a tin can next to his bunk. "What they have every Sunday, shit-on-a-shingle."

"Shit...well, I'll be back," Alton Jr. said with a grimace and a wave.

Harold waved noncommittally at his friend and pulled the blanket up tight under his chin. So far, the day was going well: He'd made his bunk but would have to make it again since he was lying in it, squared away his gear and had spent some time folding and refolding his trousers. Each item of Army gear no matter how small had its own particular place in the footlocker: Toothbrush, soap, razor, belt buckle, socks, shorts, shirts, belt and so on. It was maddeningly simple yet impossible to put every item in the right place every time to please the sergeants. The same went for the ancient Krag rifles the men had finally been allotted after training for weeks with broomsticks; they had to shine inside and out and never seemed to when it came time for inspection. Harold smiled to himself and turned on his side hoping for maybe another hour of sleep. In spite of the difficulties of basic, the army was growing on him and he enjoyed it.

The hard work and the seemingly endless amounts of pushups, marching, cleaning and other duties the men were required to do didn't bother Harold in the least. Though many men chafed under the strict routine, he and a few others quickly realized that most of these jobs were meaningless chores dreamt up to deprive them of sleep and to enforce humility. For Harold, basic training was certainly easier than living at home with his father. Sometimes in the long cold nights he dreamt of his father trying to hit or harass him now, and how he would punish him for it. The thought made him smile. "Try and bully me now old man," Harold muttered to himself. "I'll take care of you."

According to the first letter he'd received from Margaret, Frank had telegraphed ahead to every sheriff and constable in every town along the rail lines headed south to have them looking out for his missing son with orders to "drag him back in chains if need be". Evidently, his running away was the talk of the town for weeks after he had left. Harold had an idea though, that Frank had to have had some inkling of where he'd gone. His father wasn't stupid after all.

"Brooks! On your feet!" Sergeant Cox shouted as he strode into the drafty barracks.

Harold bolted to attention at the foot of his rickety bed. "Yes sergeant!"

Sergeant Cox was clearly displeased with having to go out on such a nasty day. He stood staring at Harold through dreary, bloodshot eyes. "Get your ass over to Company HQ! Get a fucking move on!" he shouted spraying Harold with breath that reeked of stale coffee and gin.

"Yes sergeant!"

"Smith and Vander Bek! Get your shit together and go with Private Brooks!"

"Yes sergeant!" the men replied jumping to attention.

All three dressed as fast as they could in their green OD tops, coats, hats and after pulling their newly shined boots on, headed for the door.

Shooting out of the barracks door with a shove from Sergeant Cox, Harold and the other two men ran through the cold rain and sucking mud towards the Company command post and the personnel office. The sideways freezing rain slashed at their faces as they ducked their heads to avoid the stinging drops of ice that was now mingling with the rain.

"What now?" asked Private Vander Bek, a slender farm boy with an enormous nose. "Surely they won't make us dig latrines in this will they?"

"Maybe they found out about what I did before I enlisted," replied Smith as he jumped a puddle. "I'd rather go back to jail than have to spend another day in this fucking place." He grimaced at what he'd said but he was serious. Harold suddenly wondered if Frank had discovered where he was and was waiting for him. The thought made him queasy. Or, perhaps the Army had discovered that he had lied about his age when he enlisted but it couldn't be, Harold thought to himself. There was a boy in his training company that had confided to him one night that he was only fifteen.

"Knock off the chatter!" Sergeant Cox growled from behind them.

Reaching the door of the Personnel office housed in an expansive wooden building, the three men paused for a moment unsure of what the Army was about to do with them. Looking at each other Harold finally broke the silence.

"Let's go," he said with a smirk. "The worst they can do is shoot us."

He opened the door and entered an expansive stuffy, smoke-filled room which was filled with other wet, sullen Privates who had also been called out of their blissful and treasured Sunday off.

"What in the fuck are we doing here?" Smith asked to no one in particular. "We goin' home or they goin' to send us to France? Goddammit I'm tired of sitting here rotting away!"

The other men milling around in the office glared at him and shuffled away to stew in their own private worlds and worries. Another fifteen minutes went by and a few more wet fearful men came in. More men were lining up outside in the rain which was now mixed with heavy, wet snow. Here and there a few tried to light damp cigarettes and threw the wet stubs dejectedly into the glowing hot stove. The uncomfortable mood broke at last as the front door flew open blasting them all with a cold wet wave. A Captain none of the men had seen around Camp Dodge before strode in followed by a Lieutenant and several corporals.

"Ten hut!" yelled the man closest to the door.

Every man immediately sprang to attention with a noisy thump as the Captain and his entourage disappeared into a larger room behind a set of double doors. After a few minutes one of the corporals emerged from the back with a clipboard.

"When I call your last name come up here and report," he announced loudly. "Aalbers! Andrews! Anfinson!"

The three men followed the corporal. Several more minutes passed and more men were called out in alphabetical order. None were coming out of the inside office. Harold grew more nervous as the time slowly ticked by. Many men had been leaving the training companies lately and Harold had noticed that Company A which was in his training group, had been cut nearly in half. Merle and T.C. had left the week before presumably to join an infantry unit being readied to ship overseas. The soldiers of Camp Dodge were rapidly shipping out to make room for the new recruits and draftees that had begun pouring into the facility.

"Baker! Bosch! Brooks!" The corporal yelled. "You're next. Get a move on!"

Harold and the other two men quickly hurried past the corporal. Yet another corporal handed them their Army files which had been started the day each man had joined the Army.

"Keep your noses out of them files," he growled. "Down at your sides." He retreated to a table where he began pulling files out of a cardboard box to retrieve the next three men. Harold held his file tightly to his side and looked around the room.

A line of men snaked around the large room, a small gymnasium with some tables set up at the front. Seated behind it were several Captains, Lieutenants and some other corporals who were busily shuffling papers. The men in line were silent, each waiting his turn to see what was going on. Harold stood patiently with the other silent men, his eyes fixed on the officers at the front of the line. As they finished with each man, a corporal stamped some papers which were then placed in the file, and given back to the soldier who exited through the side door.

After an eternity of waiting, Harold finally reached the tables. His woolen uniform had been soaked by the rain and was now moist, clammy and smelly. At the insistence of a sergeant he hadn't over his file.

"Name?" he asked without looking up.

"Private Harold A. Brooks." The sergeant continued looking through the file and scribbled some notes in it. He handed it to the next man, a Lieutenant who also began reading through it.

"It says here you did some carpentry work before you enlisted. Are you good with math?"

"Yes sir," Harold answered quickly. "Math was my best subject in school. I always got high marks."

"That's nice," said the Lieutenant making another note in Harold's file. "How are you with geometry and trigonometry?"

"Just fine sir. I've always been able to do math in my head. It's easy for me."

"We're looking for men to put in the artillery and knowing math is important in laying the guns and finding firing solutions. Says here you volunteered for Engineers when you enlisted."

"Um, no sir, the Lieutenant more or less told me I had to be in the Engineers."

"He did huh?"

"Yes sir."

The lieutenant rubbed his eyes and glanced up at Harold with a frown. "Tell me, do you really want to dig latrines and put up tents or would you rather be in an artillery outfit?"

Harold thought for a moment about this unexpected stroke of good fortune. "Will I get sent overseas sir, I mean, will I to go to France?"

"Yes," replied the Lieutenant tiredly. "We're sending a group of men to Camp Merritt in New Jersey to make up the units as soon as we have enough. You'll be going overseas while I sit here on my ass and shovel papers. Which do you want? Artillery or Engineers?"

"Artillery, sir," Harold replied enthusiastically.

"Good," the Lieutenant said scribbling on a form. "Give your file and this form to the corporal at the end of the line."

Harold took the papers grinning widely. "Yes sir!" Although he had never fired a gun bigger than a shotgun, he imagined firing big guns into masses of Germans and killing them all might be fun. How hard could it be and besides, he'd be close to the front lines.

The corporal made a few notes on the new form and loudly stamped several other forms. Handing it back to Harold he nodded towards the next door. "Congrats Private. Here are your travel orders and the other papers you need. Don't lose 'em or it's your ass. Good luck."

Harold thanked him and crossed through the door to wait with the other men who were awaiting their new orders to pack gear and report to the train station the next day.

CAMP MERRITT NEW JERSEY

March 2, 1918

Harold was thrown forcefully out of the hard seat onto the dirty floor of the train car as the long troop train lurched to a halt. His seat-mate and new buddy, Andrew Wellings, was also thrown to the floor by the sudden force of the stop and landed heavily on top of him.

"Goddamn," Wellings swore rubbing his head which had bounced off the seat in front of them. "They don't even bother to slow down before they stop." Untangling himself from Harold, who was still half-asleep, he stepped on Harold's arm and went crashing across the narrow aisle into the group of men on his who were also trying to untangle themselves. Wellings and the two men he had fallen upon all began swearing loudly at one another.

"Get the hell off of me you bugger," cried a small man with jet black hair and fine, almost feminine features.

"Jesus, I'm sorry," Wellings said pulling himself to his feet. "You little bastard."

Andrew Wellings was a large man and carried a tempter too, certainly not someone to pick a fight with on a crowded train. Standing nearly 6' 2" and weighing in at 185 pounds he dwarfed most of the other men he shared the grimy railroad carriage with. Like Harold, he was from Iowa, a small town named Montezuma and had volunteered for the army. He refused to farm with his father while his friends all went off to war. Despite the fact that both men had gone through Basic Training at Camp Dodge, they hadn't met until boarding the train to depart for New Jersey. With his easy going nature and wicked sense of humor, Wellings and Harold had become friends immediately.

"Come on," Harold said taking him by the arm. "Don't mind them."

"Yes, you might listen to your friend there," the small man said pulling himself to his feet.

"If you don't shut that mouth of yours you're going to find my fist in it!" Wellings roared taking a step towards him.

"Sit!" Harold shouted shoving his friend into the seat before turning back to the other two men. "He's done. Relax."

The other men sat down and whispered between themselves. The small fancy one made it a point to look over at Wellings and Harold and laugh about something.

Wellings wiped his mouth on his sleeve and shook his head disgustedly. "Just you wait little man, I'm going to teach you not to mess with me."

"So, where do you think we're at?" Harold asked trying to change the subject.

"Dunno. I thought I heard someone say we were in New Jersey a while back. Too dark to tell."

None of the other fifty men packed into the carriage knew either and all were straining to look out of the dirty windows. Some speculated that they were somewhere in Pennsylvania while most others tried to get back to sleep.

Harold stretched his sore body and rubbed his bloodshot eyes. "Dammit, I hope so. That means we're about there. I'm ready to get off this train."

The train they found themselves on had left Camp Dodge nearly eight days before to begin their journey to Camp Merritt and the next step in their training. At first the carriages he and the other Dodge men were assigned to had been nice and roomy and each carriage had a latrine with running water to wash up in. Despite the hard, cracked leather seats that made sleep virtually impossible, the men were excited to be moving to the East coast to be assigned to their new units which were awaiting orders to ship out for France. As the train slowly chugged on eastwards the conditions became worse with each stop. The first was Camp Grant near Chicago and Camp Sherman in Ohio. Each time more and more men were jammed into the already full carriages making the journey agonizingly slower.

The ancient coal-fired engine belched out black clouds of hot, gritty smoke that seeped into every compartment, leaving a fine black layer of soot on everything. With so many men packed onto the trains the water in the latrine had run out and the toilet was constantly plugged up. Adding to these smells, the men were hot, sweaty and perpetually dirty. With no bathing facilities and little other water than that designated for drinking the smell had ripened by the hour. A few had learned the hard way not to open the carriage windows while the train was underway – the smoke from the engine would literally fill the entire compartment adding to the overall filth and wretchedness and often as not, caused the opener of the window to get a punch in the eye.

Food was scarce too. The men only received two sandwiches of varyingly disgusting make, two apples or oranges and a pint or two of warm water once per day. Some days the sandwiches were replaced by tins of potted meat and vegetables which left a greasy, unpleasant aftertaste in the mouths and throats of the dirty men.

On top of these miseries, attempting to sleep upright in the hard, uncomfortable seats posed a real challenge. Harold and Wellings had devised a system of simply taking turns either sleeping half lying down on the bench while the other slept only a little more comfortably on the floor. However, after several days no one could sleep properly. Coupled with the bad food, this had worn the men down emotionally and physically. Fights and heated arguments filled the endless days.

Whistles and shouts could be heard outside. Suddenly, the carriage door flew open and a large Staff Sergeant squeezed himself into the mass of men.

"On your feet! Grab your gear and get moving you sons of bitches!" he shouted. "Everyone off the train and into formation. NOW!"

Harold, Wellings and everyone else jumped at the order and began rounding up their belongings and looking for lost items. It was mass-confusion and fights started as men trampled one another and got shoved into the packed doorway trying to get out of the carriage. Looking out of the window Harold could see men up and down the length of the train pouring out into the darkness hounded by the Sergeants. Suddenly he found Wellings on top of him again.

"Jesus Christ, Wellings!" he yelled at his friend. "Get the hell off of me!"

Wellings got off of Harold and began punching smaller man as they tried to get their possessions together and off the train. Harold stood quickly and tried to pull his big friend off.

"Come on Wellings. Lay off him! You don't want to get busted now! Let's go!" he urged.

"Fine," Wellings replied giving the smaller man a shove. "Where's my shit?"

"What's the matter you big oaf?" Said the smaller man in an uppity accent. "Can't take it like a real man? I'll smash that big nose of yours."

"I'm going to tear your ass apart, Romeo!" Wellings howled.

The seatmate also spoke up. "Come on George! Give it up. I'm not going to the stockade over your temper and that big dummy."

"Oh, if you say so," he replied straightening his uniform and hair. "My apologies for the pugilism." He extended his hand to Wellings who was still snorting with anger.

"The name is George Henley Wallace Goodlow the Fourth. Pleased to make your acquaintance."

Wellings wasn't in the mood. "Fuck you little man." Harold helped him round up their things and made sure to stay between his friend and George as they exited the carriage into the cold morning air.

With more pushing and shoving the men slowly made their way off of the train and onto the siding. Hopefully they would get some decent chow and a comfortable bunk to sleep in once they'd gotten to wherever they were going. Leading Wellings and carefully making his way down the narrow steps of the train car, Harold took in a deep lung-full of the frosty air. It smelled and tasted of pine and a strange dirty smell he didn't recognize. In the northern and eastern distance a soft yellow glow dimly lit the horizon for miles.

Behind him, George commented, "See that light up there. It's New York City. That's home and I wish I was there just about now. Think of it. I'd be getting ready for a night out with some lucky lady. Not here with you dirty fellows freezing and fighting." His seat mate who Harold had overheard George calling Mike laughed.

"I've never been anywhere bigger than Athens. Athens, Georgia that is. Is New York really the place all the papers and books say it is? Lots of women?" Mike asked.

"Millions," George replied. "All different sizes, colors and shapes. You want an Italian girl? A Jewish girl? I can even get you a Hindu woman if that's what you desire. Whatever you like, they're all ripe for the picking and these uniforms will get you one. If we get leave I'll find you one."

Men around them laughed and excitedly asked George to do them a favor and set them up too. He agreed but told the others it would cost them.

"Fuckin' Romeo," Wellings growled. "You can keep your harlots to yourself. I'll find my own women."

"Okay, okay, friend," George replied with a derisive smile. "But if you fail at it, which by the looks of you, you will, the offer is still on the table."

Harold made sure to stay between Wellings and his new enemy George the Fourth as the sergeants busily sorted the men out on the platform.

"All men assigned to the 65ᵗʰ get in formation over here to my left!" shouted a Sergeant with a clipboard.

Harold, Wellings, George and his seatmate Mike began pushing through the crowd of men to line up with the other new men making up their company. Other Sergeants called out looking for men assigned to the 54ᵗʰ CAC and the 60ᵗʰ CAC. As each man fell in with his assigned group he looked back and forth silently at the men he would be serving with. Some had formed friendships with other men in civilian life, basic training or on the long train ride while others knew no one. The small groups of friends talked excitedly in low voices clearly happy to be assigned with men they knew while the friendless men nervously looked down at the well-worn platform and shifted uncomfortably on their feet.

Once the men were in some semblance of order a young Lieutenant, three Sergeants, including the man who had rounded up Harold's group, stood stiffly at attention in front of them. Harold's Sergeant stood with a dark scowl on his face which was partially hidden by his low-slung campaign hat in the dim light of the platform.

"Ten hut!" he shouted jarring the tired men to attention.

"Welcome to Camp Merritt. This is 2nd Lieutenant Swanson who will be in charge of integrating you into the 65th. My name is First Sergeant Miller. In the next few days you will undergo another round of physicals, inspections and you will draw gear and clothing for overseas duty. We expect the bulk of the 65th to arrive in the next few days from the West coast at which time you will be assigned to your Company's."

The Sergeant turned and spoke quietly to the Lieutenant who had been constantly rubbing his face and eyes. He seemed to be weaving unsteadily on his feet. The Lieutenant answered sharply with a wave of his hand as though he were dismissing a child. With his scowl deepening, the Sergeant spun back to face the crowd in front of him.

"Ten hut!" he yelled again. Harold and the other men immediately snapped back to attention.

"Right face! Forward, march!"

The men were led off the platform and onto a dark gravel road leading to the interior of the Camp. Even though it was two o'clock in the morning long formations of men seemed to be marching everywhere and the endless ranks of buildings were lit up as though the day was a holiday. Harold shivered in the cold air as his new unit crunched along the graveled road.

"Damn it's cold here," he said to Wellings who was blowing on his hands to stay warm. "Can't be more than twenty degrees. I hope we can get some hot chow and a warm bed tonight."

Wellings grunted through his frozen hands. "They better feed us. I think I'm dying from malnutrition. Better not be sandwiches and that horrid potted meat either."

Harold nodded. "Yeah," he said licking his lips. "Huge flapjacks with syrup, bacon, potatoes, coffee and fresh milk would hit the spot right now wouldn't it?"

Men around them groaned at the suggestion of such a feast and began discussing their favorite meals. After being in the Army for several months they all knew they'd be lucky to get anything hot or fresh. The men continued to march through the camp releasing enormous clouds of frozen breath into the air. Suddenly the formation stopped in front of a large rectangular shaped building with light pouring out through its huge windows. Harold and the other men sniffed the air and felt their mouths water.

"Damn that smells good whatever it is!" Harold exclaimed happily.

Wellings strained his neck trying to look past the men in front of him. "Let me at it boy." he said rubbing his stomach with glee. "Let me at it!"

Soon the men filed into a huge mess hall which was packed with new arrivals. The bright lights caused each man to squint his eyes as they walked in and the warm air was an instant relief from the cold.

"Looky there." said Wellings pointing his finger to the opposite wall. "We're in Heaven. No doubt about it."

Harold, George and Mike followed his finger to a chow line extending nearly the length of the long building. A huge variety of food awaited the new men starving for a good hot meal: Piles of flapjacks, toast, eggs, potatoes, steak, ham and more all steaming in the serving lines. Harold thought he'd almost pass out from anticipation standing in the long, slow moving line. It had been months since he'd seen food this good and he felt a pang of regret for a moment over leaving home. His mother had always prepared huge, wonderful breakfasts on Saturday mornings.

After making his way through the long line, Harold paused and tried to balance his overflowing plate while he filled a cup with coffee. This done, he and the other men in his new unit quickly slid into seats just vacated by a group of other men being hounded by their Sergeant to get a move on. The men ate in silence relishing the feast the Army had provided for them. This was a treat and they all knew it.

"If we get fed this well for the rest of the war I'll be a happy man," said Wellings through a mouthful of flapjacks. "When we get to France maybe they'll let us have wine with our meals too."

Other men including Harold grunted their agreement and continued shoveling the hot food into their mouths.

George, who was seated across from Wellings and Harold, stopped chewing for a moment and held his fork up in front of his face. A twisted smile contorted itself onto his face.

"You know why we're being fed so well?" he asked looking directly at Wellings. "Well, do you?"

Wellings continued to eat and grunted at George. "No. Tell me Romeo."

"They're just fattening us up for the coming slaughter. You men just watch. We'll eat well, have a warm bed and they'll give us everything we need. Maybe even extra socks," George said dreamily. "Once we're all fattened up and start believing the Army isn't so bad after all we'll get packed into ships down in New York harbor and it's off to France to be killed like animals."

Each man at the table stopped eating and stared at George who happily dove into his scrambled eggs. He seemed to be pleased with himself.

Harold leaned across the table with anger on his face. "Is that right. What in the hell do you know about it? Been there have you?"

George stopped chewing once again and carefully wiped his mouth. "Well, as a matter of fact, I do know a little about it. I read about it in the papers. Nasty business in France. The war and all, you know."

Some men laughed and shook their heads and went back to their meals. Harold's face flushed with anger and embarrassment.

"You're a funny guy. I don't intend on dying over there and I don't appreciate you telling everyone else that either."

"Oh, calm down there, uh, what's your name?" George asked with a laugh. "Just making some simple conversation and some observations. No harm intended."

"Harold Brooks."

"I'm pleased to make your acquaintance."

Harold shook his head and went back to his meal but what George had said had bothered him. Every man knew that what he had said was probably the truth but no one wanted to admit to that it could be true. To think that the Army was just using him and thousands of others as nothing more than cannon fodder sent a chill through his body. At the profane insistence of Sergeant Miller, the men quickly finished their hurried meals and pushed and shoved their way out into the cold night. Harold sighed and stared at the piercing black sky as his stomach rumbled strangely. He could feel a small trace of fear settling deep inside him.

NEW ENEMIES

March 4, 1918

Harold staggered backwards and tried to catch his balance as the Corporal shoved the heavy coat onto the pile of clothing he was already carrying. Steadying himself, he tried to readjust his load but stumbled over someone's feet and dropping it all on the dusty floor of the warehouse. The Corporal was immediately in his face.

"What in the fuck are you doing? Pick this shit up and keep moving! We don't have all day to wait on you! Move! "

Harold blushed deeply as men around him laughed and quickly gathered up the clothing he had just received: pants, shirts, socks, underwear, new boots, leggings and the heavy all-weather coat and scrambled forward to the end of the line where he bumped into George.

"Hello Private," George said with a smile. "Come here often?"

Harold dropped his pile of clothing back down on the floor and immediately began re-folding and re-stacking it all. Finished, he picked it up and looked back at the Corporal who had just yelled at him.

"My God, what a prick," he said in a low voice.

George smiled from behind his own enormous pile of clothing. "He is most certainly from the lower classes. Reminds me of my parent's gardener. A crude man with no education."

Harold sighed deeply. "It seems like they all are."

Since he and other men destined for the artillery had arrived at Camp Merritt the week before their days had been filled with more physicals, rounds of painful shots, drawing gear and endless Physical Training. The men were roused out of their rickety cots at five in the morning and were run from one building to a next until nearly ten at night, leaving most breathless and exhausted. Most recently, the 65th had been confined to Camp Merritt and the days were spent in a tortuous agony of anticipation as the men were awoken before dawn each day for exercise with the rest of their time being spent standing in long lines drawing more gear and beat up Enfield rifles.

"What in the hell are we getting rifles for if we're in the artillery?" Wellings asked as the men sat on long benches in the armory building, cleaning sticky Cosmoline from the actions.

"Evidently, everyone gets them," Mike said. "But goddamn, I'll be upset if they tricked us and we end up in an infantry company."

Harold stopped cleaning his rifle and looked up. "I hate to say it but, two of my buddies ended up in the infantry after they were told they'd be doing something else. My friend Alton Jr. from back home was told he could take care of army horses. Another man I knew was told he was going to be a cook. A sergeant came in the day before we boarded the train to come out here and told everyone left in our barracks that they'd just joined the infantry and took them away, just like that. Hell, they're probably in a trench in France by now."

Several men groaned and swore loudly.

"Fucking army," Wellings swore. "I've noticed they tell you one thing, then do the opposite. I don't like that. I could have stayed home with my father and gotten that kind of bullshit."

"Well," Harold said, flicking a glob of Cosmoline at Wellings, "They've told us we'll get our artillery training once we get to France because we don't have the big guns they say we'll fire. I have to believe that."

"My father looked into the 65th after I'd um…enlisted," George said. "They were in charge of the gigantic coastal guns in the forts that ring important harbors. Since they're sending all of those men to France with us in tow, we'll certainly be artillerymen, won't we?"

"Hell, I'd think so." Harold said. "When I joined up they kept asking me how good I was with math and all that. You don't need to know math for the infantry."

"Yeah, me too," Mike said dejectedly. "We'll find out tomorrow when the men who've been in the 65th for years arrive."

After a march of five miles the next day Sergeant Miller informed Harold and the rest of the new men that the bulk of the 65th had indeed arrived from the West Coast bringing nearly two thousand men into the already overflowing Camp. The next morning was spent assigning men to the various companies of the 65th which needed replacements. The men were forced to stand shivering and hungry in the early pre-dawn cold as their names were called off. Harold was overjoyed to find himself assigned to the Second Battalion of Battery C along with Wellings, George, Mike and several other men who they'd begun to make new friendships with. However, the new men felt uncomfortable as they moved into new barracks with their new comrades in the 65th many of whom were Regular Army and National Guard troops who had served together in the 65th in Washington State for years.

"Just look at all the young babies they've given us to fight the Huns with!" yelled one man.

"I didn't realize they were drafting so many little school boys," yelled another. "Look at 'em all. Fresh off momma's tit!"

The veterans roared with laughter and threw insults at Harold and his group. Reaching the end of a long row of bunks Harold stopped and un-shouldered his bulging duffel bag on an empty bed. Wellings and the rest began doing the same. An older man Harold guessed to be around age thirty-five with thinning hair strode up to them with a smirk on his red-skinned face. His dark little eyes darted from man to man. His companion, a short thin man with a pitted face and narrow shoulders stood behind him chewing on a tooth pick.

"What are you doing?" the balding man asked smiling at Harold. His teeth were brown and his breath smelled of decay and cigar smoke.

Harold eyed him carefully not wanting to get off on the wrong foot with his new chums. He noticed three other men wandering over to stand along with the older man's friend. Each had the look of the hard men who had worked on the railroads or at the rendering plant just outside of Sac City.

"Just unloading my gear on this bunk," he said looking down at the older man. "Why, is there a problem?"

"Yeah," said the man. "These bunks are all taken. You boys have to find somewhere else to go."

Harold looked at the man and suddenly realized that the other men, the real veterans of the 65th were watching with great interest. Some had smiles on their faces.

Harold took a deep breath. "Is that right? By who? Sergeant Miller told us to take the first empty bunks we found in here and I guess these are it. I don't see any gear or names on any of them."

The shorter man jabbed his index finger fiercely into Harold's chest. "These bunks are taken," he said spitting on Harold. "They're for real soldiers. Not this fucking nursery school class you led in here."

Some of the men in the background laughed while others inched forward.

Harold could feel his face flush with immediate anger. He was tired and nervous and certainly wasn't in the mood for games which was exactly what these two were up too. He stared coldly at the old man and his friends.

"I think you're mistaken," he said forcing himself to smile. "We just took these bunks and if you have a problem with it you two can go fuck yourselves. Understood?"

The bald man howled with rage and drew his fist back to strike Harold who waited calmly. After years of being knocked around by his father, Harold knew how to fight. He ducked the sloppily thrown punch, turned sharply, and landed a short, hard blow to the man's midsection. He fell heavily on the floor eyes bulging, gasping for breath. The veterans in the barracks erupted in howls of laughter and slapped each other on the back. The pit-faced friend immediately ran forward and hit Harold squarely in the jaw and held up his fists rocking them back and forth.

"Come on, boy," he grunted. "I'm going to send you back to your momma in a box."

Harold shook his head, regained his feet and glared at him. "The hell you are."

The three other men rushed forward and lunged into Wellings, George, Mike and some of the other new men standing around. The remainder of the new men backed off, not wanting to get involved. Harold jabbed his fists at the pit-faced man and landed several solid punches as he did so causing him to lurch to his left before crashing into a bunk with blood streaming out of his nose. Harold didn't wait for him to recover and put all of his weight into a vicious left which splattered blood in all directions when it found its mark. Wellings roared with anger and landed a perfectly thrown right onto the face of his attacker sending the man sprawling to the floor. George, Mike and the rest of their group punched and kicked through yells and profanity and received several blows in return. In the noisy chaos of the barracks Harold's group of new men began to get the upper hand. The pit-faced man took several more well-placed facial and body punches falling to the floor in a sodden heap. Mike found himself pinned to the floor by one man who had grabbed his hair and began beating his head onto the floor. Harold took two quick strides and kicked the man from atop his friend and then kicked him squarely in the ribs. The man rolled into a ball and groaned with pain. The remaining veterans suddenly stopped fighting and backed away. One of the larger men however didn't want to quit and was latched to Welling's back choking him with all of the strength he could muster. Wellings, who was beginning to turn a remarkable shade of purple staggered back and forth trying to throw the man off. Suddenly George was on the man, tearing him from Wellings with one swift move and throwing him to the floor. The man immediately jumped up ready to take on the much smaller George who gave him a violent knee to the groin. With a smile, George strode away dusting himself off.

"Well now, that takes care of that," he said. "Who's next?"

The crowd of veterans stood silently for a moment before erupting into cascades of laughter and applause. Harold wiped the blood from his mouth and watched with amusement as the defeated veterans crawled away into the packed mass of cheering men who began berating their injured buddies with profanity and more laughter. He been afraid that more of the veterans might join in the fight and finish his small group but thankfully, they hadn't. They noisily exchanged money and derided one another with shouts and jeers.

Several other men stepped forward to Harold and his group with smiles on their faces.

"You sure as hell showed Lenny and his thugs a thing or two," the first man said extending his right hand. "My name's Walter Schmidt and this is David Poe, Amos Van Nevel and Bernie Clarke."

Each man shook Harold's hand as he introduced them to Wellings, George, Mike and the other new men. Harold smiled at the men he had just met.

"That's one helluva welcoming committee you have here."

"Don't worry about them," Walter told the group. "They're just a bunch of lousy horse's asses who are always messing with the new guys we get. They rarely get anyone to fight back. You boys just earned a lot of respect in this unit. Welcome to Second Company!"

Both groups mingled together and talked about where they were from and what had brought them into the Army. The group of new men who had chosen not to fight stood apprehensively still hanging onto to their gear unsure of what to do and where they fit in. Walter stopped his conversation with Harold and looked over at them with a smile.

"Come on, you new men. Find a bunk and stow that gear then come along and meet the rest of the men here."

A wave a relief washed over the forlorn group as they happily dropped their gear on their new bunks and crowded around Harold and Walter. Wellings stood apart from the group and rubbed his neck which was beginning to bruise and coughed. He grabbed George's arm as he walked by.

"Thanks for saving my ass, Romeo," he croaked. "I mean it. Your name is George?"

George extended his hand. "George it is. Happy to help out, Wellings."

The two men shook hands.

"Do you promise to love, obey and respect him for all of your days?" Harold said laughing.

"Go to hell," Wellings rasped to his friend.

"I do," George answered holding his hands to his heart.

The four laughed and made their way back into the crowd.

UP THE GANGPLANK

March 23, 1918

"Jesus she's big!" said Wellings cocking his steel helmet back to get a better look.

Harold and the other men swore and whistled as they marched along the busy docks to begin boarding the ship that would take them to France.

"A Cunard liner, I believe, since we are on the Cunard docks," George announced. "The officers will be going over in style while all of us are packed down in the bowels. Too bad I didn't bring my tuxedo along for dinner tonight."

The H.M.S. *Mauretania* was indeed a Cunard liner that the British Navy had appropriated for use as a troop transport when war had broken out in 1914. She had been ferrying British and Dominion troops all over the world to the various theatres of war and now she was taking the green Americans to France. Harold heard some other men with knowledge of the war discussing how she had taken British troops to Gallipoli and come through without a scratch. That was good luck.

Despite the excitement, Harold had begun to have second thoughts about joining the army and going off to the war. His restless sleep was filled with dreams of death and destruction and of finding himself alone falling into an endless, bottomless pit. He didn't talk about these dreams with anyone else but he noticed fear in the eyes of his friends too. Wellings had become unusually quiet and spent his free time lying on his rickety bunk staring away into nothingness. It seemed as though it was difficult for men to share their uneasy feelings for fear of being looked upon as a coward by the other men. Some men talked openly of their desire to run but deserters, thanks to a lecture the day before, made most of them think twice. One man, a young draftee from Washington State and a new member of the 65th had disappeared several days before. The rumor was the MP's had caught him in New York City trying to board a train for home and brought him back to the Camp in chains. And, according to the rampant rumor mill in the latrine, he sat in the stockade awaiting his court martial and sentencing. Some men in the barracks were making bets on whether or not he'd be shot for desertion.

Harold leaned forward to adjust the rest of the nearly one hundred pounds of gear each man had been burdened with. Staggering and lurching about, he was caught by Walter Schmidt who steadied him.

"Whoa there, Brooks. Are you okay?"

"Yeah, I think so. Just thinking about...things," Harold replied looking up at the ship.

"Me too. I've been in the Army for ten years but I've never been in a war," Walter replied. "But, my wife is convinced I started the war just so I could go to France to cheat on her."

Harold smiled and looked at his new friend who had pulled out a photo of his wife and children and stood gazing at it.

"She's a good girl though. And, a good mother to our two girls," Walter said putting the photo back into his pocket. "Don't know why she wanted me."

Harold nodded not sure what to say.

"You have a girl Brooks?" Walter asked.

"Sure do. Her name is Margaret," Harold answered digging in his pocket for the photo Margaret had sent him the week before.

Walter whistled as he admired the photo. "She's a beauty, that's for certain."

"Let me see her again," Wellings said from behind Harold while he reached for the photo. "Just another look? Please?"

Harold pushed Wellings' hand away. "No dice. You got your greasy fingerprints all over it the last time you looked."

Walter laughed as he glanced back at Wellings. Turning back to Harold, he spoke in a low voice. "I wouldn't let him look at her either. Dirty thoughts in that boys head."

Harold laughed as he put the treasured photo back in his pocket.

The docks resembled a huge anthill, with men swarming over crates and equipment, people yelling, and supplies being swung over to the ship by huge cranes. Harold strained to look around and saw what seemed like thousands of khaki uniformed American soldiers filling the long docks for as far as he could see. Ahead of him was a long gangplank that men were slowly walking along up to a large hatch in the side of the ship. He sighed and tried to keep his balance wondering if the sagging ropes lining the gangplank would catch him if he happened to stumble and fall. With all of the gear he was carrying on his back, Harold bet that if he did fall he'd go straight to the bottom of the harbor.

"Second Company! Stay together and get your boarding tickets right here!" yelled Lieutenant Swanson.

The men slowly shuffled forward as they had been all afternoon and began taking tickets from the Cunard employees who were too old to be in the service. Harold stepped forward, took his ticket and was handed a small postcard by one of the corporals from HQ Company. He cautiously made his way up the gangplank with his knuckles white from gripping the ropes tightly and stepped into the ship. Hot, humid cigarette smoke filled air made it hard to breathe without having to make a conscious effort to do so. With so many men packed tightly in together each laden-down with his equipment, Harold immediately felt trapped. Glancing at his ticket, he realized he had no idea where he was going either so he followed the men in front of him who kept going further and further down into the dimly lit lower decks.

After nearly an hour of progressing further down into the ship Harold could hear the unmistakable voice of Sergeant Miller somewhere ahead berating someone.

"Second Company! Second Company men! Get yourselves situated in here and don't wander off. Everyone stays put until I give the word!"

"Good lord, how in the world are we supposed to sleep in these things?" Harold asked crawling into the narrow hammock he found himself in front of. Each section of hammocks was stacked ten high from the floor to the ceiling of the enormous berth. Each one was only big enough for a small man, about five-foot-two, twenty-inches wide with only sixteen inches between.

"I don't know," Wellings grunted as he tried to climb up the side of the section and squeeze in above Harold. "Maybe they don't want us to get out of them until we're in France."

Wellings barely fit into his hammock causing his enormous body to sag nearly into Harold's face.

"I can't even roll over in this damn thing!" Harold cried. "Trade me Wellings. You'll have to go on the bottom one."

The men sorted themselves out and devised a system in which the smallest men got the top bunks with each slightly bigger man getting the next one down. Wellings swore loudly as he found himself sandwiched in on the bottom. Harold found himself squarely in the middle of the section with George's body sagging down into him.

"At least it's only six or seven days," someone muttered to the catcalls and profanity of the men.

Once everyone was as settled as they could be Sergeant Miller led the way as the men trooped back up the endless flights of stairs to the top deck and into the fresh, cold air blowing through the harbor. Harold jostled with his friends and the other men to line up along the starboard rails of the *Mauretania* to watch the dock-workers and other people wave and cheer to the men while the enormous ship shuddered and groaned as she slowly got under-way. Several tugs came along side and began pulling the ship out away from the docks while a band played *God Bless America*. People cheered and waved white handkerchiefs and small American flags. The young Americans waved and smiled back.

Harold watched as the dock faded out of sight and turned his gaze to the buildings of New York City. It seemed strange and surreal now watching as life went on in the enormous city while men were going off to fight and die in a place they'd never seen. Suddenly the tugs turned away from the ship and tooted their horns as a show of farewell. Every man waved to the tiny figures on the decks of the tiny tugs who waved back and called out encour-agement to the soldiers.

"There she is," one man said pointing. Harold followed the man's finger to a small island in the harbor.

The Statue of Liberty stood just off to the starboard side of the *Mauretania* as she slowly slipped past sloshing and churning through the dirty water of New York Harbor. Each of the men aboard was completely silent watching her as they sailed out of the harbor and towards France. Harold prayed silently as he tried to control the tears that filled his eyes and wondered if and when he'd see the Statue again. For the next hour each man aboard was lost in his own thoughts, feeling the first real tinges of fear and doubt as the last bit of home slipped beneath the horizon.

LAND

April 2, 1918

Eight tortuous days later, Harold, Wellings, Mike and George along with men from several other company's leaned on the rails and lounged about the wide decks of the *Mauretania* smoking cigarettes and looking out at the rolling gray sea that seemed to go on forever. According to the gossip they had overheard from their officers and the British crew the low dark masses stretched out along the eastern horizon were Ireland and England. For most, the horrible seasickness they had suffered through had disappeared after the fourth or fifth day as the men finally became accustomed to the endless rolling and rocking motion of the ship. Many however, lay in their hammocks below in the fetid, stinking berths unable to keep any food down.

The overcast skies were filled with thousands of sea gulls that swooped and flew about the ship annoying the sick, exhausted Americans with their loud shrieks. Wellings swore and thrashed his hands about violently after one dove close to him and left a white, egg-like mess splattered on his face and shoulder.

"You little bastard!" he yelled waving a fist at the gull. "You're going to die!"

Harold laughed at his friend and flicked his cigarette butt over the side. "I guess we all know what that one thinks of you." he said with a laugh. He was about to tease his friend more when Wellings began laughing hysterically.

"And you!" he said pointing at Harold's hat. "He must like you too, shit head!"

Harold removed his hat to see that another gull had indeed done its business on him. He smiled and began laughing with Wellings.

"They don't want us here. Maybe we should just go home."

"What? But we're almost there and I haven't seen Paris yet!"

Harold carefully cleaned the mess from his hat by spitting on it then rubbing gently with his handkerchief. He seemed to be making the spot larger. Suddenly a series of sharp whistles blew over the ship's intercom system. Most of the American soldiers had learned to ignore the constant chirping and coded whistles coming from the intercom. It seemed to be some strange language only the British sailors could understand and they would jump to work on various chores around the ship every time the whistles sounded. A voice came over the intercom next.

"Now hear this. Now hear this. All passengers are ordered below decks immediately."

Harold looked around the ship along with all of the other American soldiers. "What for wonder? A U-boat?"

Wellings pointed a finger out to the hazy sea. "Look out there about two o'clock. That's not a U-boat is it?"

Several men strained their eyes to see a small black shape bobbing and plowing through the waves towards the *Mauretania*. On the decks sergeants and corporals were busy shouting and swearing at the men milling about to get below decks and into their bunks. Harold and a few others continued watching the dark shape come nearer until they recognized it as a small patrol boat of some kind flying the Royal Navy flag from her mainmast. Soon, another joined it and sailed off in the opposite direction.

"Get below decks now!" a sergeant shouted at Harold and Wellings. "Not tomorrow. Right now!"

Harold and Wellings grumbled and turned to shuffle down the narrow steps with the other men who were all clearly displeased at being ordered below. While they waited for the line to move Harold questioned a British sailor who was walking by.

"What's going on? Are we being attacked?"

"No, mate," the sailor replied "We'll be docking in Liverpool tomorrow sometime. They just want to keep all you Americans safe and sound."

"What are those boats out there doing?" Wellings asked pointing at the small ships darting around the *Mauretania*.

"Them's just sub chasers," the sailor answered. "Once we get in close to shore they come out and try to find any subs that might be lurking about. They're not dropping depth charges, so it's your lucky day, Yank."

Harold made his way below deck to the compartment he shared with other smelly men and pulled at the uncomfortable life preserver around his neck. He was excited over finally making it to England and getting off the ship and the throwing away the awful life preserver. Maybe, he thought hopefully, mail would be waiting for them once they got to wherever they were going and the thought cheered him considerably. No one had gotten any since arriving at Camp Merritt making him miss Margaret terribly and yearn for some news from home. Was she happy? Had her parents finally gotten over the night she'd spent with him? Harold was desperate to hear from her, if nothing more than to hear that she still loved him. Pulling a leather billfold out of his inner shirt pocket he removed the photograph that Margaret had sent him in the last letter he'd received before shipping out from Camp Dodge.

He stared at the photo he'd by now memorized: Margaret's long beautiful hair was pulled up in tight braids around her head and her eyes glowed brightly in the hazy black and white photo. On her left ring finger she subtly displayed the ring he had given her the night he and Alton Jr. had left. With a smile, he gently kissed the photo and put it back in his billfold.

George tapped Harold on the shoulder. "Come on, let's have a look. They say they can see England through the port holes.

Harold and George pushed into the mass of men taking turns staring out of the tiny portholes. After a long wait they took their turn. Harold marveled at the green land rising sharply through the veil of fog. He could see a white stone house in the foggy distance and wondered who lived there. It was fascinating and exciting for the men, virtually all of whom had never been more than twenty or thirty miles from home before joining the Army. All had read about England and heard fanciful tales such as *Robin Hood* and *Knights of the Round Table* while growing up and now they were here. It seemed strange and exotic.

Deeper below decks the *Mauretania's* engines suddenly changed causing the huge ship to vibrate and groan as she slowly sailed in close to the coast of Ireland and turned into the mild swells of the Irish Sea. In a matter of hours the men of the 65th would set foot on European soil and begin their preparations for war. The thought made Harold shiver as he took his turn staring at the land rising up from the sea.

PART II

FIRST BATTLES NEAR MANONVILLE, FRANCE

September 13, 1918

Harold shivered in the darkness and blew on his hands to warm them before pulling his collar tightly around his neck to protect himself from the chilly fall wind whooshing through the camouflage netting surrounding *Dora*. He and the rest of the men who made up 2nd Company sat and stood around in the darkness of the emplacement speaking in low voices to one another about what the coming night would bring.

After months of training beginning with the 65th's first stop outside the English town of Romney in the far southeast of England, they were finally about to take their place in the American First Army's sector of the line outside of Manonville.

After leaving Romney, the men of the 65th were shuttled across the English Channel and stuffed into French rail cars built for transporting before finally arriving in the city of Limoges where their training began in earnest. It was back to the daily grind of army life complete with intense physical training and weapons schools taught by grim, battle-hardened French soldiers. In addition to running back and forth through the swampy parade ground with full packs on their backs, the men dug endless lines of trenches, filled thousands of sandbags and dug huge holes to simulate the preparation of gun emplacements. And finally, to every man's relief, they were introduced to the guns they would be working with: Enormous 9.2 Vickers howitzers used for heavy bombardments. The men trained daily in assembling and disassembling the guns, mounting them on the Caterpillar tractors that transported them, loading and unloading the rest of the equipment and tools on the gun trucks, cleaning the guns, preparing the shells for firing missions and finally, firing the guns. Harold discovered that he enjoyed this work and soon learned every detail of the guns.

Being assigned to Limoges for two months also had several off-duty distractions for the men. When their daily training was done, the men were often allowed to go into the ancient city to see the sights, eat and drink in the quaint cafes while others visited the local whorehouses. Letters from home came nearly every day too and Harold was happy with the stacks of mail he received from Margaret, Bobby and Will. It seemed that everyone was doing fine and Harold often shook his head in amazement over the worry and stress he'd put himself under before joining the army. *It was all working out.*

Harold yawned and sat down on the edge of the gun emplacement next to Mike and George. "I wish they'd let us either fire these things or let us go back and sleep for a while. I'm freezing."

"Me too," George said. "I'm tired and hungry."

"Don't talk to me about being hungry," Wellings growled. "If they feed us slum again I'm going to kill the cooks with my bare hands."

Harold and George nodded knowingly. The men had slept very little in the previous three days as the regiment had moved

148

from reserve positions several miles back to their current location. Positions prepared, sandbags filled and trenches dug before unloading and assembling the guns. After camouflaging the entire works the men had fallen down in heaps to eat greasy, watery 'slum' which was a mulligan stew generally of fairly disgusting make, bread and cheese. They'd only just started when the ammunition trucks arrived several hours late. Finally, after many more exhausting tired hours of unloading the unwieldy shells and moving them into each battery they were allowed to finish their cold and stale meals only to have more ammunition trucks appear as they sat down a second time.

Wellings leaned close to Harold in the darkness. "What time is it?"

Harold dug deep inside his coat pulling his pocket watch out of the leather bag that hung around his neck and squinted at it. "About one A.M."

"Well, hell's bells. Are we going to fire these damn things or not?" Wellings said loudly. "We've been sitting on our asses out here for two hours."

Harold looked over at Mike in the darkness and noticed that his lips were moving and his eyes were tightly closed which meant he was praying as he often did. Several shadowy figures emerged out of the darkness and spoke in animated voices before breaking up.

"On your feet!" Sergeant Miller called out. "Time to earn your pay!"

The men leapt to their feet and rushed to their assigned positions. Harold tripped and fell in his haste and scampered on his hands and knees to the breech of the enormous gun to grab the breech lock handle and pulled it back opening the gun with a loud click.

"Fire mission," Walter announced in a quaking voice. He carried a buzzer box which was connected to the man with the same buzzer box phone in the firing solution dugout where the officers with their maps and plotting boards sat and tracked the firing which was connected to the men on buzzer boxes closer to the front lines with the spotters. Lieutenant Everson, the gun captain of *Dora* listened carefully as Walter stumbled trying to relay the coordinates to him. He stepped forward with his clipboard and relayed the orders to the men.

"Listen up! Troop target fire plan. Load HE 117. Grid forty twenty-two, thirty one. Direction 3200. They've spotted movement on the roads in the German rear areas."

Wellings, Mike, Frank Neff and another man wrestled a high explosive shell from the cart into the loading tray. Another man cranked a wheel on the elevating gear to raise the shell up to the open breech where it was pushed firmly in with a long wooden rammer until the brass rifling ring surrounding the shell was firmly seated. Wellings and Mike returned with a bag of propellant and shoved this in behind the waiting shell. Harold felt around the edges of the breech to ensure that the shell and powder bag were both fully pushed in and not lying where either would be caught at an angle as he closed the breech. Satisfied it was where it needed to be, he pushed the lever hard forward and down locking the shell and powder into place. Each man in the Battery had signed the shell several hours before as their way of telling the Germans the 65th was finally in the war and ready to fight. Under the direction of Lieutenant Everson other men carefully turned the elevation and cant levers on *Dora* until they had the correct coordinates dialed in. Harold stepped back and watched Myron Worley crouch down and gently take ahold of the trigger rope.

"Fff..fi..fire!" Walter yelled.

"Fire!" Lieutenant Everson yelled allowing Myron to jerk the trigger rope back with flourish.

Dora emitted an explosion of light and sound forcing all of the men around her back several steps. Up and down the line the guns of the 65th erupted at once causing the ground to tremble and the landscape to light up as though it were daytime. Men cheered through their temporary deafness and yelled profanities into the dark night at the Germans.

"Eat that you bastards!" one man yelled.

"Go to hell you damned Huns! Courtesy of the 65th!" yelled another.

Harold leapt forward and jerked the breech open again as gunpowder wafted around the men filling their noses and mouths with its acrid scent but no one cared.

Within seconds, other artillery units began firing up and down the American lines in earnest making Harold stand back and stare with wonder at the fireworks.

"My God, look at that," Wellings said pointing to the dark eastern horizon. Brilliant flashes blossomed like strange fiery flowers as far as the men could see on the other side of No Man's Land. In the light of the explosions reflecting off the low hanging clouds Lieutenant Swanson stared at Walter waiting for new coordinates.

"M, mm, more…more 4 degrees, add one-hundred, left fif… left fifty, ou..out," Walter said continuing to stumble over the words in his excitement. "Re…repeat HE 117."

Lieutenant Everson flashed a smile at him. "Calm down, private. I'm nervous too."

Walter grinned back at him and took a deep breath. "Yes sir, thank you sir."

The men manning the gun immediately turned their levers moving the gun slightly and the strict routine of loading was repeated. Harold clanked the breach shut and stepped back making sure to put his fingers in his ears this time. Again, the guns roared up and down the line.

Walter paused, straining to listen to the new coordinates coming in and smiled broadly. "Drop fifty. Fire for effect."

Lieutenant Everson repeated the order and another shell and bag of propellant were loaded much faster this time. In the darkness the men smiled knowing they had to be close to being right on target.

"This one's dropping right on the Kaiser's head!" the Lieutenant shouted triumphantly. The men cheered and hurrahed. "Fire!"

For the next four hours the men of the 65th, one of several American artillery units stretched out along nearly eight miles of front and all of which were now part of the American First Army, fired at the German positions ranging back from the trenches to the roads and supply dumps far behind the front lines. At one point, word came down that the spotters had seen a German regiment moving up to the front lines so they shifted their fire yet again. The night skies were filled with a continuous rumble which was soon joined by German artillery batteries firing back. Several miles to the south an enormous explosion lit the night skies and caused the ground to tremble telling the men the Germans had hit either an ammunition dump or a fully loaded American artillery position.

"My God, poor bastards," Harold muttered wrestling a shell onto the loading cart with three other men.

"Bet they didn't even have time to hear it coming," Mike replied from his place next to the breech. Throughout the night the men took turns doing the battery's various jobs so that no one would be completely worn out from wrestling the shells around and so no man would become so tired or bored that he made a mistake that could kill every man in the position. Everyone's favorite job was pulling the trigger rope that fired *Dora*. "If you're going to go, that's the way to do it if you ask me."

"I'd rather not go at all," Harold grunted.

"Sorry, you know what I mean," Mike said with a shrug.

Just before dawn the orders came down for the 65th to cease fire. Every man slumped down where he was from extreme exhaustion and rubbed their dirty, powder-stained faces. A cook assigned to the regiment walked among them with a bucket full of water and a dirty ceramic coffee cup offering everyone a drink.

Harold leaned back against the sandbag walls and stretched noisily. "I can't hardly hear a thing," he said sticking a finger in each ear.

"Huh?" Wellings asked doing the same. "I can't hear you."

George and Mike lay sprawled at their feet also wiping the grime off their faces and trying to hear.

Mike stared at the faint light of morning in the east with a troubled look on his face. "How many men do you think we killed tonight?"

Harold, Wellings and George looked away not wanting to answer him.

MUSSY-SUR-MARNE, FRANCE

September 29, 1918

"Get up you goddamn schoolgirls! Get your lazy asses up out of those holes!" Sergeant Miller yelled. Taking two enormous steps he planted a boot in Harold's ribs with a sickening thud. "Get up Brooks! Up! Up!"

"What in the hell…" Harold muttered rubbing his side. "I just got to sleep."

"I don't give a damn if you've slept at all! Get the fuck outta that hole!"

Harold rubbed his eyes and coughed trying to clear his lungs of the wetness of the cold, dark mist swirling over the men in their heavy wool khaki uniforms which were now sticky and clammy. With a groan, he pulled himself up with the rest of the exhausted men of his unit who slunk on out hastily dug holes and lean-to's scattered throughout a field just outside the lonely, shadowy remains of a shattered French village.

The company had been allowed a few precious hours of sleep for a change after having spent much of the previous day and night dismantling the huge 9.2 guns and assembling the axles that they rode upon. After they had remounted the guns on the axles, everything else - tools, spare parts and gear were loaded on the huge trucks. It was a long, labor-intensive job that none of the men enjoyed. Sometime later in the day they all knew the entire process would be done in reverse as they would set up the guns in new positions further east. The short rest periods and sleep they were given never seemed to be enough as the American armies continuously slugged their way forward into German defenses. First Sergeant Miller was in a fighting mood and seemed to be even more upset than usual. Evidently Major Martin and the weak Lieutenant Swanson had been after him for something. More often than not, he was somewhat tolerable and took good care of his men but when the brass wanted something done the Sergeant reverted back to his days as a tough, demanding drill instructor.

Rubbing his bloodshot eyes and yawning widely, Harold struggled to pull himself out his shallow sleeping hole. Squinting his tired eyes to see through the piercing darkness, he quickly gathered his rifle and gear knowing that any second wasted was sure to bring down more of the man's wrath or that of Corporal Stevenson who desperately wanted sergeant's stripes and was universally hated as the biggest asshole in the unit. Harold, like all of the other men in his unit never undressed completely except for the luxury of taking his boots off some nights when a few hours of sleep offered a man complete bliss. After shoving his painful feet in the cold, stiff boots always at his side he tied them quickly, stowed his gear and swung his heavy pack up onto his back while staggering to balance himself. Yawning again, he reached into the leather bag hung loosely around his neck and pulled out his pocket watch which he carefully wound it in the light of an American signal flare.

"Four-thirty in the morning. Good lord," he muttered squinting to get a look at the time. Winding it a few more times, he held it to his ear to satisfy himself that it was ticking away before wrapping it in a soft silk handkerchief that now smelled of cigarette smoke and his unwashed body and put it safely back in the leather bag. His hands immediately went to his pocket to retrieve a bent, but intact Lucky Strike and carefully lit it under the cover of his overcoat. Other men were lighting cigarettes too and Sergeant Miller hadn't yelled at them about it so everyone assumed they weren't under black out conditions or within sight of the German forward artillery observers. Inhaling deeply, Harold leaned back and stretched noisily.

"Damn it! I'd like to just sleep for a month straight!" he exclaimed blowing a plume of smoke high into the chilly morning air while he stretched his arms.

A large shape loomed out of the darkness. "Morning Harold."

"Good morning, Wellings."

"What time is it?" the big man asked squatting down with an enormous yawn.

"Four-thirty," Harold replied wearily.

"Damn," Wellings swore. "My old father never got me up this early to work on the farm."

"Mine did."

"To work in a lumber yard?

"Hell yes, first thing in the morning I had to stoke the furnace then it was off to the lumber yard by six to stack lumber and fill hardware bins or something else. Then off to school."

"Your old man sounds like a real gem."

"Oh, he's something all right."

"Hey, you got a smoke?"

Harold pulled the pack out of his pocket and handed it to Wellings who took two.

"Thanks, I owe you."

"Ah, Wellings! You owe me at least ten packs by now!"

"Sorry. Hey, what time is it back in Iowa?" Wellings said trying to change the subject.

Harold thought a moment. Wellings had recently traded his watch for a bottle of whiskey so he was constantly asking Harold for the time and for smokes.

"It's eight hours difference so that would make it… eight-thirty at night."

Wellings lit the cigarette and exhaled noisily. "I'd be getting ready for bed about now if I were home. Son of a bitch, I'm so tired."

In a nearby hole their friend George stood and coughed finally spitting a mouthful of foulness into the mud. He stood, stretched, and looked wearily at Harold with bloodshot eyes. His blonde hair shot out in several different directions. "Have a nice night's sleep did you?"

"Not bad. Why?" Harold asked.

"You've been dreaming again," he told his friend. "All damn night talking to your girlfriend and some other nonsense. Talk, talk, talk!"

"Sorry George."

"I'll bet you are. How am I supposed to dream of my sweet Corrinne?"

Harold and Wellings cackled with laughter. Corrinne was a fantasy woman George had created in drawings he did in a note-book he always had his nose in. She changed daily depending on George's wild mood swings. Most recently he had been revising her and to the great amusement of Harold, Wellings and their other buddy Mike, she now had abnormally large bosoms that strangely resembled the 9.2 shells their gun fired.

"What did I say?" he asked now amused. "I don't remember a bit of it."

"Darned if I know. You're always talking in your dreams to someone and thrashing around. It's quite a story some nights.

157

Sometimes you hold me close and call me Margaret. I might have to find a new hole mate! You should hear yourself!" George said falling back into the mud disgustedly.

He continued thrashing around in the darkness for his gear all the while swearing and throwing things. "It's not even close to the time I should get out of bed! Damned army!"

George usually didn't come around much until mid-afternoon and thoroughly hated waking before at least nine A.M. – what he considered a civilized hour to wake. The Army and its peculiar ways had interrupted his fine, easy life as a student, self-proclaimed poet and lover at some fancy East coast college Harold had never heard of. As he mumbled to himself and continued gathering up his belongings sergeant Miller reappeared.

"Get up and get your shit together!" Sergeant Miller shouted. "We've got a lot of road to cover to get to some damn frog town called Autreville so move it out!"

Noticing that George was lagging behind the rest of the men, he double-timed his step over to his least favorite Private to give him a little extra motivation. "Let's go you fancy little prick! Get that shit together and get your ass moving!"

"Yes sergeant!"

"Not in five minutes, not in an hour…Now!"

Harold and Wellings watched with amusement as Miller stomped away to motivate some other unfortunate.

"When are you and the sarge going to just kiss and make up?" Harold asked with a big grin on his face.

"Yeah," Wellings added. "You know he loves you."

"Fuck you, Harold. And fuck you too, Wellings."

The two men laughed and knelt down to help George find his belongings. "Yeah, yeah. You'll feel better once we've had some coffee. Come on, let's go," said Harold who enjoyed toying with his foul-tempered friend early in the mornings.

With tired grumbles and muffled profanity, the other men in the Company struggled to their feet doing their best to shake off their exhaustion and stow their gear before Miller reappeared.

As he struggled to get the rest of his gear together, George continued to grumble and swear in his well-born eastern accent. "That detestable sergeant is certainly annoyed today. What are we doing now?"

"Don't know," Harold replied. "Probably another push the Frogs couldn't finish and need some fresh meat to throw at the Huns."

"Yeah," those goddamn fucking frogs. They've been trying to lose this war from the start. Now they want to kill all of us off too," George snapped.

"Or," Wellings growled out of the darkness, "The Limey's. Haig can't seem to kill enough of them neither. We're just here to fill the holes in their lines."

George angrily shoved more gear into his pack, "If they do, then maybe we can quit eating Maconochie, Bully and hard tack. What rubbish! My father will hear about this!" George exclaimed waving his hand theatrically in the air.

Harold and the other men laughed knowing George's hatred for the army and for Sergeant Miller in particular. Whenever things looked bad George would threaten to have his rich father fix things for him. Evidently he was some big shot banker who had covered George's backside and kept him out of trouble more than once during his pampered youth. His saying had become the joke of their unit, 2nd Company, Battery C of the 65th Coastal Artillery Company and when things went south men of the group would threaten to have George's father hear about it while waving a hand in the air. Sergeant Miller didn't understand the men's particular attachment to this saying and usually responded with, "Fuck your fathers!" to the great amusement of the men.

"So, tell us George, why exactly did you enlist? Couldn't you have just stayed in that plushy college you were in and lived the good life on your father's money?" Harold asked, hoping to jab his friend a bit. George sometimes told his friends he'd enlisted in the Army after a wave of patriotism, or extreme drunkenness had overcome him. Wanted to do his bit, and all of that. His stories were always different and on other occasions claimed he had been inspired by the work of Alan Seeger, an American poet who had died in 1916 fighting with the French Foreign Legion.

"Well, you know Harold, I was on the verge of being dismissed from college and was bored, so I joined up to have something to do, a Holiday of sorts." George said as he laced his boots up. "Father was certainly furious. He refused to come down and get me out of the Army. I found myself fucked once I'd um, sobered up."

"Sure George, whatever you say," Wellings grumbled. "I thought you told us you were in the pokey and the judge gave you the choice of the army or jail. What happened to that story?"

George sat back against the rim of his sleeping hole and thought a moment. "Not true. However, the real story is that the man in the recruiting office told me I was officer material and I'd go to OCS shortly after training started. The man was a liar and I intend to find him after the war and jam my bayonet up his ass."

Harold and Wellings slapped their knees with laughter.

"Imagine that will you," Wellings howled choking on cigarette smoke. "*Lieutenant* Goodlow, our fearless leader! We'd lose the war!"

"Oh, come on George!" Harold laughed. "That's not what you told us last week!"

"Go to hell, both of you," George answered as Harold and Wellings pulled him out of his hole.

"Goddamn, listen to that will you," Wellings said turning towards the east where flashes and booms began rippling across the horizon. "Someone's up early today."

160

The low rumble of British, French, German, and American artillery began pounding away at one another in earnest, slinging death and destruction back and forth through the dark morning skies. It was something that most men took for granted after so long and strangely, no one could sleep without it when they were sent to the rear for a precious day or two of rest. Silence scared them.

The dull thuds were accentuated with occasional brilliant flashes reminded Harold of the summer rainstorms back in Iowa. Storms and artillery both had something ominous and unknown about them as though God was letting loose evil upon the world and one never new if it would come a little too close. Death was a common thing to see and it happened so often the men had become callous and indifferent to it. The only way to deal with its constant reminders was to be thankful that it wasn't you who was dead and smashed beyond recognition. But, if you were dead it wouldn't really matter either way. With a shiver, Harold adjusted his rifle and gear while he and George silently fell in at the side of the road with the rest of the sleepy, swearing men in their company.

MARCHING

September 29, 1918

"Everyone here?" Sergeant Miller asked Corporal Stevenson. "Yes sergeant. All present and accounted for except for Lieutenant Swanson. Couldn't find him anywhere."

"That doesn't surprise me," the sergeant replied yawning and glancing at his watch. "Come on, get the men moving."

The corporal turned and yelled at the men of 2nd Company. "Company! Ten hut! Get those fucking smokes put out! Let's move!"

The men grumbled and shuffled to attention. Harold flicked the glowing, burning end of his cigarette off onto the ground and crushed it with his boot. The un-smoked portion went back into the pack of Lucky Strikes in his coat pocket for later.

"Left face!" the corporal yelled. "Fo'wrd march!"

The tired men slowly trudged uphill through the sucking mud towards the main road which was already alive with traffic.

"Dammit!" George exclaimed angrily. "The gun trucks have already left. We're walking again!"

"And they'll probably get stuck somewhere and show up about the time we get there so we'll do all the work again!" Wellings grumbled from behind Harold. His opinion was greeted with more swearing and threats.

"Those sons of bitches," Harold grumbled. "And, you can bet they won't start any of the work until we all get to wherever the hell we're going to."

"You're right. Those lazy bastards are probably having a nice hot breakfast about now," Mike said from behind Harold and Wellings.

"I'd like to beat on a couple of them," Wellings said balling his fists up. "Especially Corporal Hansen, the chief idiot in that crew. He doesn't know his ass from a hole in the ground."

Corporal Stevenson led them up to the road where they joined in with other units headed east towards the front lines. Horse-drawn wagons slipped back and forth in the mud while their drivers yelled streams of profanity at the animals to keep them moving. The occasional crack of a wet whip rang out indicating those not going fast enough. A long line of mules from the States plodded along carrying their precious loads of ammunition, food, and medical supplies. Trucks rumbled along beside the men and animals splattering everyone with mud and water.

"Now, that will wake you up!" Wellings said covering his mouth with a handkerchief. "What is that smell?"

"Jesus, are we walking through a latrine?" Harold asked catching his breath.

Other men were choking and complaining about the sickening smell in the air. Some tore off chunks of cigarettes to stick in their noses.

"We're outside of Verdun," Sergeant Miller informed the men.

The 65th's sector of the battlefield was on what had been the far left of the French defensive line during the enormous battles around Verdun in 1916. The men remembered reading about the Germans and French fighting here for ten horrible months as the German Army had attempted to "bleed the French white" and ultimately win the war. The German plan, they knew, had failed as the French held their ground and fought the Germans to a standstill.

"I heard over one million men were killed around here," Harold said.

"Yeah, I heard that too. Most of them never got buried. Just ground up by artillery and mixed in with the mud," Sergeant Miller said grimacing.

"Is that what we're smelling?"

"More than likely. Probably a mass grave got opened up by the shelling."

"Good lord…"

The bones and rusted equipment littered the devastated battlefield and seemed to be everywhere. In addition, millions of unexploded live shells of all sizes and caliber littered the ground, now rusty and black from age but still enormously lethal to the unfortunate man or animal who happened to stumble in the quagmire and set them off. The men had learned from experience to dig slit trenches and holes carefully.

"Remember that kid…what was his name? The one who got blown up digging a sleeping hole," Harold asked pulling a cigarette from his pocket.

"Which one?" Wellings answered. "Couple of them clipped it that way."

"The one from Iowa."

"Oh yeah, I remember him. He was short and had kind of a round face and a little nose. You know, he looked like a fat mouse. Where was he from in Iowa?"

"I thought he said Hastings."

"No, I thought he said over around Iowa City somewhere, my neck of the woods. We all told him not to dig in that field."

"We did. Don't dig where there's been a recent bombardment. You never know what didn't go boom," Harold replied breaking a cigarette in two and shoving the pieces in his nose.

"Yeah, he was what? Four or five feet down, just hacking away."

Harold laughed. "Remember what he said?"

Wellings nodded and chuckled with a few other men who remembered the day. "Hey! You guys have a pick? I think I hit a rock. Then, BOOM!" he replied throwing his hands in the air. "I had bits of that guy stuck all over me for weeks."

"Me too," Harold replied shaking his head. "Poor bugger."

The men all knew if they were forced to dig in disturbed ground to do so carefully. German artillerymen were notorious for setting their artillery fuses to detonate at different altitudes and depths to increase the kill ratio on the battlefield either instantly or later on. The power of the explosion had turned the young man and the man next to him into a red jellied mass of bone and gore.

Millions of broken shards of jagged shrapnel were everywhere and still inflicted wounds on the men and the service animals when stepped on. They crunched and clinked metallically under the heavy, wet boots of the Americans.

"*Guten tag*, asshole," George said with a mocking salute to a skull complete with tufts of brown hair and putrid, mummified skin covered by a dented German *Stahlhelm* helmet some American jokester had propped on a rusty screw picket, or pigtail as the men called them, by the side of the road for fun. It glowered at them with dark, vacant eyes while its skeletal mouth was opened wide in a silent scream of discontent. Bits of rotten flesh, bones, uniforms, leather, and smashed weapons littered the ditches around it. Rusty barbed wire wove through the ground in deep, torn up belts that only added to the discomfort of the men and animals trying to move towards the front. It reminded Harold of the junkyard back at home except for the proliferation of fat grinning rats that populated the dead ground.

Hundreds of men from several half-destroyed American infantry units also trudged toward the front lines in the sucking, nearly frozen mud. Dark curses and laughter revealed men who slipped and fell. On the left, a steady procession of wounded made their way to the rear each hoping his injury was bad enough to merit a ticket away from the death and from the mud. If they were lucky, a hospital near Paris with a wound bad enough to be sent home. Many didn't care if they lost a leg or an arm anymore just as long as it got them out of the war. Wounds, the men knew, weren't always lucky though: If a man developed gas gangrene in their wound which was an easy thing to do because of the filth they would slowly rot to death.

Suddenly, a series of German flares popped overhead illuminating the road and surrounding fields in their ghostly shimmering light.

"Take cover! Incoming!" yelled Sergeant Miller ducking his head and running for cover at the side of the road. Everyone along the road scattered hearing the high pitched whooshing, screaming sound slicing through the air above and knew what it meant: German 77 mm shells, the infamous "whiz bangs". Men scattered everywhere jumping into ditches and shell holes as the shells began pounding the road and surrounding fields.

"Fuck!" Harold shouted ducking low and running. "Every goddamn day!"

More shells came thundering in followed by an ominous shriek.

"Here comes the devil!" George shouted as he ran beside Harold. "Bastards!"

Harold ducked his head a little lower and ran as fast as he could despite the weight of his rifle and gear dragging him down all the while jumping over men who had fallen in their haste to find cover. After falling twice and shoving another man out of his way he finally lurched headlong into a ditch half full of fetid water with George at his side. Curling themselves up and hugging their knees they prayed and tried to keep their mouths open.

"Our Father, who Art in Heaven," Harold murmured to himself. "Hallowed be thy..."

One shell exploded dangerously close to the ditch blasting them with its shockwave and covering them with mud. Someone cried out in fear.

"Hallowed be thy name, Thy Kingdom come, Thy will be done on Earth..."

More shrieking shells exploded around them and several smashed to their right into an American field kitchen and mess area in a field next to the road. Kitchen equipment, pots, pans, field ovens, heaps of dirt and several body parts were strewn about haphazardly. Harold could hear a number of men screaming in pain. The others must be dead he thought.

"Dammit all to hell!" exclaimed Wellings as he peered over the edge of the ditch at the shattered mess area. "I was looking forward to breakfast today. I heard they was havin' oatmeal and biscuits. Maybe even bacon. Hell's bells!"

"Get your head down you big dumb son-of-a-bitch!" Sergeant Miller barked. "More incoming!"

Several more German shells roared over and tore into the field where Harold and the rest of his company had just spent the night causing everyone to press themselves deeper into the ditches.

And suddenly, the barrage stopped. The men all waited, afraid to leave the relative safety of their cover. The Germans would often wait several minutes between barrages to lure men out of their hiding places. Then they would suddenly open fire again to try and kill more men out in the open.

After what seemed like hours Sergeant Miller climbed cautiously out of the mud, dripping with filth. "Spotter team somewhere over there must have seen all this traffic. Bastards have good eyes. Everyone alright?"

A few men answered the sergeant with weak voices.

"Good, let's move out. "Doesn't look like we're getting hot breakfast today."

As the men struggled out of the wet ditches and got moving again, Harold looked ahead into the eastern sky. It was burning with the pinkish, hazy light of dawn.

"Damn Boche," said George to no one in particular. "Don't they know they've lost this war? Why don't they just give it up so we can all go home?"

"I don't know," replied Harold. "Maybe they've been doing it so long they can't do anything else anymore."

"Well, I for one wish the bastards would find something," Wellings swore wiping red liquid from his coat and pants. "That bottle of wine I had in my pack broke. Goddamn son-of-a-bitches!"

Ahead of the men an American mule shrieked and thrashed about violently in the middle of the road. It had been wounded by the shelling and was trying to stand despite the wicked injuries it had suffered from the shrapnel. The mule would half-stand, then fall back into the muddy road with another horrible shriek, it's feet wrapped up in its intestines which hung from its bloody, torn open stomach. The load of bandages and medical supplies the animal had been carrying were scattered about indiscriminately in the filth of the road. The creature's eyes were huge and white with fear and pain as it continued its' dreadful shrieking. The muleskinner who had tended this poor animal lay face down in the road still clutching what was left of the leather harness he had led his wounded charge with. His dark blood steamed in the frosty morning air as it ran in tiny rivers down into the deep water-filled ruts.

Harold and the men gave the dying animal a wide berth as they slowly marched by. Each man stared on with morbid, though indifferent, fascination. A mud-encrusted Lieutenant from one of the infantry units walked over to the wounded mule and produced his .45 pistol. Pulling back the slide to rack the weapon, he lowered it and fired two quick shots into the animal's head. It fell heavily onto the road, its blood mingling with that of its master. Holstering the weapon, the Lieutenant rejoined his men. Harold had looked at the man as he walked by and was struck by his eyes which were dark and lifeless. His face too, had been completely devoid of any expression. Harold coughed and looked away wondering if he looked like that now himself.

AMAZING GRACE

September 29, 1918

As the sun began peeking over the eastern horizon Harold and his friends came upon a maintenance company of black men who were busy filling shell holes and potholes along a stretch of torn up road. Most used shovels and picks while a lucky two manned the horse drawn road grader which smoothed over recently filled holes. None spoke and all were giving careful looks to a white corporal who was busy screaming at a black private the corporal had just knocked to his knees by the side of the road. The man was holding his stomach and breathing heavily while spit and vomit hung from his mouth.

"You goddamn colored son of a bitch!" he yelled at the defenseless man. "I ought to have you skinned for speaking to me that way!"

He raised his hand to strike the man again when a voice behind Harold spoke up.

"Hey asshole. Why don't you leave the man alone!" It was Mike Wilson, who surprisingly was a Georgia boy, a true southerner.

The corporal strode angrily across the muddy road while the black private made a run for it. "What did you say to me?" he demanded pulling a trench knife out of its sheath.

"Why don't you pick on someone who will fight back? Like me, you fucking white trash son-of-a-bitch!" Mike roared.

The corporal smiled showing brown, tobacco stained teeth and took a step towards Mike when suddenly a green uniformed blur knocked him down onto the muddy road.

"Get your ass away from the men in my company! Move!" Sergeant Miller growled standing over the man.

The corporal's white buddies who had been sitting around watching the black men work were now lining up across the road from the company ready to fight. The black soldiers stopped their labor and immediately stepped back curious to see what would happen next.

The corporal breathlessly picked himself up out of the mud glaring at Mike and Sergeant Miller. "You fuckers watch yourselves," he drawled holding a hand to his eye. "If I find you in the dark sometime, I'll cut both ya's up! You can count on that!"

"Go to hell," Sergeant Miller said shoving the man out of his way before turning to get his men moving down the road.

Lieutenant Swanson unexpectedly appeared and glared at his men through bleary, bloodshot eyes. "Sergeant Miller!" he shouted. "What in the hell is going on here? Get these goddamn men moving. They don't have time to play grab-ass with the Engineers!"

"Yes sir!" the Sergeant answered turning away from the Lieutenant. "Move it out! Now! Double-time!"

The men quickly began striding out down the road, each holding his head a little higher and with all in step while they laughed and made obscene gestures at the corporal and his cronies.

"Well, that was fun!" Harold laughed after the men crested a small hill leaving the Engineers behind. "Leave it to Mike to say what we were all thinking."

When Mike had something to say, which wasn't often it was usually very direct and most importantly, to the point. George smiled and looked back at Mike who still scowled with anger. "I think his hair is turning redder. It always does when he gets angry."

"Shut up, George," Mike grumbled.

The men around them laughed knowing the depths of Mike's particular temper. Educated to be a Southern gentleman from the day of his birth, Mike had gone to an expensive boarding school as a young man and gone to the University of Georgia for two years before enlisting in the Army as a common private in 1917. He, like so many others, wanted to escape his father and live an adventure before he had to become the responsible adult everyone said he should be.

"Those men," Mike drawled. "I see the same thing at home in the chain gangs on the side of the roads and even in church. It's just legalized slavery now and I'd bet every one of those white boys back there is from the south too. Fuckers."

"Come on Mike," Wellings said with a smile. "They're your Rebel brethren."

"Haw!" Mike spat. "They're all ignorant white trash. Definitely not my sort of people. They're why we lost the war to you Yankees."

"Didn't you say your grandfather was a Confederate General?" Harold asked lighting a cigarette.

"Yes, he was, and he personally owned slaves. After the war he changed his ways, saw the light of God and became a Baptist preacher. He freed all of his slaves," Mike said proudly. "I don't care for people who can't get over the Civil War. Especially the ones who wear bed sheets."

"But what can you do about it?" Harold asked exhaling smoke.

"I'm going to run for office someday once this is all over with. You know, try to change things from the inside."

Several men laughed and muttered to themselves.

"We already have a President Wilson," Wellings replied with a smile. "And I don't care for him a bit."

"If I ever got to the White House I'd change a lot of things in this country," Mike said with determination. "I'd help blacks get more rights and education. I'd help the poor."

"Would you keep us out of wars in Europe?" George asked.

"You're damn right I would."

"You've got my vote then!"

The main topic of conversation quickly turned to sex as it often did. A voice from behind from the rear of the column spoke up.

"Hey Wellings! Getting any?"

"Only your mother," Wellings responded without missing a step.

"Fuck you!" the voice answered.

Wellings smiled and turned his head. "Nah, your mother wore me out. I need to stay fresh. Your sister is coming over tonight." The men laughed even harder as Wellings was showered with mud thrown from the man behind them.

"When do you suppose we'll have to sit through another 'How to fuck in the army,' lecture?" George asked. "I'm personally looking forward to more stories about Private Johnson and his diseased escapades in the French whorehouses."

The men groaned and booed in unison. Every time they received a few days of R and R in the rear they were forced to sit through sex education and health lectures which became a source of great amusement to some and an embarrassment to others. Recently, the Army had begun cracking down severely on men who found themselves infected so the health lectures were now mandatory for everyone. Harold had thought about visiting some of the French brothels in the rear areas on two different very drunken occasions when the 65th was training in Limoges but he hadn't been able to bring himself to do it. He simply loved Margaret too much and besides, he didn't want to take a turn after God-only-knows how many men had been there before him. George and Wellings had no such qualms though and loved to regale many of the non-participating men with vivid, often shocking tales of their newfound prowess. Harold still laughed at what Wellings had first thought was a nasty new strain of viciously biting cooties that had taken up residence in his pubic hair but in reality had been a fearful dose of crabs. Some of the more daring veterans called Wellings "the fisherman."

The march continued as the first light of the morning sun popped over the horizon. Harold reached into the inner pocket of his coat and carefully touched his now well-worn packet of letters just to reassure himself if only for a moment. He suddenly wanted to throw down his rifle and all of his equipment and run all the way to Brest and a board a fast ship home. His worry over Margaret's strange letters and more recently, the lack of any writing at all, tore at Harold's mind.

As the men crested a small hill groups of soldiers were seen in the nearby field digging and moving things about.

"Look, over there. What are they doing Harold?" asked George.

Looking to their left Harold saw another company of black soldiers digging what looked like a long trench. The men dug in rhythm; each spade full of mud was dug and thrown out of the trench in a cadence sung out by a young black Private with a particularly beautiful voice. His song sounded strange and haunting while they performed their unappreciated labor. Harold listened closely, inhaling deeply then carefully tearing the lit end of the cigarette off and repeating his habit of putting the butt in his pocket for later. The song sounded strangely familiar and stirred something within him. It sounded like something from home.

"What is that," muttered Harold. "What is that song?" He tried to listen above the distant din of artillery, the boots of thousands of men tramping in the mud, the trucks and the careless banter of his comrades. Behind him, Harold could hear Sergeant Miller yelling blindly at Wellings and someone else who had stopped to relieve themselves by the side of the road.

"What in the hell are you two doing!" he shouted. "You men don't have time to take a leisurely Sunday morning piss. There's a war on!"

He stomped through the mud towards the two. "I said move!" he snarled with his mouth almost touching the new guy's ear.

"Can't even take a leak in the army without written permission!" someone yelled.

Another man answered, "Flies spread disease. So keep yours closed!"

Wellings went ahead with his business and began whistling a tune as he gazed unhurriedly into the sky. Unnerved by Sergeant Miller's outburst a new guy fresh from the Replacement Depot tried to get back into formation while pulling his trousers up but they fallen down around his ankles. After taking one shaking step he tripped and fell face first in the mud which brought howls of laughter. Wellings, a veteran like Harold and most of the other men knew Sergeant Miller had been trying to scare the new guy a bit and ignored him. He casually finished the job and shook himself vigorously while looking around for encouragement from his buddies.

"Sergeant Miller!" he called out in a feminine voice. "I have something for you. It's very special!"

Someone yelled, "Shake it for him Wellings! I heard you like the sarge!"

Sergeant Miller strode off without a word looking for some of the other new replacements to the great amusement of his men. Wellings buttoned up with obvious disappointment and ran to catch up with Harold, George and Mike.

"Maybe next time," he grumbled as he fell in line with his smirking buddies.

All of the men loved to get a word in on their first sergeant when he was unprepared for it. He was used to the old army standards of ruling through absolute fear with men who were volunteers and actually wanted to serve in the peacetime army. Mike noisily cleared his throat and threw his shoulders back doing his best impersonation of Sergeant Miller, a favorite among the men.

"All of you goddamn glory-seekers and draftees really chap my ass!" he bellowed. "And none of you scumbags seem to worry much about the chain of command or army discipline at all. I think you're all here to work me into an early grave! You sons a bitches! Get on your faces and give me twenty-five!" The men roared with even more laughter and several patted Mike on the back.

Sergeant Miller cast a dirty look at Mike and stomped away. The young boy still tried in vain to button his trousers up.

"You know he won't forget that," Harold said turning to see where Sergeant Miller had gone.

"I don't give a damn," Mike replied. "What's he going to do? Send me to the front?"

"Yeah, good point."

On the side of the road the moaning cadence continued, every now and then another voice would add a beautiful harmony or a completely new line.

The glory of the Lord. He will forgive.
Glory be to the true believers.

Harold strained his ears to listen, trying to remember. As he kept marching he came upon Padre Fred, the unit chaplain, a Catholic priest from Portland, Oregon.

"Hey Padre," Harold called out to the short, stocky priest who stood watching the grave diggers sing. "What's that song? I can't quite place it."

Padre Fred turned and looked at Harold. "Why, that's *Amazing Grace* Private Brooks. A beautiful rendition I must say. Just beautiful."

Harold cocked an ear to listen and also smiled. It was a favorite of his mother's so he quietly hummed along as he fell back in with George.

"Why the hell are they digging a trench back here?" asked George pointing. "We're two or three miles from the front."

After a few steps it became obvious what the trench was for. Marching up another small rise in the road gave them a perfect view of the muddy field and the miles of open country beyond where the front lines snaked around endlessly. Row after row of smashed, disfigured bodies lay silently in the field wearing identical American dark green wool uniforms and brown boots wrapped with puttees. Some had been hastily covered with any available material, tarps, old tents, pieces of boxes, anything to give them some kind of dignity.

"It's a mass grave," Harold said casing a long glance at the field.

"Oh, Jesus…there are hundreds of them."

Two men moved among the dead squatting down at each to look for identification tags. All men carried two identical tags hung around his neck with his name, rank, and service number. One tag went into the dead man's mouth, if he still had one, for future identification, the other into bloody leather bags carried by the men in Graves Registration so the man's family could be notified of his death.

"Holy mother," George said looking away.

"I'll never get used to seeing that," Mike said with a shiver.

"No, not when they're young like all of us are," Harold answered.

Every man in Harold and George's company continued marching steadily along staring silently at the dead. One man turned his head to spit a large stream of brown tobacco juice which splattered noisily on the muddy road. They had all seen enough bodies since arriving in France and as long as the body wasn't a particular buddy it didn't matter much.

Harold thought about the only dead person he had even seen before he had come to France. The memory of his Aunt Olive had given him nightmares when he was younger. The woman was shrunken and white in death and her tiny body had barely filled the shiny wooden coffin in the Sac City funeral home. He then thought of one other new soldiers sent to their unit two weeks before. A young boy no one had taken the time to get to know was about Harold's age had been an ammunition loader in their neighboring gun crew. Harold and his friends in 2nd Company had just finished assembling *Dora* and had camouflaged the entire gun position behind the ruins of a French village where the 65th was digging in. As they were walking back to the old French trenches and dugouts which were their billets for the next few days the Germans began shelling the village hoping to destroy the American artillery they had observed digging in. Harold, George, Mike, Wellings and the other men heard the first few coming down and had luckily made it into the trenches in time. The twenty minute barrage hadn't done much damage with most of the German shells falling short in the already smashed village. As other men yelled the all clear Harold and his group emerged from their trench to see a small group gathered around a lifeless form next to the neighboring gun emplacement. It was the new guy. There were no noticeable marks anywhere on his body and his uniform was still fresh and new, a kid who had gone straight from the transport ship to the outfitting depot and then directly to the front. He looked like he had just slipped and fallen into the mud. His rifle lay across his chest hooked around his neck by the sling – it was pristine and virtually unscratched, and still had a thick wad of greasy Cosmoline smeared across the action. When the shelling had started the boy had panicked and was frozen in place while the rest of the men in his unit had run for cover. He was the only casualty that day.

"High explosive shell," Sergeant Miller explained as they stood looking at him. "The concussion killed him. Dumb bastard never knew what hit him."

The image still haunted Harold because the boy's bright green eyes were eerily reminiscent of Bobby's. It was strange; he didn't look dead, he looked as though he were simply resting and there wasn't the old smell of death like Aunt Olive had in Harold's memory. And despite what Sergeant Miller had said, he was just dead due to no particular act of stupidity on his part.

"Just like blowing out a candle," Harold muttered quietly to himself as he and his comrades turned to walk to the chow line. Someone had told them they were having beef stew, cornbread and real coffee. More than likely it was goat flesh stew and moldy bread with fake, lukewarm coffee, but the promise of a hot meal made them forget about the nameless dead boy.

Wellings stopped to light a cigarette. Holding the match out in front of his face, he blew it out quickly. "Jesus, I just can't get used to it. Just like that, one second you're here, the next...poof."

Harold and every man in his company knew their odds of survival weren't that good even if they were in an artillery unit. Death seemed to spare no one who found themselves in France.

Continuing on their slow march forward, the men pulled to the side of the road as a wagon approached. Three blacks rode on the front bench smoking cigarettes to dull the stench of what they were carrying behind them.

"You boys gonna kill some Germans?" asked one with an expressionless face. "They been killin' the shit outta you boys at the front."

"Yeah," cried another. "I wish they'd let me kill some of them Huns. Just look what they done! Son of a bitches!"

Harold and George looked into the back of the wagon as it rolled and meandered along in the mud. It, and the other five wagons in their column were full of body parts that these poor men had been sent to collect for burial. Arms, legs, torsos, hands, feet, whatever was left of men who had been shattered by the incessant

German shelling and couldn't be identified were being brought back to be dumped in the huge trenches in the field. The cart hit a deep rut in the road left by American traffic and a severed arm fell out into the mud. Despite the cold air, the smell soon overwhelmed them as the sad procession bounced by.

"Jesus Christ," choked George. "It's like a rendering cart!"

He stopped in mid-step and vomited. Harold slowed to wait for him. Other men were gagging and vomiting in the road as well.

"You okay?" he asked his friend.

George wiped his mouth and shook his head. "I hate this place."

Harold helped his friend along and adjusted his pack and rifle and kept walking down the muddy road digging in his jacket for his precious cigarettes. One for him and one for George. "Yeah," he said. "Me too."

MAIL

"Mail call! Mail call!" Corporal Stevenson shouted waving a handful of letters in the air. Harold and every other man his Battery immediately stopped what they were doing and pressed in tightly around him jostling and elbowing one another good naturedly.

"Please God, let me get something from Margaret this time. Please..." he mumbled while wiping his greasy hands on his trousers.

After what seemed like an eternity Corporal Stevenson finally called his name. "Brooks!"

"Yo! Right here!" Harold answered pushing his way through the crowd of men with his hand in the air before snatching the letters from the corporal's outstretched hand. Once clear of the crowd he leaned back against a wall of sandbags and began thumbing through the three letters he'd received. One from Bobby, another from Mr. Caldwell his high school principle and the last from the men at the GAR unit in Sac City but nothing from Will who always forwarded Margaret's letters on to him in a new envelope.

"Dammit!" Harold cursed. It had been several weeks since he'd gotten anything from her and he was beginning to become angry over her silence.

Other men talked excitedly and sat down in and around the gun emplacement and happily tore into their mail while Harold dejectedly sat down on a wooden shell crate and opened a letter he'd received from Bobby. Even though Margaret hadn't written in several weeks he was always happy to get a letter from the boy, misspellings, wrong words and all.

> *Dere Harold,*
>
> *I hope you are killing lots of Germans. Theyr bad. Will says you shoot big guns. How big are they? Can you shoot skwerls with them? I shot one down at the river. He was big and my frend Billy and I skinned him and made a hat. It stinks now. Will said I'm a good worker. I help him do chors. Miss Allen says I'm good at math. When are you coming home? I think dad misses you. I wish I could talk to Margaret. I bet you do to. I made a pole for you with a neat stick I found the oter day. You can have it when you come home.*
> *Love,*
> *Bobby*

Harold smiled and read the letter again. Bobby's penmanship wasn't very good and Harold always had to squint when reading them several times to make sure he'd understood what the boy was telling him. When he got to the line about Margaret he stopped cold. What did he mean when he said that he wished he could talk to Margaret? Wasn't she still walking him to school and helping to keep an eye on him?

Suddenly Sergeant Miller interrupted the letter reading. "Get back to work, goddamn you all!" he shouted. "This gun ain't going to fix itself and those fuses won't just jump into the shells. Let's move! You can read them later after chow!"

The men grumbled and stuffed their mail into pockets and pulled themselves back to work amidst a chorus of profanities and thinly veiled threats. Harold took a deep breath and squeezed his shut wishing suddenly that he'd never joined the Army and come to France. "How could I have been so stupid? I'm gone and she's done with me. Shit!" Wiping the beginnings of tears from his eyes before Wellings or anyone else saw them he quickly read back through the letter hoping somehow to see the true meaning in it as though the child were leaving him a cryptic message.

"Get your ass back to work Brooks! Move it!" Sergeant Miller yelled in Harold's ear causing him to nearly fall down with surprise.

"Fine!" Harold shouted wadding up the letter into a ball before throwing it to the ground. Wiping his eyes again, he stomped through the mud back to the makeshift table where he'd been cleaning *Dora's* firing mechanism.

Sergeant Miller marched angrily over and grabbed his shoulders wheeling him around to face him. "Pick that up Private," he snarled pointing to the letter.

Harold glared at the Sergeant, his face pinched with anger and embarrassment. Many choice words came to mind and for a moment he considered telling Miller exactly what he thought but he knew better than to push the man. "Yes sergeant," he replied in a wavering voice. As he stood and pressed it into his pocket Sergeant Miller was immediately in his face again. He looked at Harold with dark piercing eyes.

"I don't know what in the hell's been going on with you lately but you better un-fuck yourself and do your job. Understand?"

Other men in the Battery suppressed laughter as they went about their work. Harold stared straight ahead. "Yes sergeant."

Sergeant Miller continued eyeing Harold, his tobacco and stale coffee tinged breath blowing in Harold's face. Behind the Sergeant, Harold could see Wellings thrusting his hips out as though he were having wild sex. A few men laughed quietly but the rest watched to see what would happen next. Emboldened by his luck of getting away with what he was doing, Wellings grabbed his crotch and began thrusting even harder bringing more stifled laughter. Sergeant Miller finally did an about face and glared at Wellings who immediately went back to work.

"Come with me," he growled.

Just as they were about to step out of the gun emplacement Sergeant Miller stopped and turned. "Private Wellings!"

Wellings bolted to attention. "Yes sergeant," he answered with a smirk still plastered on his face.

"You have latrine duty for the next week. You'll begin after we've gotten our work done on the gun and shells. Those shitters better be fucking spotless."

The entire group of men in the Battery erupted in laughter. Wellings threw his wrench to the ground with disgust. "Yes sergeant," he answered dejectedly.

Harold followed Sergeant Miller out of the ravine where the 65th was dug in and then back down into a field where several makeshift tents had been set up. They stopped under the shelter of one set up for storage of the Company's spare parts and other assorted Army crates. The musty tarp covering the piles flapped and swayed in the wind. Sergeant Miller sat down on one of the boxes and removed his hat.

"At ease," he said in a tired voice.

Harold relaxed from attention but feared the ass-chewing and punishment he knew he'd probably receive would be coming. After digging into a trouser pocket Sergeant Miller pulled out a pouch and filled one side of his mouth with chewing tobacco.

"I don't know what's going on with you but you've gone to hell in a handbasket lately. Anything you'd like to talk about?" he asked spitting tobacco juice into the mud at his feet.

Harold lowered his eyes and kicked at the ground. For some reason he couldn't explain he'd become surly and angry lately.

The week before he'd been put on latrine digging duty for fighting with Howard Neff during a day-long firing mission. The two had accidently run into each other causing Harold to fall face first to the ground as he and other men were wrestling the big shells into position for the loaders. Even though it had been an accident and he considered Howard a friend, Harold punched him. Howard of course, returned the favor and the fight was on.

Harold shifted on his feet and felt the lump around his bruised eye which was now a strange green color. "Nothing much, sergeant. Just some trouble at home."

Sergeant Miller leaned back against a crate. "If it's trouble at home then it shouldn't affect you in the least. There's nothing you can do about it."

Harold nodded and looked away. He'd heard this from his buddies, too, and was growing tired of it.

"Wouldn't happen to be a woman problem would it?" the sergeant asked. "Because if it is, that's the worst kind of trouble a soldier can have while he's fighting a war."

Harold smiled sarcastically. "Yes sergeant, that's it. Dumb woman problems," he blurted out but quickly turned more serious. "What does a guy do when they quit writing and there's no way to know what's happened? It's making me crazy thinking about it all, sergeant. That's what's eating at me. That, and this all, here...it never ends. I feel hopeless."

Sergeant Miller leaned forward and spat into the mud again while scratching vigorously at his armpits. "I'll tell you what that means Brooks." he said. "It means that there isn't a damn thing to be done about it, especially worrying yourself to death with it. You need to focus on your job and the men you're with here. This is the only reality you have now."

Harold eyed him curiously.

"That's right," he continued. "The only things that are real are what you're living and doing right now. And that's the War and our

185

part in it. You have to find a way to take home and loved ones and tuck it away somewhere and keep it put away. When you get back to the States, then you can let all of it back out. This shit here," he said waving his hand around, "the mud, the killing, the exhaustion, the fucking cooties...all of it, will be the things you'll have to put away once you're home."

Harold stood with his brow creased trying to take all of Sergeant Miller's advice in. It was certainly a lot to think about and he was surprised at the depth of the man that was Sergeant Miller.

Sergeant Miller stood and extended his hand which Harold took and shook firmly.

"Get yourself together, Brooks," Miller said. "You're a good soldier and you shouldn't be letting something at home kill you inside. She'll be there for you when you get home."

"Thank you Sergeant," Harold answered earnestly. "I'll try my best. I really will."

"Good," Miller said. "On another note, I have a little job for you to do over in HQ Company. Shouldn't take more than a week or two but if you like it you can stay with them. Call it a little change of pace for a few days. I think you need one."

Harold thought for a moment. He welcomed a change, anything that would break up the grinding monotony of the unremitting life he endured as an artilleryman. He didn't want to leave his friends but doing something different might possibly be nice for a while.

"Yes Sergeant. If I may, what is the job?" he asked.

"HQ needs someone to act as a messenger to run orders to and from the batteries in the Company. I think you'll get to drive a car too," Miller explained. "You want it?"

"How's the chow? And do I get a bed? Harold asked with a smile.

Sergeant Miller smiled back at Harold with brown, tobacco-stained teeth. "All the amenities of home," he replied. "I'll run you over tomorrow."

FIRST BRUSH WITH DEATH

October 4, 1918

"Faster, Private! Goddammit, faster!"

Harold smashed his foot down onto the accelerator causing the motor in the car to jump while he gripped the steering wheel tightly as the vehicle bounced and slid along the torn up road. The Captain riding with him gripped the door and the dash while trying to duck lower in his seat.

"Sir! Shouldn't we stop and take cover? We'll get blown to hell!" Harold shouted as he drove.

"No! Just keep driving! Don't stop!"

Another German shell came shrieking down landing just behind the car splattering Harold and the Captain with mud and tiny bits of white-hot shrapnel which tore into the flesh on the back of his neck. Ignoring the pain, he kept his eyes in front of the car and kept his foot on the accelerator while weaving in and out of abandoned wagons and trucks. Ahead, infantrymen were busy taking cover in the ditches and shell holes more shells came roaring down. Suddenly an enormous explosion ripped into the road directly in front of the car throwing it into the air. Harold felt himself suspended for just a moment before crashing forcefully into the muddy field to the side of the road.

"You okay?" a voice asked in the darkness. "I don't see any holes in him."

Harold slowly opened his eyes to see a dirty, partially bearded American soldier looking down at him. He tried sitting up but the man held him down gently.

"Don't move Mac. Doc's coming over to take a look at you." The soldier said keeping his hands on his shoulders. He turned to another man in the hole with them.

"Where's that fucking doc at?"

The man pointed and grunted something to his friend and leaned back against the side of the hole to light a cigarette.

"What in the hell were you two doing up here?" he asked Harold.

Harold turned to look at the man. He was just as dirty as the other.

"I was bringing the Captain up. He's an artillery observer." Harold croaked through his pain. "Wouldn't let me stop and take cover when the shelling started."

"That's fucking stupid," the man said looking away. "Don't have to worry about him anymore though. He's a fucking mess."

"Yeah, you're lucky," said the man helping Harold. "That dumb son of a bitch took the full effect of the blast from that shell."

Another man jumped into the shell hole and immediately began looking him over. "Can you sit up?"

Harold sat up slowly with the help of the first man while pain shot through his ribs and back. The medic probed him and gingerly felt along his ribs. "You've got a couple broken ribs and some cuts but nothing more. It's your lucky day."

"Lucky, my ass," Harold replied angrily.

The medic and the first man pulled Harold's coat and shirt off spilling his precious letters and the faded handkerchief into the muddy water at the bottom of the hole. Harold grunted and reached for them.

"Here," said the first man. "I've got them." Using the sleeve of his coat, he wiped the mud and water from the bundle while the medic quickly wrapped Harold's torso. The pain was almost unbearable and Harold let out a moan. Finished, the medic pulled out a small card and began writing while the first man helped him back into his shirt and coat. He then leaned over and pinned it to Harold's overcoat.

"Let's get back up to the road and we'll load you up with our wounded."

The first man and the medic helped Harold to his feet while the other man sat silently smoking his cigarette.

"So long," he said indifferently.

The two men helped Harold through the mud and debris each taking care not to jar his ribs too much.

"There's your Captain," said the medic.

Harold looked down at the Captain he'd known for only a few days since being assigned as a runner for HQ. He lay splayed out in the filthy ditch, the entire right side of his face gone leaving a gaping red hole ringed with teeth, bone and hair. What was left of his brain had oozed out joining with the polluted ground while his bright red blood colored the muddy water in the ditch in a macabre shock of color. His right arm had been ripped away too, leaving a horrible, huge tear down the right side of his body exposing a rib cage and the smashed organs inside. Flies were beginning to busily gather. Harold stopped to vomit.

The men waited for him to finish.

"Come on. Don't need to see that. Friend of yours?"

Harold coughed, spit and shook his head. "No."

The three climbed onto the road which was filled with men and vehicles busily moving along before the Germans began shelling the road again. After waiting for a group of infantrymen and a truck to pass they walked across to another truck waiting with its engine idling. The medic and the first man carefully lifted Harold into the back where other men with fresh, bloodstained bandages lay about and sat.

"Almost forgot, here are you letters," the first man said handing the stained bundle to Harold.

"Thank you," Harold croaked. "And, thank you for helping me."

"Any day," said the man extending his hand. "Take care of yourself."

The man and Harold shook hands.

With a smile, the man re-shouldered his rifle and join in with the rest of the Americans marching towards the front lines as the truck joined the exodus of those lucky enough to be going the opposite direction.

"You take care as well," Harold muttered softly.

TOTAL WAR

October 15, 1918

The tiny kerosene lamp sputtered and the flame went out for a moment but suddenly flickered with a snap and slowly came back to life. Harold lifted his weary head from the letter he had been trying to write for days but couldn't seem to finish. He coughed hard and painfully into the handkerchief that was now his constant companion. It was wet and sometimes frozen with the sludge he coughed out of his sore lungs. Holding it to his mouth, he took several breaths to try and restore his normal breathing. If he let it go, the coughing wouldn't stop and he'd often find himself frightened and choking for breath after an episode.

Beside him, Wellings and George were sound asleep, buried deep in the damp, pungent straw that they'd been lucky to find in a neighboring destroyed farm after moving *Dora* up with the rest of their regiment earlier in the day. Other men, his friend Mike, the new guy from Virginia who they all called the Kid and the remainder of Battery C laid about in the straw some snoring and others talking in their sleep. The ancient stone farm building the men had taken refuge in had certainly been a cow enclosure for much of its hundreds of years of existence as evidenced by the streaks of dried manure on the gray block walls. No one minded however and they considered themselves lucky; the building still had most of its roof still intact and was remarkably dry.

Clustered around the barn was a typical French farm of a type the men had by now become used to with its enormous pile of manure taking up most of the front yard of the house and surrounding barnyard. The French farmers never ceased to amaze Harold or the other men in the AEF, with the piles of shit they so carefully built and cultivated in front of their homes which some of the more knowledgeable Americans said was a display of wealth and prosperity. And what was worse, the manure didn't all seem to be from the livestock the French shared their homes with. Wherever the men were assigned, whether in the towns, the farms or the obscenely dirty French trenches, it seemed as though the French people lived in filth and shit and didn't seem to mind.

Harold coughed several more times, finally caught his breath and looked around at his sleeping comrades to make sure he hadn't woken any of them. After weeks of moving, setting up, tearing down and firing the guns the men were exhausted. The previous days had been particularly grueling with 2nd Company firing almost continuously from early morning until well after dark, the only break coming for an hour while they waited for more ammunition to be moved up.

For Harold, the past week had been particularly harsh: Following a several day long stay in the hospital to only slightly mend the broken ribs and the various cuts and bruises he'd received in the shelling, he'd requested to be sent back to 2nd Company and his friends. *The hell with you HQ buggers,* he thought spitefully to himself. Despite Sergeant Miller being kind enough to put him on easier duties, he knew there were no easy jobs in an artillery unit and soon found himself immersed in the backbreaking labor it all entailed. But, he was happy to go back despite his injuries and sickness.

During his five-day stay in HQ, Harold had done nothing except drive the spotters to and from the front. And each of the five days he'd driven back and forth to the front lines they'd been shelled. Another day after dropping off the spotter, Harold had spent much of the day crouched in a shell hole up to his waist in filthy water hiding from a German sniper somewhere across No Man's Land who seemed to see, and shoot at his every move. His sole companion that day and into the night in the hole was a smelly, decaying German corpse which had been disinterred from the constant shelling. Now back where he felt he belonged, sleep only seemed to come in bits and pieces here and there with a good night's rest amounting to perhaps three or four hours. The rest of their days and nights were spent unloading the shells from the transports, setting fuses in them, cleaning *Dora* and her enormous barrel and firing mechanisms, shoring up the sides of the gun emplacement with sandbags, digging trenches, finding and building up sleeping shelters while finally covering the entire battery with camouflage. There were rumors that the Germans were almost finished and were on the verge of surrendering at any time. For Harold and his friends, the bastards couldn't quit soon enough.

Outside and down the lane from the farm where Harold and the men in 2nd Company were billeted, guns in other batteries of the 65th fired randomly in the night at unseen German targets over the horizon. The thumps and booms from the never-ending noise of the front lines had become an all-too familiar sound for the young men whose only wishes now revolved around food and thoughts of actually going home.

Harold suddenly scratched deeply and viciously at his armpits, his coughing forgotten for just a moment. "Damned cooties."

In the weak flickering light of the lamp he could see the tiny gray lice swarming over the fabric of his heavy overcoat despite the cold weather. He, and everyone else, had discovered that once the temperature plummeted to near and below freezing the lice simply moved further into their clothes in search of warmth and no one was immune from the tiny insects burrowing deeper and deeper into their underclothes only to lay more eggs and produce even more biting, uncomfortable young.

Harold coughed, scratched and slapped at himself until he had finally put the cooties into submission for the time being. Picking up the worn paper and nub of a pencil he'd been writing with, he looked over the letter he'd been so carefully crafting.

Dearest Margaret,

I sincerely hope this finds you well. You know that I love you more than life itself and the only way I can get through the days is knowing that you still love me. I've been worried about you for several months now and I want you to be completely honest with me. I realize the mail is awfully slow but I need to know where you are and why you haven't written me since July. It's now October. Are you through with me? Has something happened? Please, I need to know. This is all making me go insane not knowing why you've been so silent. Please, write me and tell me what's going on.

Harold leaned back against the dirty wall and thought. This letter was a good one and it had taken him several days to get the words on paper without being angry. He'd written horrible things to her. Things he'd never imagined he'd ever have said or written. One by one, he tore them up and fed the scraps into the kerosene lantern. It felt good to get it out.

Harold felt trapped and completely isolated because he knew there was no way he could contact her except through the mail. Taking a couple of months off and sailing the thousands of miles home to find her was simply out of the question. Even if he were to try, he knew the Military Police prowled the rear areas looking for deserters who would be locked up for a time in the stockade, then sent right back to the front to fight and die with the rest of their units. If a man were lucky enough to make it all the way to the Channel or Brest would still never have a chance to board any of the transports or cargo ships heading back to the States because papers were doubly checked there. The rumors swirled about desertion becoming such a huge problem in the AEF that General Pershing was having deserters tied to poles and shot to improve discipline.

While in the hospital Harold had seen men shipped out every day to a transitional hospital at Brest to be sent stateside. He couldn't understand why some who didn't seem to be too badly wounded were going home while he was being shipped back to the front. The memory of pleading with the doctor still burned inside him.

"If I sent you home with some broken ribs and some cuts and bruises they'd lock me up. Are you crazy, Private?" the doctor had exclaimed incredulously.

"You fucking son-of-bitch," Harold muttered.

Watching so many men leave made him despondent and for a time, Harold even considered switching papers with someone, anyone, to be sent back. He had also considered hurting himself so that they'd have to do something with him. Despite these thoughts, he couldn't bring himself to do any of it for fear of the MP's and the Army's brutal system of wartime justice. Most importantly, Harold knew he could never leave his buddies behind. They had become brothers to him.

Mike stirred in his sleep and began scratching at his own batch of cooties and mumbling in his southern drawl. "Ya damned critters. Get the hell off of me," he moaned quietly. "You're eating me up."

Harold watched him in the flickering half-light and smiled. His friend had a soft, gentlemanly voice and it was always amusing to hear him swear because it certainly didn't fit him. Suddenly, his throat constricted causing him to cough violently into his sopping handkerchief.

"You okay?" asked a voice in the darkness. It was Mike.

"Yeah, I think so," Harold answered. "Sorry I woke you up."

Mike yawned widely. "Oh, it's okay. The cooties have set up house on me. Makes it kind of hard to get any sleep."

He looked at Harold, his eyes shining in the dim light. "You're getting sicker aren't you? That pneumonia won't get any better until you go see the doc."

"I know," Harold replied. "We're so busy and all and I don't want to leave the rest of you short-handed. I'm just glad that I didn't have to stay with HQ. That was damn near a death sentence."

Mike sat up to lean on an elbow and began scratching his head. "You're sick and you're worried about your lady at home. You need to see doc and rest for a few days. Hell, your ribs and your back haven't even healed have they? We can manage," he said softly. "So, when was her last letter?"

Harold looked away. It embarrassed him to know that other men knew of his problems. "July. I know it doesn't take that long for mail to come here from home. Makes me wonder if something's happened."

Mike slithered through the hay and nestled in close to Harold. "Hell, maybe the mail's just slowed down because of the war and the trains and ships and everything. Maybe she's just writing you a big book of a letter to send over or maybe some of them just got lost in the mail. Look how many letters get lost when a ship gets sunk in the Atlantic. It could be a lot of reasons. Don't lose faith."

"I know, I try to think about it like that," Harold said wiping his eyes. "But, I feel like I'm going insane over here. I really do, and her letters are the only thing that keep my dreams of her and home alive."

"Your family, your brother-in-law, Will, he knows her and surely he'd let on if something had happened wouldn't he? From what you've told us about her, she loves you. She doesn't sound like the sort to run off with someone else and simply forget you. You'll see."

"It's funny, I have asked Will about her but told me that he hasn't seen her for quite some time," Harold explained. "He doesn't know if she's locked up in her parent's house or what's going on. And, my brother hasn't seen her at school either. They've been asking around but no one seems to know a thing."

"I'm sorry to tell you this, Harold, but you just have to have faith like I said. God works in mysterious ways. Maybe it's all a test in some way."

Harold nodded but before he could reply he coughed again, this time so hard he felt as though his eyeballs would pop out of his head. *That would be one way to get sent home* he thought to himself.

Once the fit subsided he laid back down and pulled his blanket tightly around his shoulders. "Thanks, Mike. I'm grateful to have you as my friend."

"Hey, any time," Mike yawned.

Harold reached over and turned down the lamp until it was a tiny blue flame and curled up next to Mike in the straw.

After only a few minutes of sleep, the men were suddenly jarred awake.

"On your feet!" Sergeant Miller bawled. "Everybody out. Right now!"

"What in the hell?" Mike asked looking up at the sergeant.

"Firing mission! Let's go, get a fucking move on!"

The men jumped to their feet grumbling and swearing as they jumped from their warm beds and searched for their boots and overcoats in the cold air. Wellings was clearly angry as he pulled his boots on.

"This is bullshit!" he grumbled. "We've worked for two days straight without hardly any sleep. Goddamn fucking bullshit!"

"Shut up and move your ass, Wellings, you fucking crybaby!" Miller barked.

Outside the stone building the men could hear other sergeants yelling and men running through the darkness. Below the farm an orchard bordered the long depression where Harold's battery was located one of the guns suddenly boomed out. Harold and the men ran quickly through the darkness down the path where *Dora* waited. Guns in other batteries began firing too lighting up the sky and causing the earth to tremble.

"What in the hell is going on?" Harold wondered out loud. "Everybody's up."

"Damn Boche, that's who's up!" Mike yelled as he ran along with Harold.

Reaching the gun emplacement tired and out of breath, the men immediately took their positions while Lieutenant Everson stood quietly talking with Sergeant Miller and Corporal Stevenson who was manning the buzzer box. Miller nodded and strode over to the men.

"Brooks, you and the Kid are setting fuses. Can't do much with those broken ribs and the pneumonia. Wellings, Goodlow, Van Nevel and Worley, you're loading," He quickly walked away and gave sharp orders to the rest of the men.

Despite the pain cascading throughout his body Harold ran to the toolbox, picked out a wrench, a hammer and crow bar and immediately went to work opening the wooden crates containing the fuses. With the help of the Kid, a new man fresh from the replacement depot who appeared to be barely even sixteen, he carried the crate back to the waiting shells and began carefully screwing the fuses into them. Immediately after completing the first shell and fuse, four other men quickly wrestled the shell onto the cart and took it straight to the gun. After several tense minutes of preparation, *Dora* began firing into the night.

"Hey sarge, what's the word?" Harold asked Sergeant Miller who had come to help Harold set fuses.

"The Huns broke through the lines up north of here somewhere. They hit the French left with a shitload of artillery and troops and the Frenchies pulled out leaving the 47th Division's right flank wide open."

"Jesus," Harold swore. "Leave it to our fearless French allies."

"Yeah," Sergeant Miller replied. "Don't know what we'd do without them."

Harold shook his head and began coughing again. His lungs back ached from the effort and he found he couldn't draw a breath. After several uncomfortable seconds he was finally able to breathe again. Directly in front of the Battery several large explosions began tearing into the fields slowly walking their way in closer and closer. After several more explosions they suddenly stopped. Sergeant Miller stood and turned to watch where the incoming shells had come down.

"Fucking Hun artillery is looking for us!" he yelled, running towards Lieutenant Everson.

Harold continued to work, quickly setting fuses but watching the field where the German shells had landed. Sitting amidst nearly one hundred, two-hundred and ninety pound shells filled with highly explosive Amatol he didn't want to think about what happened when the Germans shelled American artillery batteries especially when they were fully loaded with ammunition and men as his was now. He and his friends had seen the results several weeks before while they marched past the remains an American 155mm artillery battery that had been hit by German counterbattery-fire. The rumor was over thirty men had been killed instantly while the crater left from the explosion was nearly twenty feet deep and fifty yards wide. Small bits of men's remains were scattered all around the site, some hanging from trees and others lying as red jellied lumps in the fields.

Harold and the Kid continued to work when suddenly a high pitched moaning sound could be heard over the firing of the guns. The men knew trouble when it came looking for them.

"Oh my God!" Harold said looking to the sky. "That one's coming in close!"

The shell screamed down exploding only yards in front of *Dora's* emplacement showering the men with dirt and powder.

"Come on Kid. We're going to get plastered!" Harold shouted beginning to run. They joined in with Lieutenant Everson and everyone else who were running towards the line of trenches dug further up the hill well away from *Dora* and her stocks of ammunition. Behind them, German shells began exploding in and around all of the guns of the Company. Harold ducked his head and ran as fast as he could praying he wouldn't be hit. Another explosion ripped the ground to his left throwing him forcefully down to the ground. He scrambled, stood, and kept running until he reached the trenches where he jumped in feet first landing heavily on top of several other men. The Kid followed kicking Harold in the face as he belly flopped into the trench. Harold rolled away from and curled himself up into a ball with his hands holding the helmet down on his head. The German artillery pulverized the ground all around the trenches uprooting trees and destroying the farm buildings where they had been quartered. The ground shook violently while the night was filled with fire, noise and flying debris. In the bottom of the trench Harold and the men huddled low, some crying and others silent and completely lost in their own fear.

Suddenly, an explosion louder than anything Harold had ever heard before enveloped his body crushing him with its violent shock and was immediately followed by an eerie, muffled silence. He tried opening his eyes but saw nothing but blackness and as he attempted to reach up and wipe his face he discovered he couldn't move. Instinctively, he panicked and his body writhed: He was buried alive. Harold clawed at the heavy dirt and slowly suffocated while his mind raced remembering the stories he'd heard about men dying in trench cave-ins. It was terrifying. Just as he felt himself slipping away a pair of hands pulled dirt from in front of his face. He gasped for breath as more dark hands and shapes pulled him out of the grave.

"You okay?" shouted Wellings.

Harold nodded, breathing hard. "Yes. I think so."

"Come on then, help us dig! That shell caved in the other side!"

Harold slowly stood and spit mud from his mouth and blew his nose to clear it. The German shells were still falling but they were slowly shifting their fire further away to the north. In the light of the many small fires started by the barrage he could see men desperately digging in what was left of the trench with their helmets and bare hands. Stumbling forward, he fell to his knees between Wellings and the Kid and began digging furiously with his hands.

"Good thing we were in the other traverse," Wellings said breathlessly. "This side got creamed."

Harold nodded. Then men had been taught to dig trenches in a zig-zag pattern where one section of trench would be dug for twenty or so feet, then another section dug in a line and at the opposite angle. This was done to minimize the blast effect of shells and to contain explosions, and cave-ins to a smaller area.

"Who's in here?" Harold asked.

"Don't know," was all Wellings could say.

Harold continued scraping away until he felt something soft under his hands.

"I've got somebody!" he yelled.

Wellings, Mike, the Kid and several other men leapt to his side and began digging frantically. After several agonizingly slow moments they were able to pull the man out. It was George.

"Is he still alive?" Mike asked.

By the light of the fires the men could see that George was a ghostly pale white. He didn't seem to be breathing. Harold forced his mouth open and pulled out dirt.

"George!" he screamed. "Wake up!" he screamed slapping and shaking his friend. George unexpectedly took a loud, deep breath and opened his eyes and stared with horror at his friends for a moment before sobbing hysterically.

"Someone help us get him out of here!" Wellings yelled to the men who were standing off to the side tending the wounded and dead. Padre Fred and another man came forward and hauled George out of the hole while he continued to sob and scream as though he were an insane man.

The men continued to dig until dawn but found only two men left alive. Five others had suffocated or been crushed by tons of earth. The men looked down with sadness at the body of Myron Worley who they had just uncovered. Sergeant Miller quietly ordered them to stop digging.

"Everyone's accounted for now. You can stop."

They looked on silently as Myron's body was carefully pulled out and laid out with the other dead men including Amos Van Nevel and Lieutenant Everson. The only sound was the thump of artillery fire in the distance. Harold crawled out of the remains of the trench and collapsed to the ground on his knees and held his face in his dirty hands fighting back the urge to cry. Wellings and Mike both knelt down beside him.

"Goddammit," Harold choked. "I want to go home."

ALWAYS MOVING

October 21, 1918

The train gently clacked on eastwards through the beautiful French countryside, ignored by for the most part by the war since 1914. Harold dozed off and on enjoying the rare fall sunshine warming his face. After a long march along the muddy roads and a brief artillery barrage, the men of the 65th made their way to a tiny rail siding near a surprisingly intact French town which still had a few French civilians living in it. They were a sullen, sad collection of people who had suffered through four years of German occupation and brutality. Not sure of when the next invader would arrive, they went about their daily business with a grim, silent determination. Several of the women were seen to have healthy blonde haired babies despite the fact that no men within marrying age were left in the town. Harold had heard Lieutenant Swanson discussing the French Army reserve garrison from this town which had been completely wiped out during the French foray into Alsace early in the war. The other men left in town, the very old and the very young who weren't in the army had been put against the wall of the church and shot by the Germans as suspected spies.

The previous evening, Harold and his comrades were given a rare treat; a hot supper of beans and ham and bread with plenty to go around along with an extra ration of chocolate and cigarettes. After weeks of eating potted meat and slum everyone gorged themselves on the hot food only to find themselves desperately searching for the latrines in the middle of the night. The Germans seemed to know of their discomfort and fired artillery at them sporadically through the night keeping everyone awake and on edge. Harold smiled remembering Wellings joking about how he didn't want to die sitting on a shitter.

The men rode in open rail cars that had been modified to support the heavy 9.2's, all of their necessary equipment and tools along with the gun crews. They usually had to march or ride the uncomfortable carriages with the guns whenever they moved so riding the train was a real luxury. Harold leaned comfortably against *Dora's* big barrel where it was warming in the sun and simply sat back to enjoy the ride. Neither he, nor any of the other men had had a chance to relax for weeks because of the German Army's headlong retreat and the never-ending forward movement of the 65th and this was a welcome change of pace after working so hard for months.

A road ran along the side the rail lines and was choked with American and French troops and support vehicles of all descriptions. Harold and Wellings lazily watched the men, vehicles and animals as the train swept past.

"Look at those trucks," Wellings said pointing to a ditch between the road and rail line. "I wonder if we did that."

Harold turned to look as they rolled by. The black, smoking remnants of several German trucks lay on their sides and in pieces along the road and in the wide ditch. Large, fresh shell craters surrounded them and the field beyond where more craters and scores of dead German soldiers lay scattered about. The trees lining the road, once so ancient and mighty, had been blown in half and their trunks and limbs still smoldered from the firestorm. French service troops were busy throwing the dead Germans into one of the shell craters while others struggled to clear the road.

Harold and Wellings stared silently at the carnage. Other men did too.

"I'm sure we did," Harold finally answered. "We were firing into this area several days ago."

"Hmm," was all Wellings could muster. Shaking his head slowly from side to side, he turned away not wanting to look anymore.

Harold pulled his blanket tightly around his head and shivered from the cold air. George who sat on the other side of *Dora's* barrel from him. "Hey George, how are you doing? Want something to eat? I snatched some of that bread last night."

George ignored his friend and stared straight ahead, his face showing no emotion. Harold, Wellings and Mike had been worried about him since he had been buried alive in the trench. Once lively and spirited, George had stopped talking and rarely ate anymore. In fact, he'd lost so much weight that his uniform hung baggy and loosely from his body while his eyes seemed to stare off at nothing.

Several days previous, Harold had tried talking to Lieutenant Swanson about George to see if his friend could possibly be sent to the rear for a few days to rest and clean up. The men all knew that getting back to the relative safety of the rear areas could work wonders on those who were suffering mentally. Even if only for a day, a man could sleep, eat and wash without the fear of being found by a sniper's bullet or a shell. Many times, a man would often return unit completely refreshed and recharged.

Harold burned with rage remembering the conversation with Lieutenant Swanson who, after the death of Lieutenant Everson, was now in charge much to the chagrin of every man in the battery.

"Fuck no he ain't going back. He's just trying to get out of doing his duty."

Harold persisted. "But Lieutenant, I'm with him all of the time. He needs a break. Just for a day or two. He's not right in the head, I can tell."

The Lieutenant spun around with anger and jabbed a finger into Harold's chest. "Oh yeah?" he snarled. "I didn't realize you were a fucking head shrinker! Not another word about it, or I'm putting both of you son of a bitches on report." He pressed his face close to Harold's until he could smell the liquor on his breath. "You fucking get me, Private?"

Harold glared back with hatred in his eyes. "Yes sir," he answered, his voice deep and menacing. Swanson stared at him for a moment before spun stomping away in the mud leaving Harold shaking with anger.

"Bastard," he muttered.

The men didn't have much respect for the Lieutenant and hadn't since their days at Camp Merritt. When things got tough he simply disappeared. He was a weak man who couldn't, or wouldn't, deal with his responsibilities or his own fears preferring to spend his days alone somewhere with a bottle. Sergeant Miller, Harold and everyone else knew, somehow always managed to get the men through the toughest days. He found food for them, broke up their fights, told them what to write home to unfaithful wives and girlfriends and never took their money in poker games. Outwardly, the men made a show of disliking the Sergeant but deep down, they respected him enormously.

After his failure with Lieutenant Swanson, Harold sought out the advice of Sergeant Miller. He explained George's problems and to his satisfaction, the Sergeant had agreed to help.

"Yeah, I've noticed he isn't doing so well ever since he got buried a while back. But you, Wellings and Wilson are doing the right thing for now. Keep him away from the Lieutenant too. I'm working out a deal to have Goodlow shipped back to Battalion mess where he can peel potatoes and wash dishes for the rest of the war."

The train continued slowly on throughout the day stopping at small villages and remote sidings to take on water and allow the men a latrine break. Harold tried to lie down and sleep more comfortably but the pain in his ribs brought on by his constant coughing prevented it. By afternoon the landscape changed again as the train entered territory where the Germans had been only days before. The landscape here changed dramatically back to what the men were accustomed to: The retreating Germans had burned and destroyed everything they couldn't carry away leaving a burned, ruined landscape. The bodies of French civilians littered the roads, fields and villages where they had been cut down. Harold felt rage burning inside him at the sight of the tiny bodies of dead children, some of whom were still clutching their dead mother's skirts. His rage turned even worse at the sight of the babies the Germans had killed. All of the men stared silently at the carnage quickly losing any feelings of remorse they may have had for the Germans.

"I'd kill every one of those fucking Huns with my bare hands if I could," Mike swore as they slowly rolled through a flattened, still smoking village. "Jesus. Look, the kids..."

"I hope they don't surrender like the rumors we've been hearing say," said Wellings. "We should keep killing all of them until we get to the Kaiser, even if they do quit."

Harold sat shaking his head, taking in the carnage.

"Nah," said the Kid. "Let the Frenchies have the Kaiser. They should hang him from the Eiffel Tower for everyone to see. They've earned that."

The train slowed and lurched to a stop. Ahead, several sergeants were jumping off shouting instructions at the tired men. Sergeant Miller soon joined them.

"Everybody off and into formation!"

"Where are we, Sarge?" someone asked.

"France," exclaimed Sergeant Miller. "Get the fuck off the train."

Harold jumped down with Wellings and Mike and together they waited for George to join them.

"Feeling okay, George?" Wellings asked.

George shook his head and looked away. The dark circles under his eyes were becoming larger and his skin, now gray and flabby, hung from his face.

Harold again offered George the bread he'd been saving since the previous day and to everyone's surprise, he reached over and tore away a sizable chunk. Taking an enormous bite of the bread, he silently chewed while looking straight ahead. Wellings leaned forward and whispered in Harold's ear.

"At least he's eating something. That's a good sign."

Harold nodded and shushed Wellings. "Let's leave him be for a bit. See if he's feeling better."

The men in front of Harold's group began to slowly march forward, urged on by the sergeants further up the line.

"Moving out boys!" Miller yelled. "Get a move on. We've got new positions to prepare!"

The men groaned and swore in unison as they wearily stepped out with the rest of the regiment onto the well-worn road beside the railroad tracks. There had been rumors of a few days of R and R complete with showers, de-lousing, food and hopefully, French prostitutes and gallons of the rough *vin* in the *estaminets* found everywhere in the rear areas. But to their dismay, it was back to the hellish, backbreaking work that all had begun to hate in earnest. Everyone wanted to get the war over with and go home but there seemed to be no end in sight. More trenches to dig, more guns to set up, more sandbags to fill and more sleepless, hungry nights followed by more endless firing. And many more Germans to kill. For Harold it all had crossed the ever thinning line to complete insanity.

MEUSE-ARGONNE

October 31, 1918

"Let's take a break," Lieutenant Swanson shouted through the deafening din of guns firing. His voice sounded weak and wavered as he spoke. "The 530th is digging in near the village, so we've got a few minutes to rest."

This was good news and meant that at least some of the day's attacking American forces had reached their objectives and had taken the Bois De Forges, a ruined forest which overlooked yet another utterly destroyed French village. Other batteries down the line stopped completely while a few others continued sporadic firing while the front line observers moved up with the infantry and settled in to calculate new fire missions.

Harold and the men slumped down where they were each reaching eagerly for his water and carefully saved scraps of food amidst the bits of rubbish that littered the position. They were exhausted and hadn't eaten much all day due to the offensives launched earlier in the morning. And worse, water and cigarettes had been sparse too. Harold coughed wetly but reached into his grimy overcoat to pull out his Lucky Strikes and discovered he only had one badly mangled cigarette left.

"Fuck," he muttered lighting it. He wadded up the empty pack and threw it viciously to the ground. "Anybody heard anything about getting some chow or more supplies?" he asked no one in particular. He was answered with a few half-hearted grunts and some muted profanity. Glancing around, he noticed every man's face and clothing were covered in a grimy combination of sweat, dirt and gun powder.

Lieutenant Swanson, who was leaning against the sandbags of the position with his arm over his face, replied: "I sent an order back last night to have extra food, water and cigarettes sent up this morning before the attack. All this firing must have scared the ass-holes away," He slowly got up, his face wan and haggard and put his smudged steel helmet back on. "I'll go see what I can round up."

The men's eyes followed the Lieutenant as he slowly his way out of the sunken gun position and back to the battered old stone farm buildings that made up the HQ.

"Funny that," said Wellings. "The Lieutenant's not looking good. You all see his eyes? He ain't in there anymore. Why's he trying to be nice to us now I wonder? Out of booze and wants some of ours?"

Mike shrugged. "Who around here is? We're all tired, sick and starving, and all we do is move these damn guns from here to there and fire them full time. Don't the fucking Germans know they've lost? I'm so sick of this shit."

Wellings leaned back covering his eyes with his helmet. "You'll see. He's got that look about him. I'd bet money he's out of booze so the bastard better not do anything to get any of us killed. And I'm not sharing any of mine with him either." Wellings gleefully held up his canteen and sloshed the wine he always carried.

Harold was only half-heartedly listening to the conversation and was doing his best to make his last cigarette last a little longer.

The Lieutenant did worry much more than he should he knew, and when things got tough, he simply disappeared. The men had noticed that both of his hands shook and were getting worse by the day.

Harold closed his eyes tightly and tried to think good thoughts but they rarely came to him anymore. It seemed as though his head was full of nothing but nightmares about watching men die and all he could see was the damaged world he and his friends inhabited. It was as though home had never existed. Only this.

Other things rattled away in his waking mind and not getting any letters from home for the past two weeks were slowly making him angry and cynical much of the time. Maybe, he wondered, Bobby was so upset about Harold leaving that he didn't want to see his brother again. What if Margaret had found a new man but hadn't told him about it? The only thing Harold thought about now was going home to Sac City to find out for himself where she was. But other days, he wasn't so sure he could go back. Perhaps Margaret somehow knew how much he had changed and how much the war had made him into someone he never thought imaginable.

Harold smoked his cigarette down to the very nub and carefully flicked the hot glowing cherry off and pulled the usable tobacco out to make up part of a smoke later. There never seemed to be enough of anything, especially food, sleep and cigarettes, the three things every man treasured above all else. After carefully putting the tobacco in his left shirt pocket, he was surprised to hear someone crying and looking up, was startled to see it was George. This was the first time he'd shown any emotion or much of anything else since his brush with death.

Harold and the other men stared at him unsure of what to do. Most looked away uncomfortably. In the past two months no man had the strength or mental ability left to show any sort of emotion whatsoever.

When no one else made a move, Harold gently slid over to George who was sobbing uncontrollably now. His hands covered his grimy face, the tears leaving long black streaks which dripped off his chin and fell silently into the mud.

"Hey, what's the matter?" Harold asked softly.

"This fucking place," George stammered between sobs. "I'm sick of being tired and sick all the time. I'm sick of being afraid all the time. I can't take it anymore. I wish I could die and get it over with."

Harold wrapped an arm around his friend's shoulders and held him. The other men acted as though nothing were happening. They were afraid that George had lost it and to get involved with him only meant that they could be next.

"Hell George, the Huns are done for. You've heard all the rumors. It's going to be over soon. Trust me. Then we can go home and forget any of this ever happened," Harold said trying to sound convincing.

"Home to what?" George spat. "Home to my rich fucking father and mother and their big house on Long Island? They wouldn't understand what we went through. They think this is a summer camp! I can see myself now telling my father 'Be a good man and have the butler clean up the sheets I just shit myself in. War nerves you know. And get me a drink and a cigarette while you're at it you rich twit. There's a good man now. Hurry before I have another one of my episodes.'"

"But we're still alive," Harold said. He knew exactly how George felt. "It'll just take us a little time to go on once we're back."

"No!" George yelled wild-eyed. "I'm not going home! I tease you about your dreams and how they keep me awake at night. If only my dreams were that pleasant you fucking bastard! Dreaming about your sweet Margaret and little Bobby! I have nightmares about killing myself. I wish I had the courage to do it but I don't!"

George pushed away from Harold breathing hard, his eyes wild. Everyone stared on with horrified looks. They all suffered from awful dreams but they hadn't allowed them to surface as George's had.

"Come on, George," Harold said slowly rising to his feet. "Maybe Wellings will share some of his wine with you."

"Yeah," Wellings said jumping to his feet. "Just sit down, George and have a drink. It'll help."

Ignoring his friends, George tore into his pack pulling out the notebooks that he'd so lovingly written and drawn in for the past six months. Holding them high he began tearing the pages out and throwing them at his friends. He screamed at them. "You all know who Corrinne is? Sweet Corrinne? Do you?"

No one answered but stared on in disbelief. Lieutenant Swanson returned with an armload of supplies but stood on the edge of the sandbags watching.

"Corrinne," George said weaving about like a drunken man, "Was the daughter of my parent's maid. She lived in our house with us. I knew her for years."

He stared coldly at the men.

"Do you know why I joined the Army? I joined the Army to escape my parents, their maid, the coppers and some nasty Italian boys. I...I got her pregnant. Well now boys, a rich ass like me isn't supposed to breed with the help so I took her into the city. To have her and the baby...taken care of."

Several men gasped in horror. Harold and Wellings tried to grab George who spun away from them in a rage.

"I took her to a back alley doctor in the city, some slimy Italian bastard, to get an abortion and she died right there on his table. The fucking butcher pulled out her insides and she bled to death right there in that dark back room. I ran away and...I left her there." He sobbed uncontrollably falling to his knees.

Harold, Wellings, Mike and several others tackled him and held him down. Wellings looked up at Lieutenant Swanson hoping for some kind of answer. Instead, he dropped the supplies he'd found and walked away.

"You son of a bitch!" Wellings yelled at him. "Get back here and help us!"

The Lieutenant turned and disappeared into the stone huts behind the emplacement. George continued thrashing and fighting Harold and the other men desperately trying to hold him down. In his rage he broke free of their grip and punched Wellings so hard the large man went flying.

Suddenly Sergeant Miller had both of George's arms pulled up tightly behind him and forcefully wrestled him down to the ground. "Grab that rope up there. We need to get him tied up."

Several of the men leapt out of the gun emplacement to gather strands of rope that had previously held the shells in place on the traveling racks. In an instant Sergeant Miller had George's arms and legs tied up. George let out a fearful wail that shook every man's nerves.

"Let me die you bastards! Kill me!" he screamed.

The Sergeant stood and looked over at Harold. "Brooks, you and Wellings give me a hand here. We're taking him back to the medics."

Harold and Wellings, who had blood running from his mouth, silently helped the Sergeant pick George up and began to carry him out of the emplacement. Men in the other gun emplacements stood and quietly watched the procession. A few coughed and turned away.

The three men grunted with exertion as they dragged George to the rear along the muddy path.

After a time Sergeant Miller spoke, "I think your buddy has lost it completely. I didn't think it was this bad."

"We didn't either," Harold replied. "I hoped he'd get a few days of rest then he'd be fine. The Lieutenant told me last night he'd bring charges up on George if he didn't get it together."

"That fucker of a Lieutenant," Sergeant Miller said, "Has no business out here and certainly no business looking after men. But don't either of you repeat that. The Army frowns on dumbass enlisted men bad-mouthing officers, even worthless assholes like Swanson. Understood?"

"Yes sergeant," Harold and Wellings replied.

"Well damn," Miller said, "I had it all worked out with the Captain. Your buddy was going to be sent to the Division hospital outside of Paris tomorrow for a little rest."

They carried George on to the aid station silently below a cold gray whirling sky. He was only whimpering now and thankfully, had stopped flaying about. Harold had known for some time that George was losing control. In the dark never-ending nights he would talk in quiet, animated tones to people who weren't there and often laughed hysterically at the jokes these phantoms told him. It was evil, demonic laughter. Just days before, Harold overheard him discussing the best ways to kill himself with one of them. It was strange: George always displayed very vivid, manic emotions when he was feeling good. He'd laugh and joke with everyone and he would be on the go for hours. But other times, he would suddenly, and for no reason, sink into a dark, far-away depression where he refused to eat or have anything to do with his friends. It seemed like he would sometimes become someone else. He told incredible stories that made the men laugh but they could never tell if George was telling the truth or not, as his stories contained many holes.

The aid-station was set up in a former school building of some sort. Like the other buildings in the area, it was sturdily built of the local stone but the wooden roof had been destroyed in an artillery barrage at some point. Several tarps meant to provide some shelter from the rain and the elements flapped and swayed in the cold fall wind that was beginning to spit pellets of frozen rain and snow. Outside a series of ambulances sputtered and choked as medics and other men carefully loaded wounded men to be transported back to the hospital. Scores of other wounded and sick men filled the building and lay about in the run-down school yard and along the sides of the road. Screams and frightful moans filled the air. Some convulsed in severe pain clawing and kicking at the air with their shattered limbs and gaping wounds while others lay still and silent waiting for death to finally deliver them from their pain and suffering. As Harold, Wellings and the Sergeant crossed the congested road and came to the front yard of the building they came across a pile of dead, disfigured American soldiers heaped up nearly five feet high, to Harold strangely resembling an Iowa haystack as though a farmer had recently worked his hayfield. A river of blood ran from the pile out into the road where the ambulances splattered it on the still-living men lying helplessly on their stretchers.

The three carefully set George down on the ground just outside the aid station and gasped for breath. Sergeant Miller disappeared into the building for a few minutes and came back out with a doctor who he exchanged a few muffled words with. The doctor's heavily lined face was gray and flabby with fatigue. He nodded and called a medic to come with him to examine George.

Harold looked on helplessly. His mind was racing with emotion and fear. "Should we untie him doc?" he asked.

"No," the doctor answered rolling up George's sleeve. "Not until we get him back to the hospital. I don't want him coming back around in the ambulance and getting loose. He'll hurt himself and the others." He pushed a syringe into George's arm while the medic filled out a cardboard tag to pin on his grimy overcoat. George whimpered quietly and suddenly went silent. The doctor scribbled a note on the tag and nodded to the medics who loaded George into the waiting ambulance.

The doctor rubbed his creased forehead and turned to the Sergeant. "That's the fifteenth shell shock case I've seen today," he said wearily. "They keep coming and coming. Almost as many of them as there are wounded men. He's lucky he doesn't have the flu. That's killing more men than the war is now."

"Thanks doc," said Sergeant Miller. "What'll they do with him?"

"Well," the doctor answered. "They'll keep him sedated for a few days then keep him under observation for a few more days. He might be back in a week."

Sergeant Miller turned to leave. "I don't want him back. I hope they just send him home and away from this hell. The boy has worse problems than the war."

As the sky began to grow dark and unleash more flurries of snow and ice, Harold and Wellings followed Sergeant Miller back down the darkening muddy road they'd just brought George on and headed back.

PHOSGENE

November 4, 1918

Harold and the men slogged through the mud struggling to move the heavy shells but they were exhausted and on the verge of collapsing. They'd been firing continuously for more than four hours and their fear and adrenaline were the only things keeping them going to load and fire *Dora* as fast as they could. In between shots they could clearly hear German advance getting closer. Every third shell, Lieutenant Swanson would run to each gun making careful corrections and then instruct the men to elevate and cant each gun more. Evidently the French regiment to their left had retreated leaving the American flank dangerously exposed once again. Harold's battery was firing into the place where they should have been holding the line.

"Keep it up boys! The Huns have broken through the line!" Sergeant Miller screamed above the din.

Harold peered over the edge of the emplacement and was horrified to see infantry troops falling back through the open fields quickly. Some were running directly through their battery of guns.

One man was frantic and had lost his helmet and rifle. Now he was running for his life, his eyes wide and crazy with fear.

"Fucking Huns are comin'! Run! Run for your lives! They're comin'! You're all gonna die!" he screamed as he passed through. He was soon followed by others but many were stopping in front of the gun emplacements to shoot at the deluge of Germans flooding across the open ground.

"Don't look out there, keep loading and firing!" Sergeant Miller shouted throwing Harold into the Kid. They ran blindly with the empty cart to gather another shell while Mike, Wellings, the Kid and Padre Fred muscled the next one into the loading tray. The air was heavy with acrid gun smoke burning and filling the backs of their throats with black sludge. Fire again. Lieutenant Swanson stopped his work and stared out to the front of the gun emplacement. He wavered for a moment, then suddenly turned and began running up the small path away from the gun. As he ran by, Harold reached out and grabbed him.

"What in the hell are you doing Lieutenant?" Harold yelled above the sound of the blasting guns.

Harold noticed the Lieutenant had complete fear in his eyes. "Just keep loading that son-of a-bitch and keep her firing! I have to...find help!"

"You fucking coward!" Harold screamed. "You goddamn worthless coward! If we survive this I'll kill you!"

"No!" the Lieutenant answered swinging his fists wildly at Harold. "But they will!" Harold turned and saw gray uniformed Germans swarming more quickly across the open ground towards them. They paused only to fire their rifles while they followed their own artillery barrage that was walking closer to Harold's battery with every shot. The noise of the battle continued to increase as an American machine gun rattled continuously to their left and the infantry up and down the makeshift line began pouring rifle fire into the Germans. Many Germans fell but on they came, their NCO's and officers made their way forward through the torn ground over the dead and wounded men in front of urging their *Soldaten* on toward Harold and the American rear areas. Harold pushed the Lieutenant's hands away, grabbed him by the collar and forcefully shoved him to the ground while his right hand reached down for the pistol on his belt.

"If you try and run away I'll put a bullet in your back! You fuck-ing bastard!"

Lieutenant Swanson looked up at Harold with teary eyes and whimpered.

Several explosions followed by loud pops could be heard over the pandemonium somewhere in front of the gun position. All of the men, both in the defending infantry and in the artillery bat-teries began to panic knowing what those peculiar sounds meant.

"Gas! Gas! Gas!" someone yelled. Up and down the line Harold could hear men yelling out the same chilling word while others banged furiously on their "Gas Bells," old shell casings and their helmets to get the warning out. More Americans turned and be-gan to run away.

Almost immediately, a white fog began hissing furiously out of the half-buried containers, filling the air. The Germans were shelling them up and down the line with Phosgene gas which caught the wind and began blowing directly into the American lines. Most of the infantry in front of the battery were fumbling for their gas masks while trying to continue their fire on the advanc-ing Germans. Still more broke down in panic before the white mist enveloped them. Harold could smell the chemical through the smoke and burnt gunpowder as it made its way towards them ever so slowly in the gentle breeze. As the bullets and artillery fire whistled over his head Harold panicked while trying to get his gas mask out of its case around his neck. He began coughing and his eyes burned. If only he could get the mask on.

AEF HOSPITAL, REIMS

November 7, 1918

The huge hospital stunk of gangrene, urine, feces, blood and antiseptic. Men lay wherever the overworked staff could put them while some were simply left to die. Once they did, they were carried out and immediately replaced by another pathetic wreck of a young man. Some lay on the bare floors between beds, others were propped up in chairs in the hallways. Everywhere men screamed in pain and everywhere men died.

Harold lay quietly in the bed he'd been moved to only that morning after spending his first three days in the hellish hospital lying on a stretcher out in the busy hallway with many other wounded men. His head and body throbbed with searing, burning pain from the wounds he'd received in the German attack. He'd always thought himself as tough but he couldn't stop himself from crying out in agony. Even if he managed to get the attention of the orderlies or a nurse he was lucky if they'd do anything to help him. The pain medication they gave him worked well and allowed him to sleep but it only came occasionally as did food and water. According to the doctor, Harold had a fractured skull and the wound had required nearly twenty stitches to close. This, along with the phosgene that had burnt his already sick, pneumonia-filled lungs and the broken ribs from his last trip to the hospital virtually guaranteed him a ticket home. Harold didn't care. He had come to believe that he had nothing to go home to and he didn't want to go back to the front. He simply wanted to die in the hospital and be free of the pain and misery that he felt his life had become.

"Hey buddy. Hey, you there."

Harold turned his head painfully to look at the man in the bed next to him.

"Got any smokes?"

Harold looked at the man through his cloudy, distorted vision. Half of his face was covered with a thick white bandage with blood seeping through and he was missing half of his left arm. "Sorry. I don't have any."

The man fell back on his bed and gently touched the wet bandages that covered his broken body. "Damn it." he said. "Nobody does. I'm dying for a smoke."

"Well, I could use a smoke and a shot of morphine myself," Harold replied. His voice grated against his throat as though it were full of sand. "And maybe even something to drink."

The other man snorted and gurgled through his bandages. "Good luck with that, mac. The service in this joint leaves a lot to be desired, if you ask me."

Harold smiled until head begin to throb more violently. He had to be careful too. If he laughed or talked it made him have to cough which was excruciatingly painful and he discovered to his horror, he coughed up blood and bits of black, burnt lung tissue.

"You're new," stated the man. "My name's Wendell Anderson from Bloomington, Indiana."

"Harold Brooks from Iowa."

"Welcome to death's door."

Harold wished the man would shut up and leave him alone. The pain in his head had settled in now and thumped with every beat of his heart. Squeezing his eyes shut, he covered his face with the thin blanket which smelled oddly of death, desperately trying to shut out the world and his talkative neighbor but the man continued droning on.

After several hours of lying still Harold felt a hand gently touch his arm. Pulling the blanket back, he shielded his eyes from the bright hospital lights and saw a young nurse sitting on the edge of his bed holding a tray in her lap.

"Hello Private," she said smiling. "How are you feeling?"

"Not worth a darn," Harold rasped. "I could use a drink and another shot of morphine though ma'am."

"Well it's your lucky day. I have both and even something for you to eat."

Harold stared at her with not quite focused eyes as she rolled up the sleeve on his hospital pajamas and injected him with the morphine. The warm, wonderful effects of the drug immediately coursed through his veins forcing the pain away. Through the fog he noticed the nurse had very long blonde hair that was tied up in a bun on the back of her head. She was very pretty he noticed; her bright blue eyes caught his attention.

"Margaret?" he asked reaching a hand out to her. "Margaret? Is that you?"

The young nurse laughed quietly and took Harold's hand. "No Private. I'm sorry. My name is Bernice. Is Margaret your wife?"

Harold continued to stare at her while she gently caressed his hand. "No," he choked. "I wanted her to be before..."

Bernice continued to smile at Harold and held his hand softly. Her eyes gazed into Harold's soul. "I understand."

She gently raised Harold into a sitting position and helped him drink and eat the food she'd brought. While he ate, he noticed she was a little older than he was, probably twenty-one or twenty-two and she was very beautiful despite the fact that she wore no makeup and her mouth and eyes were lined with wrinkles. Her job tending to wounded and dying young men must have taken a toll on her, he thought to himself. Harold finished eating in silence while she quickly changed the bandage on his head.

"You're healing wonderfully," she said helping him lie back down. "They'll be sending you on to the convalescent center at Brest in a few more days."

Harold looked at her with surprise. "I'm not going to die?"

"No, of course not!" Bernice said with a smile but her face quickly turned dark and serious. She had tears welling up in her eyes. "You're one of the lucky ones. I've seen many, many boys die here."

Bernice gathered up the tray and dirty bandages and stopped to look back at Harold. Again, her eyes sparkled at him just like Margaret's had. There was something different about this woman that he couldn't quite figure out. There was a strange radiance that surrounded her and set her apart from the horrible, stinking hospital.

"You know Private, once you get healed up and go home you should find her," Bernice said in a soothing feminine voice. "Just forget about everything you've seen and done here."

With that, she turned and walked away into the mass of wounded men to tend to the next man on her list. Harold watched her every step until he couldn't see her anymore. For some strange reason, he felt a hopeful feeling come over him. If they were sending him to Brest, that meant he'd be going home soon, much sooner than he'd anticipated. He knew he would live and once he was home he *would* find Margaret.

Harold turned to his neighbor Wendell who had been unusually quiet.

"That nurse is really something isn't she? She reminds me of my girl back in Iowa."

Wendell gurgled and turned uncomfortably to gaze at Harold with flat, lifeless eye.

"What nurse?" he asked. "I didn't see anyone."

ARMISTICE

November 11, 1918

Harold sat on the edge of his bed going through his possessions feeling anger consume him. He hadn't felt well enough to check while he'd been in the hospital near Paris but since arriving in the Convalescence Center he wanted to make sure he still had his things. His head began to throb again making him even angrier still.

"Goddamn thieving bastards!" he shouted throwing the empty bag to the floor.

After being wounded in the German counterattack and sent up through the confusing, varied torments of aid stations, field hospitals and finally the huge divisional hospital, Harold hadn't ever had complete possession of his bag. Several things had been stolen from him, his shaving kit, the treasured pocket knife that he'd received from his father on his tenth birthday and a handful of French coins. It infuriated him to know that American medics and orderlies stole from their own wounded and dying men. At least they'd left his bundle of moldy, dog-eared letters and the .45

pistol he'd stolen from Lieutenant Swanson. And most thankfully of all, Harold had always kept his cherished pocket watch in its' small leather pouch tied around his neck along with his identification tags the entire time. He could vaguely remember a man pulling at it while he lay in the stinking, freezing aid station he'd gone to first after the battle. If he hadn't shouted and slapped at the man he knew it most certainly be gone too.

Harold was glad to be in the Convalescence Center but his wounds and sickness left him little energy or enthusiasm. There rumor was that a ship would be going back to the States in a few days and he prayed that he'd be one of the lucky ones to be sent home. After being in Brest for two days he knew that the thousands of more seriously wounded men would probably be sent home first but he still hoped he might be given a slot. At least the ones who were expected to live were going home. There was a huge building near the entrance of the enormous camp where the most seriously wounded men had been unloaded after the train had first arrived from Paris. Most of these men had absolutely horrific wounds from which they would never recover. Often, they were missing multiple limbs or half their faces. Once they were unloaded the train slowly made its way farther into the camp giving Harold and the more-fortunate soldiers who were expected to live a good look at the stacks and stacks of wooden coffins piled up behind the cold gray building. It was the death house as many now called it. Harold's neighbor in the divisional hospital near Paris, the talkative Wendell Anderson who just wanted cigarettes hadn't made the journey with him. The morning Harold had slowly walked out of the hospital to the waiting hospital train Wendell had been wrapped up in his soiled sheets and carried away to the morgue by two silent orderlies. Harold hoped now that he hadn't had anything for the orderlies to steal.

The train ride to Brest meant six hours of agony for the wounded, shattered men. The French rail system had fallen into disrepair because of the war and the tracks were being repaired with whatever scrap metal the overworked rail workers could find leaving the lines uneven and susceptible to breakage. It was a rough, sickening ride that caused many wounds to re-open and drip on the floor of the carriages. Harold and the other wounded men had been tied into their bunks and simply left to their own devices for the duration of the trip. With a shortage of nurses to tend so many men, the six hours was a hell of screaming men who writhed and lashed about in pain. At least two men in his carriage died during the trip west.

Throughout the long hospital building, the wounded and the medical staff buzzed with excitement about the rumors of an Armistice. Evidently, the Kaiser had abdicated the German throne and fled to Holland leaving chaos behind in Berlin while the German general staff was sending out peace feelers to the allies. But, he and most of the other men doubted the rumors: How could they just quit after fighting for four years when they hadn't actually been defeated? No matter the rumor, Harold didn't care any longer. Let the bastards surrender if they chose to.

Harold slowly gathered up what was left of his belongings and carefully put them back into his bag. His head pounded from the work and he carefully lay back on his bed wishing he could get another shot of morphine, which he had discovered he liked very much but the medical staff weren't too liberal in handing it out. The silver flask he'd bought the previous summer while on a short but very drunken leave in the city of Limoges with Wellings, Mike, George and Walter had also been stolen during his recent painful travels. Sadly, it contained some very fine and extremely powerful French Brandy that Harold and the men in 2nd Company had found in several huge wooden casks in a dank cellar in one of the ruined villages they'd set the guns up in. *Bastards* he mumbled to himself. It was good Brandy and a couple of shots would have been a perfect substitute for morphine.

"Private Brooks! H.A.! Brooks! I've got mail for Brooks!" a voice shouted.

Harold immediately sat up in his bed despite the pain in his head and shoulder and looked for the man calling his name.

"Private Brooks! Mail!"

"Right here!" Harold shouted waving his arm. "I'm Private Brooks!"

The man threw a bundle to him and in his excitement Harold dropped it scattering letters on the dusty floor. After picking it all up, he sat on the edge of his cot and smiled. Five from Bobby. Two from Irene. One from Edith in New Jersey. One from Will. One from the Masonic Lodge in Sac City and finally, one letter with no return address. Harold turned it over examining it carefully not recognizing the handwriting. The postmark was nearly six weeks old but it was from Sioux City, Iowa. He tore into it and felt his heart stop.

My Dearest brother Harold,

It's been many months since I've written and I must apologize to you for the long delay. This was certainly not my intention and it seems that my absence has caused you a great deal of grief. My new school has grown on me and I've found it hard to write for all of the work we are required to do and Miss Billings our headmistress makes sure that we are good, Christian young ladies at all times. But as you are a soldier, my work cannot begin to compare with that of yours. I want you to know that I love you dearly as any good sister would do and that I pray for your return to me and our family as soon as possible.

We have much to discuss as we look towards the future our family has always dreamed and spoken of. I hope this war ends soon and you come to stand by my side again my dearest brother.
Always yours and with love,
Margaret.

Despite his aching body Harold let out a whoop and danced around his creaky hospital bed to the amusement of the other wounded soldiers in the building. Some cheered and whistled but a few others swore and told him to shut up. He read and re-read the letter wondering why it had a Sioux City postmark and why she referred to him as her brother. New school? It didn't make any sense but he didn't care. She was still alive and she claimed she still loved him wherever she was. Harold kept reading the letter over and over again. He could tell that she was telling him something cryptic because of the way it had been written. It was as though someone were censoring her letters.

At the far end of the building a man came crashing through the door shouting excitedly. A crowd gathered, their voices rising until the entire hospital building was full of cheering, dancing people. Harold stopped his own dance wondering what he'd done to provoke such an outburst from everyone. Then he heard it passing down through the crowd.

"The war's over! The Huns signed the Armistice at eleven o'clock this morning! It's over! The war's over!"

Harold and the other wounded, damaged young men were stunned and silent not quite believing what they were hearing. So, it was finally over. The insanity, the killing, the destruction. He felt a shiver go through his entire body and sat heavily on his bed. Despite the cheering and the festive atmosphere in the hospital, Harold felt empty inside. It made him sick to think of the things he'd seen and done, things too horrible to contemplate. As with Harold, most of the wounded men were quiet and didn't join in the celebration. Some cried while most stared silently into the distance each lost in his own dark thoughts. He knew he should be happy but he just couldn't find the feelings. He felt only sadness.

LOST FRIENDS

December 8, 1918

Wounded men from throughout the 65th recently released from the hospital milled about on the edge of an enormous parade ground smoking cigarettes and stamping their feet to keep them warm in the biting cold. They had been waiting for days for the main body of the 65th to arrive from the interior of France to take up residence in the hundreds of empty tents that ringed the ground. All looked forward to reuniting with their buddies and catching up on the latest news and gossip.

"Got a light?" a man asked Harold.

"Sure," Harold dug in his pocket and carefully lit the match in the wind, cupping his hand as he did so. As he lit the cigarette he glanced down at the man's leg which had been amputated just above the knee.

"Thanks," the man said shifting his weight on the crutches he used. "Think the boys will show up today?"

"I hope so. What has it been? Three or four days since they should have arrived?"

"At least. Typical fucking army. Hurry up and wait."

"Yeah, you know it. I wonder how long we're stuck here before they send us home?"

"Shit," the man snorted. "I'd rather not go home. What fucking good will I ever be? I can't farm anymore without a leg and that's all I ever wanted to do."

To Harold's relief, the man turned on his crutches and hobbled away.

In the distance Harold could barely make out the sound of tramping feet. He hoped it was the 65th and not another regiment marching into camp instead as had been the case for days now. The men with him also heard the marching and turned their eyes towards the long avenue which intersected the huge camp. As the long column turned and came into view, the men squinted their eyes trying to catch a glimpse of the tiny regimental flag at the head of the column.

"Who is it?" one man asked.

"Damned if I can tell. I only have one eye," another man answered.

After several minutes Harold and several others let out a whoop.

"It's the 65th!" some shouted. Within minutes the long column of tired, dirty men came streaming into the parade ground where they were given orders to form up by company. Harold walked through the crowded ground looking for his group and finally glimpsed some familiar faces.

"Wellings!" Harold called.

Wellings raised his head and smiled at the sight of his friend. He took several steps forward and embraced Harold.

"Harold! Good God! Look at you!"

"How are you?" Harold asked pumping his friend's hand.

"Good enough. You doing okay? You were a mess the last time I saw you."

"Ah, doing better. I still get headaches but they're not so bad. And, the bayonet wound in my shoulder is pretty painful but it's healing."

"I'm glad!"

"So, where have you all been? They said you'd be here days ago."

"We've been all over northern France," Wellings replied with a laugh. "Right after the Armistice we had to stay in position for almost two weeks in case the Huns decided to start up again. Then, we took all the guns to an artillery park in Limoges where we trained last summer. I was lucky to find Madame Maureen in the whorehouse there and she remembered me. Boy, did we have a lot to talk about! But, we've been moving all over. Every place we've been quartered has been worse than the previous. Bad food too."

Seeing their friend, the men of 2nd Company led by the Kid came over and greeted Harold with handshakes and smiles.

"There he is," the Kid said shaking Harold's hand with obvious gratitude. "My savior. Brooks, I can't thank you enough for saving my ass the night you were wounded. That fucking Hun had me dead-to-rights until you did him in. Thanks."

"My pleasure," Harold answered remembering one of the German's he'd beaten to death. "I guess you owe me."

The Kid laughed and patted Harold on the back. "Sure thing."

"Hey, where's Mike?" Harold asked looking around. "He must have found a wine cellar somewhere. Or, he's praying again."

The Kid's smile immediately faded. He looked away and glanced at Wellings.

"About Mike…" Wellings began. "He uh, um…he didn't make it. He was killed that night in the gun emplacement. When you were wounded."

"What?" Harold asked with disbelief. "It can't be."

Wellings put his hands on Harold's shoulders. "Yeah, I'm afraid so. He was bayonetted to death by one of the Huns, right through the heart."

Harold closed his eyes tightly, gripped Welling's hands, and shook his head. "My God…"

"Yeah, I know. It's been tough for me without you, Mike and George. But at least you're okay Harold. Thank God for that," Wellings said earnestly.

"I'm happy to see you too," Harold answered. "I truly am."

Once the 65th settled in camp Harold and the men discovered that the Army was in no particular hurry to let them go home as everyone wished. With little to do other than line up in formation every day and slog through the knee deep mud. Everyone became surly and chafed at the rigid Army rules that held them in place. Each day became more boring and more awful as the temperature would fluctuate between freezing and just above freezing. The weather was made worse by the proximity of the Atlantic Ocean to the camp. Rain, snow and gale-force winds forced the men to set up their tents anew every few days. Other than this, the only thing left to do was march to the chow hall three times a day, read, and write letters and sleep.

Harold continued to read and re-read the mysterious letter he'd received from Margaret. It had been the only one he'd gotten from her since the previous July. He prayed that it wasn't a vicious trick of some sort but the handwriting was definitely hers. According to the letters from Will earlier in the fall, in the weeks before she had gone missing her attitude had completely changed and his last sight of her was in church one Sunday sitting not in the choir where she had always been in Harold's memory, but with red eyes and her head down and crying, sitting between her scowling mother and sister Judith in a pew. Will wrote that she seemed to be crying all of the time and he hadn't seen her in public since that day. The rumors in Sac City, always abundant but never quite entirely true, said that her sneaking around with Harold had enraged her parents enough to send her away to a girls school much like the one Frank had planned to send Harold to until he had run away. Other rumors had her running away and joining the Salvation Army in order to go to France and find Harold while she worked in one of the canteens they had spread all over France serving the Doughboys doughnuts and coffee.

Harold knew her father, Reverend Nicholson, could be a fearsome man in stature and voice but Margaret's mother was the true disciplinarian who like Frank, had a heavy hand and an uncontrollable temper. Will's letters raised many other questions in Harold's mind. If Margaret's parents were so upset about her night with him back in January why did they wait until June to send her away? Had she completely rebelled against her parents as Harold had done which was so out of character for her? Why didn't they keep her locked up in the house months after their secret tryst? Why did she seem to be crying every time Will saw her in May and early June and not before?

Harold thought he might know the answer though: In a dream he'd had earlier in the fall, he had had a vision of a very pregnant Margaret crying and reaching out to him but the more he tried running to her, the further away she went. He'd awoken from this dream with a start and immediately began counting back the months to the night they had spent in the cannery office before he and Alton Jr. had left to join the Army. Harold prayed this wasn't the reason for his concern and misery but as time went on, it seemed to make more sense. And, if this were indeed the case, he trembled at the thought of what she was going through.

"Hey, Harold."

Harold turned his attention from the letter to see Wellings standing over him.

"Hey, what's going on?"

"Nothing much. I thought you and I would go snoop around to see if we can find George. Sergeant Miller thinks he might be over in the Psych hospital here."

Harold smiled, sat up quickly, stopped and held his head in his hands. Quick movements still gave him uncontrollable, searing headaches.

"Oh, no," he groaned gripping his head.

"You okay?"

"Yeah, give me a minute."

After several moments Harold recovered and was on his feet. Just as he and Wellings were about to duck through the open flap on the tent Sergeant Miller appeared in front of them ashen faced.

"Ah, Brooks, Wellings. I was just coming to find you."

Harold's heart sank thinking Miller had an unpleasant job for them to do. "Great."

"No, it's not what you both think. I...I have some information about Goodlow," Miller said reaching into his overcoat to produce a folded piece of paper. "Here. I'm sorry."

Harold took the paper and unfolded it feeling his stomach lurch as he read the words scrawled in pencil.

Pvt. G.H.W. Goodlow IV 206872

65th CAC, 2nd Company Battery C

New York, NY

Committed suicide in the psych ward, First Army Hospital, Brest, France

Cause of death – asphyxiation (hanged with his shirt) November 5, 1918

WAITING

December 25, 1918

"Boy what a feast!" Harold exclaimed falling back into his cot with a crash. "I think I'm going to be sick."

Wellings groaned and belched with discomfort as he too fell face-first into his cot. "I think I ate more today than I have since we've been in Europe. Wasn't that ham something? I mean, it was real meat not that shit in a can!"

"And the potatoes. And the pies. I can't think of it anymore," Harold grunted and covered his eyes with his arm. The thousands and thousands of Americans waiting in Brest to be sent back to the States had been treated to an enormous Christmas dinner courtesy of General Pershing and his staff. It was a huge affair, even better than the Thanksgiving feast they had been treated to with food most of the men hadn't seen since before joining the army. Hams, turkeys, real potatoes, fresh milk, pies made with real fruit, cakes, candies and more. Unlike the typical army meals they were accustomed to, the men were allowed to take as much time as they wished to eat and were even allowed back for seconds and thirds.

Harold and every man he knew had indulged themselves knowing they would pay for it later.

"The only thing that would make today better would be if someone came in here right now and gave us our travel orders," said Sergeant Miller who along with the rest of the men, had flopped onto his cot and unbuttoned his pants.

"What are you going to do once we get home Sergeant?" Harold asked.

"I'm not sure. The first thing I want to do is go home and spend a little time with my wife and daughter," Miller replied. "After that, I don't know. Hell, I've been in the Army for ten years."

"I never knew you were married and had a girl. We always thought you were just another old career man whose life revolves around the Army," Harold said with surprise.

"No, I've been married for eleven years and my daughter is ten. I joined the Army to take care of them and to get as far away from my father as possible. It was either that or work with him and my brother in our family printing business in Ohio. I never was one for sitting in an office and having fancy little pricks in their nice clothes telling me what to do all day. I certainly couldn't take it from my father."

Harold laughed and rolled over to make himself more comfortable. "I know exactly what you mean. I was supposed to go to college and go back to help my father run his lumber yard but I sure as hell will never work for him again. He beat me senseless most of my life."

"Yeah," Sergeant Miller replied, "My old man liked to beat on me too. I hated the bastard until the day he died. Don't have much time for my brother either. He's a very rich, important fellow who thinks a little too highly of himself."

They drifted off into their own thoughts for a while. Beside them, Wellings snored loudly.

"What are you going to do when you get home? Still going to marry that gal you've driven yourself nuts over?" Miller asked.

"Well, that's the plan. After that, I don't know. As long as we can get far away from our parents and be together, I'll be happy."

"Have you thought about staying in the army? You could take your gal and live all over the world like my family and I have. It's not a bad life."

Harold thought a moment. "Nah, I've had enough of the Army. If Margaret and I want to simply pick up and go somewhere I want us to be able to just go. Besides, I don't ever want to fight in a war again. It's all just too horrible. I don't think I could ever tell anyone about the things I've done and seen."

"I know exactly what you mean," Miller answered staring at the gently swaying ceiling of the tent. "I've thought about what my wife and daughter would think of me if they knew what I'd done here. I can't tell them about it either. They just wouldn't understand."

"I remember you telling me to put it all away somewhere deep once we're home. I just hope I can."

"You men want some great Christmas news?" asked a cracking voice. Harold lifted his arm to see young, bespectacled Lieutenant Fleming standing in the open flap of the smelly tent.

"Only if it's my discharge!" yelled one man.

"No!" Harold and many others shouted. The Lieutenant had recently come to replace the dead Lieutenant Swanson and he relished in taking the men on long hikes and running them through their paces on the parade ground. To him, the Army seemed like one large Boy Scout camp. Even Sergeant Miller had joked that their young Lieutenant was earning a merit badge as some sort by getting to play soldier. All of the men agreed the boy wouldn't have lived long if he'd arrived in France a year sooner.

"Well, if you don't want to know that you're all being shipped home in two days then I won't tell you," the Lieutenant said with a grin. "Start packing!"

PART III

THE LONG RIDE HOME

February 9, 1919

Harold coughed and shifted uncomfortably in his seat as the empty snow-covered Midwestern fields rolled by. Beside him, Wellings sat with an unlit cigarette in his mouth and stared out through the frosted windows of the train carriage. Neither man had spoken since the train had rolled across the Iowa border thirty minutes before and both felt a tinge of excitement and fear as they rolled nearer and nearer to home. Harold read through a letter he had received from Margaret the day before the 65th had boarded their ship for home. The new letter, only the second he'd gotten from her since July, was much like the first one he'd gotten in November. Margaret still referred to Harold as her brother and wrote that things were fine and how much she missed him. But, this letter like the first didn't reveal any information as to where exactly she was, or how he could reach her.

The previous weeks had been a fast, confusing time for Harold and the men of the 65th. Once the huge transport ship bringing them home, the *HMS Haverford,* docked in Philadelphia after a long, monotonous two-week voyage, the men found themselves quarantined aboard the smelly ship for another four days as a precaution against the flu epidemic. Next, they disembarked onto the huge docks of the Navy Yard and marched to a cavern-ous building where every man stripped for showers and delous-ing. Their uniforms were washed and deloused in huge wash tubs then treated with several chemicals to kill vermin and bacteria. This left the men's uniforms a size too small, itchy and stinking from the chemicals. The 65th then marched in a victory parade through downtown Philadelphia with other returning Army regi-ments on their way to the train station and the ride west towards home. After a demobilization ceremony in Kansas City for all of the Midwestern men of the regiment, Harold and Wellings sud-denly found themselves discharged from the army and riding the northbound train towards Iowa and home. Harold had been over-joyed to receive $42.17 in convalescent and discharge pay and was careful to put the money in his small leather pouch containing his precious pocket watch.

While the train crept slowly westward men with the same thoughts and fears left the Company for good and faced the rest of their lives without death, decay and the war's world of absolute ter-ror. They feared to go back to the alien world that had been their lives before the Army and the war. Many grew silent and distant as they approached the old familiar towns and fields of home. How could they ever tell their wives and children that they had killed other human beings in brutal macabre ways and how they had looked upon the dead and mangled bodies of their comrades with relief just because it wasn't them?

"What time is it, Harold?" Wellings asked breaking the silence.

"Just after two," Harold replied looking at his watch. "We should be in Des Moines in two more hours."

"Are you still going to find Margaret once you get home?"

"Yes, that's the plan. I'll try and find out some more information once I get home. The letters are from Sioux City so at least that's a start."

"Hell, if I were you I'd just march right up to her parent's house, knock on the door and ask, 'Where in the fuck have you sent Margaret? I've come to retrieve her."

Harold laughed at his friend. "They'd probably call the constables on me and not even open the door. It might work though."

"It would if you kicked the door in and held your .45 to her fathers' head. Just be sure to ask them nicely and say please before you start shooting. God, how I hate men of the cloth. Pious, morally corrupt sons-of-bitches, the whole lot of them."

"If I did that I'd never find her because I'd be on another train right back down to the prison in Fort Madison," Harold said with a laugh. "You're right though, it has crossed my mind."

The two men rode along in silence for several more minutes.

"So, what are you going to do once you're home?" Harold asked his friend.

Wellings shook his head. "I don't know. Hell, I haven't even thought about it. I'm not farming with my father, I do know that."

"What about that girl you told Mike, George and me about? Are you still in contact with her?"

"No," Wellings replied with a smile snaking across his face. "She decided she couldn't wait for me to come home from the war so she married some scrawny little mutt who was 4-F. He's a Benchley, the son of the local lawyer with all of the money."

"Are you going to beat his head in? Because I wouldn't expect any less of you."

"Nah, she always was a whiny little thing who henpecks nonstop like her mother. I guarantee young Mr. Benchley didn't pop her cherry on their wedding night though," Wellings said with a big rumbling laugh. "Too bad I didn't get one last chance to give her some French crabs. She deserved them."

Wellings lit his cigarette and quickly became more serious. "You know Harold, I was thinking. Maybe you and I could do something together, maybe we could go into business together."

"I like the idea. What would we do?" Harold asked.

"I don't know. That's the problem."

Harold thought a moment. "Why don't we just wait a while and get settled back in. In a few months we can meet in Des Moines or Margaret and I will come visit you in Montezuma. I'm sure we'll both have a lot of ideas then."

"That sounds good. Everything is so confusing right now anyway. I have terrible nightmares. I see Mike and George in them."

Harold pulled out a two cigarettes, one for him and one for Wellings, and looked at his friend realizing he looked small and helpless for some reason. "I have them too. Hell, I've been having nightmares about the war, home and everything else since before we went to France. But, they're worse now. They scare me."

"Yeah? What do you dream about?"

"The war. I always see dead men, men we killed. The Germans are always after me too. I keep seeing you, Mike and George, Sergeant Miller and my little brother all getting shredded by artillery and machine guns. I try to help but I can't move."

Wellings leaned back in the hard seat staring at the ceiling of the carriage. "Me too. My dreams are about the men we killed coming back from the dead to drag us to Hell. There are some others I have too but that particular one haunts me."

The two sat talking about their hopes and dreams until the train slowly lurched to a stop.

"Des Moines! Des Moines, Iowa!" shouted the conductor.

"We're here already?" Wellings asked with surprise. "Well, next stop Montezuma for me then."

Harold stood and helped Wellings pull his gear together as many other men did the same.

"I'm going to miss you Harold," Wellings said sadly with tears in his eyes, something Harold had never seen before. "I've never had a friend or anyone else in my life I've ever cared about so much."

"And I'll miss you, my friend," Harold answered. "I don't know how I'd have made it through all of that without you there."

"Same here. I don't know how I would have either. And we had George and Mike too," Wellings said stifling a sob. "You have my address?"

"Yes, right here," Harold answered patting his coat pocket. "Like I said, write to my brother-in-law's address and he'll send them on to me wherever I'm at. I'll write to you too. Once I find Margaret and we get everything settled I'll let you know where we're at."

The big man suddenly hugged Harold crushing him with his enormous strength as the two said their final goodbyes.

"Make sure you stay in touch," Wellings said through his tears. "And if anyone asks, you never saw me cry."

"You've got a deal," Harold answered through his own tears.

The train suddenly lurched again as it started forward.

"Take care of yourself Harold. I hope you find Margaret soon."

"You also take care of yourself friend," Harold answered shaking Wellings' hand. The train continued to gather speed before Wellings and several other men ran to the doors and jumped off onto the platform. Harold sat back in his seat waving to his friend until he was out of sight. He continued staring out of the frosted window into the coming darkness as Sac City drew nearer and nearer feeling more alone than he ever had before.

HOME

February 10, 1919

The train pulled noisily into the Sac City station belching steam and stench as it screeched to a halt. Harold sat silently peering out of the window to see if he recognized anyone thinking back to the day so long ago when he had left, how busy everything had been and how he and Alton had walked the lonely country roads in the middle of the night when they had run away from Sac City. Now, it was almost deserted as if half of the world had simply gone away. Wednesdays had always been the big day in town when supplies and mail came in. Now, there was virtually no one.

Picking up his tightly packed heavy Army bag containing all of his worldly belongings, Harold made his way slowly to the end of the carriage. The few returning soldiers and sailors shuffled silently down the steps onto the platform into the bright, warm sunshine. Harold recognized most of the Sac City boys among them. There was Robert Hansen a classmate of Harold's and a soldier. There was Paul Wenden two years older and a Navy man. And Eugene Norton who had been the star outfielder on the baseball team with Harold when they were younger, also in his Army uniform but with the right sleeve empty and pinned up to his shoulder. There were a few others too. Harold had grown up with most of them and had attended school with them as well. Each man looked nervously at what was the end of the line and home.

Harold knew that his boyhood friend Alton Jr. wouldn't be among those returning home. In a pack of worn, smelly letters he'd received while recovering in the Convalescent Center, Will had written that Alton had been declared missing in action and presumed killed sometime in October during the enormous Meuse-Argonne offensive. Harold had cried at the news and was surprised by it thinking he was incapable of remorse or tears anymore. Harold would always remember his oldest friend's smile of joy and his stupid laugh lighting up the dark night when they had finally made their way out of Sac City in the middle of the night. Alton Jr. had truly believed the war would be a fun time like their summer days fishing on the river or the thrill of delivering his father's moonshine in the night had been but he'd found out otherwise. Harold's unit had taken part in that one last horrific battle to finally break the Germans and end the war. He'd seen the thousands upon thousands of bloody, disfigured American bodies strewn in the fields and stacked neatly along the sides of the roads as they continued their march forward to new firing positions during those two terrible months. Now, he wondered if Alton Jr.'s body had been among them.

In a later letter from Will, Harold learned that Alton's death had been a surprise to his parents who had never known their son was in the infantry. Evidently, the boy had written letters home telling his family how good his job was tending the animals in the safety of the rear areas as he had promised his mother he would do despite the fact he was in the hell of a front-line infantry unit. The word in Sac City, according to Will, was that his father, Alton Sr., was determined to hunt down and kill Harold for taking his oldest son away to war and allowing him to die. Harold shuddered at the thought knowing he had indeed been partly responsible for his friend's death.

Harold and the other uniformed men had grudgingly taken account of one another after the train had left Des Moines for its long trip north and west stopping in every little town along the way. A few nodded at one another, a few shook hands and spoke some words with those they knew from home and from a life so different from the ones each had left. Men in uniform got off at every stop, most taking a deep breath before striding confidently at first, then more slowly towards the doors and the mostly empty train platforms that welcomed each home. Some had a few family members waiting for them waving tiny American flags while they cheered and cried for their returning heroes. Others simply stood on the platforms and looked back at the departing train with fearful faces and hesitation.

Walking down the steps of the carriage, Harold stopped and squinted in the bright sunlight and adjusted his heavy pack. He sighed deeply knowing that within the hour he would have to face his father for the first time in nearly a year.

As he walked slowly across the platform, he saw a man he knew. It was Stan. He looked older somehow, his face was gray and flabby and he seemed to labor with each breathless step. Harold walked up to him.

"Hello, Stan."

The old man turned and looked at the strange man in the army uniform speaking to him. Harold could tell that he was quite drunk already. He continued to stare at Harold, not sure of who he was.

"Stan, its Harold. Remember?"

Stan's eyes immediately lit up. "Harold Brooks!" he exclaimed taking Harold's hand. "By God, boy, it's good to see you!"

The two men shook hands smiling at each other.

"You're back! I knew you'd survive. You're tough, like your father." Stan said continuing to pump Harold's hand. "This calls for a celebration. Buy me a drink?"

Harold laughed but thought a drink might be just the thing to calm his nerves. "Sure Stan. Just one."

As they slowly walked out to the street Harold saw several people he hadn't seen in a long time. Some stared at him while most didn't give him a second look. They were used to men in uniform coming and going but it made him feel uncomfortable, as though he weren't welcome here anymore. He tugged at the tight collar of his uniform hoping to get a little more air. Next to him, Stan chattered away filling Harold in on everything that had happened since he'd left. He talked of the few boys from Sac City who had been killed in the war including Alton Jr. and of Harold's father Frank not having much business because of wartime rationing. According to Stan, he only worked two or three days a week now. That explained his mid-day drunkenness.

Harold stopped in front of the tiny liquor store and peered in.

"What's the matter boy?" Stan asked with a smirk. "Afraid your father might see you?"

Harold flushed, pushed the door open and entered the brightly lit store. He'd never set foot in this place until now. A voice spoke up from the back room.

"Can I help you?"

"Yes sir," Harold replied. "Do you have any Brandy? French stuff?"

The bald little man eyed Harold curiously. "Sure do. But are you old enough to buy it?"

Harold felt anger coursing through his body, something that he'd never had a problem with before the war. Now, it often consumed him and drove him to desperation. He'd spent a year in France where no one had ever asked him if he were old enough to drink and he certainly didn't feel like explaining himself to this man. Unconsciously, his hand went to his belt before he remembered the loaded .45 pistol he carried was tucked away inside his duffel bag. He smiled wondering how the shop-keeper would react to having the loaded gun shoved under his chin. "Yes, I think I'm plenty goddamn old enough," Harold said glaring down at the man.

The smaller man stared back at Harold for a moment. "You're Frank Brooks' son aren't you? The one that ran away and joined up. I have a good bottle right back here," he said scurrying to the back of the store. He returned with a square bottle wrapped in newspapers.

Harold pulled out his discharge pay and began to count until the man stopped him.

"No charge for you son. On the house."

Harold opened his mouth to argue but the man cut him off.

"You had the guts to run away from your father and fight in the war for all of us back home here. You've earned it. Besides, your father's tried to have me shut down for years being on the city council and all. Here take it."

Harold extended his hand. "Thank you. Don't worry about my father anymore. I'll come back and pay the next time."

The men shook hands and Harold walked out into the cold winter afternoon. He and Stan stepped into a side alley while Harold unwrapped the bottle. Stan let out a whistle.

"Look at that. Real French Brandy. Damn boy, you got yourself some culture over in the war!"

Harold handed Stan the bottle and he immediately had the lid off and the bottle raised to his lips. He suddenly handed the bottle back to Harold.

"You first. You're the war hero and...Welcome home. I mean it."

Harold took the bottle and drank deeply feeling the liquid burn down his throat and into his stomach. He shivered as he handed the bottle back to Stan who also drank deeply.

Stan handed the bottle to Harold and paused. "You know, your father is a good man. I know he was awfully tough on you. He's bullheaded and stubborn and a tee-totaler but he loves you."

"Yeah," Harold replied gazing at the bottle. "He had a funny way of showing it. How's my brother? Dad didn't beat on him did he while I was gone?"

"Ah, Bobby's fine. He learned how to side step the old man from you and I think he's given up with the boy. Frank and your mother don't pay much attention to him. I doubt you'll recognize him. Boy's grown but he talked and bragged about you since you left."

Harold eyed Stan with curiosity. He had to ask the old man something he'd wondered about his entire life.

"Stan, why does dad let you get away with drinking when he can't stand anyone else doing it? Hell, you two have been together for years and you've always drank and he knows it."

Stan lowered the bottle and thought a moment. "Well, when he was homesteading out in South Dakota all those years ago he was out there with your mother and Irene who was a little thing then. There was a big blizzard, one of those bad ones that last for days. Your father was driving his wagon back to the homestead from town when the blizzard caught him. He damned near died. All of the horses had frozen to death and he knew he was next so he tipped the wagon over one of the horses that was still warm, slit her open and crawled inside her," Stan said before taking another drink. "Anyway, I'd been out hiding from the Army after I'd decided to leave them and was living in an old abandoned sod place. After the storm let up a bit I could see the snow had drifted around this wagon and some dead horses down a ways from there. I was hungry so I was going through all his supplies when I found him frozen and mostly dead under the wagon inside that horse. Dragged him back to the house and nursed him back to health on horse meat and some buckwheat flapjacks I made from his supplies. There was some whiskey too," Stan added with a smile.

Harold stared at Stan wide-eyed. He'd never heard this story before and it fascinated him to think that his father had been so weak and vulnerable so long ago. Frank certainly didn't act that way now.

"He was with me for over a week. Once he'd come around and got his health back I took him back to your mother and sister. Told me he owed his life to me and that he'd always give me a job and a place to live. We've been together ever since."

Stan offered Harold the bottle but he waved it away. "No, thanks. I need to go home and face them. And I need to find out where Margaret is."

Stan put the lid back on the bottle and quickly slid it into his coat. "Your father will be glad to see you, son. He's missed you and worried about you. Believe me, he has a tough outside, but he's been worried since you left. He knew you'd left to join the service too and he never came looking for you. That's why you got away so easily. As for your lady friend all I know is that her parents sent her away last year. Don't know where."

"Thanks Stan," Harold said extending his hand. "I hope I can find her."

Stan shook Harold's hand and put his other hand on Harold's shoulder. "You will. You're the most determined person I've ever met before."

Harold gathered his heavy bag and turned to make the long walk up the hill towards home. Despite the warm Brandy in his belly he shivered in the freezing cold air out of a strange uncertainty he hadn't felt in a long time.

The late afternoon sun began to set on the world while he walked home along the rough, cracked sidewalk that was crusted with ice and chunks of hard snow. After readjusting the heavy duffel bag slung over his shoulder he tugged at his collar hoping to release some of the warmth from his stained, odd-smelling uniform that itched uncomfortably and rubbed his body raw. He wouldn't unbutton it however, he felt he had earned the right to wear it and he wouldn't let his father or anyone else see him as any less of the man he believed himself to be now. Harold wondered how his father would greet him and had thought about this moment of his homecoming since before he'd left. It didn't matter to him if Frank were angry or not and Harold had learned during the war that he had changed a great deal from the innocent young boy who had allowed his father to beat and harass him as a child. His wartime experiences had proven that he was capable of doing whatever he felt necessary in order to survive. If Frank tried to hit or attack him once he reached home, or any time from now on, Harold knew for certain he would kill him.

After slowly walking and silently talking to himself Harold finally reached the front gate of his family's house out of breath. It didn't look as though it had changed other than the paint being a little more faded. An American flag hung lazily from a pole affixed to the front porch and stirred gently in the continuing cold of the coming night. He could see Bobby's treasured assortment of sticks jammed into the snow around small holes and forts the boy had dug along with his homemade toys which were scattered haphazardly around the yard. A large black dog Harold didn't recognize slunk forward to examine the new stranger in his yard with a growl. He kicked at the dog which retreated with a yelp into the growing darkness towards the back of the house. For several moments he stared at the home he had grown up in trying to work up the nerve to walk up to the door. His feet seemed to be frozen to the ancient concrete walk keeping him from taking another step. After what seemed a lifetime of watching his friends and strangers die horrible deaths and living in the surreal world of shattered France, Harold didn't know how he felt. He suddenly wished he hadn't come home.

"Harold?" a voice cried from the back yard. "Harold? Is it you?"

Harold looked towards the voice. It was Bobby. Or, at least he thought it was. This boy was much taller, seemingly very muscular through the old stained coat that had once been his, staring at this familiar stranger through his odd-colored green eyes that shone in the half-light of the evening. The boy stood uncertainly by the huge trunk of the ancient maple tree patting the black dog on the head. His face was longer and thinner and his breath came in quick, short breaths steaming off into the cold air. Somehow Harold could recognize his features but, he still wasn't sure. The boy carried a long stick, a homemade fishing pole attached to a line of fresh, frozen fish behind lying in the snow behind him. His hair was long and greasy, shooting out of the faded blue stocking cap, also once Harold's and hanging low over his eyes.

"Bobby?" Harold asked. "Is that you? It's me, Harold. I'm home."

The boy shifted uncomfortably, his feet crunching in the snow, his green eyes piercing this stranger who had appeared out of nowhere.

"Harold?" he asked again.

"It's me Bobby. It's me. I'm home."

After entering the house with Bobby in his arm's Harold's mother crushed him with a hug and buried her face in his chest, her tears running down the front of Harold's long army overcoat dripping silently onto the floor. She cried and moaned and prayed in a succession of short, labored breaths thanking God for bringing her son home from the War. Mary too, hung on Harold's left arm screaming excitedly jumping up and down. Bobby stood with his arms wrapped tightly around Harold's waist crying too...he hadn't let go of his brother since meeting him outside and Harold had carried him quietly into the house to the utter surprise of the family who were just washing up for supper. The boy wailed and tore at Harold's uniform still not believing that his brother had finally come back to him.

Frank approached Harold and stood looking him up and down. Harold thought he looked older somehow as his skin wrinkled and hanging loosely from his cheeks. He looked tired and stooped like a man much older than his fifty-nine years. Frank coughed quietly and straightened himself up pushing his chest forward with his hands firmly planted on his hips as he had always done.

"Well son," Frank began. "I see you've decided to come home."

Harold paused, glowering at his father. "Yes sir. It's been too long."

Frank sniffled and removed his glasses. He pulled a handkerchief from his pocket and dabbed his eyes. "Indeed."

The two stood and looked at one another while Nina, Mary and Bobby continued to scream, cry and tug at Harold. Frank too paused a moment and spoke up as he pushed his chest out further.

"Did you accomplish what you set out to do?"

Harold thought a moment about the war and everything he'd done. He knew he couldn't ever explain it to anyone and the all-too-fresh memories he carried inside his head had to stay locked up and hidden away forever.

"Yes sir, I did. Things I don't ever want to see or do again. But most importantly, I got the hell away from you."

Frank took a deep breath, clearly not expecting Harold's answer. He again cleared his throat and looked away. Harold continued to stare at him without moving. After a moment, Frank turned his gaze back to Harold, straightened himself again and extended his hand.

"Yes, well then. Are you okay?"

Surprised, Harold took his father's hand and squeezed like he'd always been taught and looked directly into his father's eyes.

"I believe so, other than a little pneumonia and this scar," he said pointing to his head.

"Very well then. Very well," Frank said pumping Harold's hand. "I'm glad you've come home son."

FINDING MARGARET

February 13, 1919

The Sioux City train station was crowded with people hurrying to get to their destinations and seek shelter from the frigid air gusting in from the north. Harold wrapped his scarf snugly around his neck and turned the collar of his army greatcoat up and moved along with the crowd of people towards the main entrance while he shouldered his heavy duffel bag. Several returning soldiers, sailors and Marines were met with loud cheers, crying mothers and girlfriends and stern fathers trying their best not to break down as their men stepped off the dirty, snow- and ice-encrusted train. Harold smiled as he watched these small family reunions taking place remembering reuniting with his family only a few nights before. It had been an awkward affair that Harold hadn't enjoyed much. For reasons he couldn't understand, there seemed to be a pall hanging over the house leaving him feeling as though he were an outsider, someone not welcome there anymore.

After the initial joy his family had shown after his arrival home, things soon became quiet and tense. Even Bobby seemed afraid of

Harold and the boy had told their mother he didn't want Harold sharing a room with him as he had his entire life. Not wanting to upset the child, Harold slept on the large sofa downstairs with his army duffel bag containing the always loaded .45 pistol close to his side at all times. His second day at home was spent with Will and Irene but like the rest of the family, he also found it difficult to talk to or be comfortable with them as well. By the third day Harold decided to leave and find Margaret with the little information Will had managed to find for him. Leaving Sac City the second time had been a relief. He was looking for a Girl's school north of the river in Sioux City but he didn't have the name or address.

The crowd on the platform soon thinned out leaving several lonely soldiers who stood uncertainly for a time in the station looking for a familiar face and finding none, wearily gathered their bags and shuffled to the main doors with everyone else. Harold could see the disappointment in their faces and the stooped, more rounded shoulders as they stepped out towards an uncertain future.

Harold moved through the crowd out to the sidewalk in front of the old station, once the gateway to the Dakotas and the endless prairies being sold to white men to farm, men such as his father, who had found nothing but dry, untenable soil and life-taking pain and misery in their search for independence and new wealth. Reaching deep into his coat he pulled out a cigarette and continued digging in the pocket for his matches.

"Dammit," he swore. "Must have left them on the train."

He looked left and right for someone else smoking and saw one of the lonely soldiers he'd seen inside the station who hadn't had anyone waiting for him standing alone smoking a cigarette.

"Hey buddy," Harold said walking up to the soldier who was nothing more than a teenage boy just like him. "Got a light?"

The young soldier nodded, reached into a pocket and handed Harold his matches. Harold turned away from the cold wind that howled along the busy street and quickly lit his cigarette, still care-ful to cup the burning end inside his hand as he had learned to do in France to shield the glowing end from the always-present and forever-watching German artillery spotters. Handing the matches back, he noticed the young soldier held his cigarette the same way.

"Thanks," Harold said exhaling into the wind.

The young man took the matches and quickly put them back in his pocket. Harold looked him up and down and his eyes settled on the shoulder patch of his uniform, then to his coat collar which bore two crossed rifles.

"Rainbow Division huh?" Harold asked. "Infantry?"

"Yep," the boy answered looking at Harold's worn shoulder patch. "Artillery?"

Harold nodded. "We did quite a bit of firing for you infantry boys in the Meuse-Argonne. 9.2's, the big heavies."

"You should have fired more," the boy answered taking a deep drag on his cigarette. "Most of my company got killed when we attacked into the hills because no one bothered to hit the Hun's pillboxes."

Harold felt his face flush red with anger. "We did our best. But, you know better than anyone what a fucking mess that all was."

"Yeah," the boy answered flicking his cigarette into the wind. "It *was* a fucking mess. But, you saved our asses a few times too. You guys with the heavy's took out an entire Bavarian regiment that counterattacked us outside of Autreville. Blew the son-of-a-bitches to high hell, every goddamned one of them. There wasn't anything left for us to kill."

Harold looked away and fumbled with his cigarette. "Yeah."

The two stood silently in the cold watching people come and go in their horse-drawn carts and rumbling autos, each shivering and gripping their coats and shawls tightly in the cold. Specks of snow flitted and swirled to the ground only adding to the agony of the hurried civilians desperate to scurry home to seek warmth and comfort.

The young soldier turned and eyed Harold again. "My name's Sam McGowan."

"Harold Brooks."

The two shook hands and nodded to one another. Sam was just a little shorter than Harold and looked as though he were just about the same age, eighteen or nineteen. Thick, dark hair shot out from beneath the wrinkled, faded army cap he wore pulled low over his forehead.

"You from Sioux City?" Sam asked.

"No. I'm from a little town called Sac City, just east of here. You?"

"Born and bred in Sioux City," Sam said proudly. "My daddy works for the packing plant up on the river. We live up on the northwest side by the packing houses with my momma and my little brother.

"Looking for work?" Sam asked.

Harold shuffled and looked away. "No, I'm here to look for my fiancé. I was told that her parents put her in some all-girls school last June. I'm hoping I can find her but I don't have much to go on."

Sam turned and looked up at Harold with a squinted eye revealing the pink, jagged scar that ran from his forehead down around to his nose.

"Girls school huh? There's a Catholic one up close to where I live called Briar Cliff and another Christian such and such school north of the downtown here."

Harold thought a moment and realized that since Sam had been raised in Sioux City he could possibly help him find Margaret faster than he would have been able to on his own. He had only been to Sioux City twice in his lifetime, once as a small child and the most recent time had been when he was around twelve or thirteen when he had come along with Frank to buy a stock of west coast lumber and that trip had taken only a day. Compared to Sac City, Sioux City was enormous.

"Well, my girl is the daughter of our local Methodist minister. Do you think she'd be at the school north of here?"

"Could be," Sam answered squinting his bad eye again. "We could find out but I'm getting cold and I'm hungry. Why don't you come home with me for tonight and tomorrow we can start looking around. Besides, I haven't seen my folks or my brother for over a year."

Harold wasn't sure what to say but the offer interested him. He'd brought one hundred dollars of the army pay he'd carefully sent home to Will and had planned on finding a hotel for the evening while he looked into the girl's schools in town and tried to figure out what to do next.

"Come on," Sam insisted. "You and I were in the war together. The least I can do is give you a place to stay and a hot meal. I don't have any friends here. The one's I had are buried in France."

"I have a few that got left over there too," Harold replied sadly dropping his cigarette to the sidewalk and crushing it violently with his boot.

The two young men stood silently, not moving despite the freezing wind and snow blowing around them, each lost in his own thoughts of the dead buddies they had left behind.

"Well, what do you say?"

"You've got a deal," Harold finally answered with a smile. He and Sam set off walking through the late afternoon crowds towards his new friend's home exchanging war stories and talking about where they'd been and what they'd done.

Harold immediately felt at home with Sam's family who welcomed him into their home, treating him as though he were a long lost member of the family. He found Sam's parents to be very hospitable, loving people who laughed and did the best with what they had. During their walk Sam described his brother as little but Harold was surprised to meet an outgoing fifteen year old boy who was nearly six feet tall and very muscular. He'd recently quit school and now worked with his father at the packing plant giving their small family a much needed boost in income. After a huge meal, laughing, much conversation and a bottle of home-made wine Harold, lightheaded and red faced, gladly fell asleep on the family's couch which Mrs. McGowan had made up as a bed for him.

The next morning to his delight, Harold realized that he'd slept for nearly thirteen hours straight through, something he had never done in his life. More importantly, he hadn't been both-ered by the dreadful dreams of home and of the war. After a huge breakfast with the McGowan family he felt alive and happy and ready to continue his search for Margaret. Mr. McGowan drew a map on a scrap piece of paper showing Harold and Sam where the girl's school was on the north side of Sioux City along with its name: The Florence Crittenton Home.

With full bellies and the map carefully folded and inside his coat pocket, Harold and Sam set out into the cold sunny morn-ing to find the school and hopefully, Margaret. While the two walked and visited Harold could feel his heart beating a little fast-er with each step and a strange tingling sensation jolted his body. He hoped that this would be the day that he would finally find Margaret after so much had happened.

Sam eyed Harold curiously as they walked along the busy street. "I shouldn't say anything but I have to."

"About what?" Harold asked taking a drag on his cigarette.

"Well, my father said that this girl's school we're looking for its...it's not what you think."

"What do you mean?

Sam took a deep breath and stopped walking.

"What? Tell me Sam!"

"My father said that this place you're looking for is a home for wayward girls. You know, um, girls that get pregnant before they're, um, married. The babies are put up for adoption."

Harold stopped and stared at Sam, his eyes and mouth wide open in disbelief. He felt as though Sam had punched him in the stomach as it knotted up tightly. *It couldn't be! Could it?*

He'd thought about it for months now. Yes, it all made sense-- that was why she disappeared in June, she would have been very pregnant by then and showing so her parents sent her away to save themselves from the embarrassment and shame. That's why she couldn't write directly to him.

"Hey Harold, it's none of my business. Things happen and I understand that. I'm not judging you."

"Oh, my God, no..."

Reaching deep inside his coat, Harold pulled out a small bottle of Brandy he'd bought from the same man in the Sac City store before leaving for Sioux City. He removed the cap and took a deep drink. "I knew it! I just knew it!" he cried tipping back the bottle to drink again.

Several people walking by on the sidewalk gave Harold and Sam a wide berth while Harold tried to get himself together. Two older women walked by shaking their heads and scowling.

"Just look at that will you? Drunk already and it's only ten in the morning," said one loudly.

"It's just shameful. All of these troubled young men drinking and carrying on. You'd think the army would have taught them better or would keep them locked away," chirped the second woman.

Sam turned angrily towards the two women. "Get the hell out of here damn you!" he roared.

The two women gasped in horror and ran wild-eyed and fearful down the sidewalk shrieking for help. Other pedestrians crossed the street to avoid Harold and Sam while others stopped to see what was going on.

Sam grabbed Harold by the arms. "Come on, let's get going before the Constables show up. They're not the nicest bunch in this town and I'm on the wrong side of the tracks over here."

Harold stood, wiped his eyes and straightened his coat and pants. "Yeah, good idea. Let's get going."

After walking for nearly two hours in the bone-chilling cold the two men stood on the sidewalk in front of an enormous Victorian house surrounded by oak and maple trees. A small sign fastened to the front wall of the house read, *The Florence Crittenton Home for Wayward Girls.* In the rear of the house stood two other large brick buildings with a large courtyard area in between. The entire property was surrounded by an imposing wrought-iron fence nearly ten feet tall. Harold noticed that the top of the fence balusters had been forged into lethally sharp pointed ends that were carefully crafted inward and slightly downward. He had seen defenses like these in France with barbed wire and the evil sharpened sticks hammered into the ground to keep the Germans out of trenches and gun pits. Here at the girl's school, the inward bent points on the fence meant that instead of trying to keep people out of the grounds the people running this place intended that none of the girls try to leave.

Harold and Sam looked the house and grounds over carefully with the trained eyes of soldiers.

"Place looks like a prison," Sam said. "All they need is some barbed wire around the inside base of the fence with K-ration cans strung up for alarm. That rise along the back side of the house there would make a great defensive position too. It overlooks all of the grounds down into that ravine and timber."

Harold could feel the ever-present anger in himself again. It did look like a prison, someplace awful he was sure free spirited Margaret would struggle with.

"I'm going to the door," Harold said unlatching the heavy front gate. "Wait for me down at that restaurant we just walked by."

"You sure?"

"Why not? I need to find out something."

"Okay. Come get me if you have trouble."

Harold nodded and walked slowly up the steps to the house. His entire body tingled with uncertainty and apprehension. Clearing his throat he knocked loudly. Hearing someone approach inside, he quickly removed his hat and stood at attention.

The door opened and a mousy little woman with hollow cheeks stared up at Harold. "Yes. May I help you?" she asked in a squeaky, child-like voice.

"Yes ma'am," Harold replied with a smile. "I'm here to visit my sister who is staying here. A Miss Margaret Nicholson."

The small woman stared at Harold for a moment then opened the door fully. "Please. Come in."

Harold stepped into the warm house and immediately began sweating. He thought he'd ask for Margaret by name before introducing himself just to see what would happen. If they told him they didn't know her then he'd have to try somewhere else. But, he hoped he was right.

"Wait right here...um, who should I tell Miss Hanlon is calling?" asked the girl.

"Harold Nicholson ma'am," Harold answered trying to sound confident. "Margaret's brother."

The girl scurried down the wooden-floored hallway with her wide skirt swishing back and forth. Harold stuck his finger into his uniform collar and tried to catch his breath hoping to let a little heat out of his shirt. After a moment the small girl came back following an older woman.

"Mr. Nicholson. I am Miss Elizabeth Hanlon and I am in charge of the young ladies here."

Harold nodded and bowed slightly to the woman. The stiff collar on her dress tightly covered her neck forcing the flesh on her face out which was taught and pale white while her hair was pulled tightly back into a Victorian style bun. She looked harsh and certainly frigid reminding Harold of Mrs. Sanderson, the high school secretary in Sac City whom everyone despised.

"Miss Hanlon, it is a pleasure to meet you. I've just returned from the war and I've missed my sister terribly. After finding out what had happened to her I was beside myself with worry. Our father, Reverend Nicholson, told me of her plight and that she had come here. If it's not too much trouble could I see her? It's been over a year Miss Hanlon. Please, is my dear sister here?" Harold said trying to be as formal and dignified as possible. This stuffy old spinster obviously demanded respect and manners from everyone she met so Harold laid in on thickly.

The woman squinted her eyes and raised her chin as she took in the man in front of her.

"Well Mr. Nicholson I can appreciate your love for your sister but we do have rules here. Very strict rules that your father should have informed you of. We do not allow visitors on non-visiting days and even then we could not permit you to see your sister privately. You must be accompanied by your father and mother if you wish to see her."

"I see," Harold said trying to keep his composure. "I apologize for barging in on you today Miss Hanlon but you see, I just got off the train from my demobilization ceremony and I haven't even been home yet. I was passing through Sioux City on my way home and thought I'd surprise Margaret. I am sorry."

The woman smiled sardonically and clasped her hands tightly together. "That's wonderful of you, Mr. Nicholson. Our next scheduled visitation day is this coming Saturday and you'll be happy to know that your parents are coming to visit Margaret then for the first time since we admitted her. They wrote that they would arrive around ten o'clock this Saturday morning. Perhaps you can come back then."

"Yes ma'am, that sounds wonderful," Harold said bowing slightly. "I look forward to our family all being together and praying for Margaret. It's been much too long I'm afraid."

Miss Hanlon moved towards the door which the young girl held open for Harold.

"It was truly delightful to meet you Miss Hanlon," Harold said. "I shall look forward to seeing you again on Saturday."

Miss Hanlon nodded imperceptibly and scowled. "Yes Mr. Nicholson. It was nice to meet you as well. Goodbye."

Harold stepped back out into the cold, glad to be out of the stuffy, hot house. He replaced his cap and quickly walked down the sidewalk careful not to look back feeling Miss Hanlon's eyes burning holes in him from inside the house. Margaret was here. Now he had to figure out a way to get her out of the awful place before her parents came to visit on Saturday when Miss Hanlon would presumably tell them of Margaret's long lost brother Harold coming to visit. He had four days.

BREAKOUT

February 19, 1919

Harold and Sam leaned forward to speak in low voices to one another about the plan they'd spent two days working on in small rundown café directly across the street from the girl's home. It was a perfect place; they could scope out the buildings and grounds from a booth they'd taken over next to a window. Most of the people frequenting the place were laborers and workmen with a fair smattering of men who'd been in the service so their presence wasn't considered out of the ordinary. "Wow, we have a lot of info here," Harold said sipping tepid coffee from a chipped mug while looking through the notes he and Sam had been keeping.

"We do, but the more intelligence we gather before we jump off the better," Sam replied. "I can't believe that place isn't guarded. Hell, it looks imposing but it's really not."

Both had kept detailed time tables for class changes when the girls were let out in the yard to exercise, when the deliveries came and when the day staff left in the evening. Their military training proved invaluable because they understood extreme patience, how to read the lay of the land, how to devise plans and to how solve problems. Each one agreed what they were planning would be easy compared to the war because no one inside the school would try to kill them. Harold wasn't so sure about Miss Hanlon though.

"The day guard leaves the same time every day and through the same gate too," Sam said pointing to a lonely gate at the rear of the school property. "Sometimes it's locked sometimes not. Just depends on if he remembers to do it."

"Good. We have two ways to either get in or out. The hole in the back fence is well-hidden in some old brush and the ground drops off into a ravine. Perfect cover that goes east for a mile. That's where we'll go once I get her."

Sam smiled and laughed. "I'll cause one helluva ruckus to distract whoever's in there watching those girls and you and Margaret get away back there. It's brilliant. You know, we should have been officers. We could have finished the war in three months. Not like those fucking college boys who played soldier with their commissions and got all of their men killed."

Harold laughed as well. "So are we on?"

"You bet. This is going to be fun!"

Harold swirled the coffee around in the mug feeling excitement radiate through his body. The day before he'd snuck onto the school grounds through the back fence in the late afternoon and hidden in some thick bushes next to a small brick pump house sitting in a deserted corner of the grounds. The girls who were residents of the school were brought outside by Miss Hanlon and three other stern, unhappy looking women, presumably teachers, and allowed to walk and play games for an hour. Two of the teachers would walk the inside of the fence line of the huge grounds looking outward while the other two kept a close eye on the girls who weren't allowed within ten feet of the fence.

"It's about dark. I'm going in," Harold said pulling his coat on.

"Don't get caught," Sam said lighting a cigarette. "I'll wait for you here."

Harold walked down the street as the late winter sun began to settle low in the sky. From his observations the previous two days he knew the girls schedule. The day before he'd been on the grounds earlier in the afternoon hidden in the dusty second story of a rundown building housing the boilers for the campus. He still shivered with excitement remembering seeing Margaret. Peering through a broken section of a smudged window, he'd recognized her the moment she walked out of the door of the large brick building in the center of the grounds. She still had her long lovely blonde hair and had gained a little weight but as he watched her from his hiding place he could see the unhappiness on her face and in her movements. It seemed to pull her down as she shuffled along the worn sidewalk with the other girls, some of whom were very pregnant. After their hour of outside recreation the girls were herded back into a smaller brick building which Harold and Sam guessed was a barracks. The smells of food came from this building too and once darkness settled in Harold could see the girls preparing for bed on the second floor.

Harold waited down the street until the sun was completely down bathing the entire area in darkness before running through the woods and slipping through the hole in the fence he'd discovered earlier. From here, he ran from tree to tree taking great care to stay in the shadows. Upon reaching the building he walked around to the side and discovered a metal fire-escape that went up to a second floor window. He climbed it silently and brought his face up to the bottom corner of the window and peered in to see a long hallway with doors on either side. Girls walked about in their nightclothes preparing for bed and going to and from the washroom. As he watched Margaret exited a room and walked down the hall directly towards him causing his heart to skip a beat as she looked out the window into the darkness. He hadn't been that close to her in a year and he felt goose bumps all over his body. His hand ran over an envelope in his pocket containing a letter for her with his detailed plan to get her out the next night wondering how he he'd be able to get it to her.

While he sat contemplating the window was suddenly thrown open.

"Oh, shit." Harold froze hoping one of the girls had opened it just to get a little fresh air. Leaning back to press himself flat against the wall he felt himself teeter precariously on the edge of the fire escape. A leg suddenly shot out of the window and a girl lowered herself to the fire escape just inches from Harold. She leaned back against the wall and lit a cigarette taking deep drags. She continued smoking the cigarette until her eyes adjusted to the darkness until she saw Harold sitting just next to her. Just as she opened her mouth to scream he leaned over and covered her mouth.

"Shhh!" he hissed holding her tightly. "I'm not going to hurt you. I'm here to find Margaret Nicholson. I'm her fiancé."

The girl continued to squirm and kick at Harold.

"Goddammit," Harold whispered loudly. "I'm not going to hurt you! Stop it! I'm just here for Margaret!"

After what seemed like hours the girl calmed down. Harold slowly removed his hand and backed away from her now raising both of his hands. "It's okay. Honestly. You know Margaret don't you? I'm Harold from Sac City."

The girl glared at Harold in the darkness. "You scared the hell out of me!"

"I'm sorry. But tell me please, do you know her?"

"Sure," the girl answered insolently. "You're the soldier boy that got her in trouble. A minister's daughter too." The girl laughed and sucked on the cigarette. "Come to take her away have you?"

"Yeah, I have as a matter of fact. Listen, will you give her this letter for me? I'll make it worth your while."

The girl thought a moment before answering "Sure. Give me a carton of cigarettes and get me out of here with her and I'll give it to her and I'll keep my mouth shut."

Harold opened his mouth to argue but knew this girl wasn't kidding. She could ruin everything. She sat smiling at Harold. "Well? We got a deal or not?"

Harold shook his head and handed the girl the letter. "Deal. Tomorrow night. Ask Margaret for the details.

Once the girl disappeared back into the building Harold scrambled down the ladder and took the long circuitous route back to the café.

"You did what?" Sam shouted at Harold. "That little harlot could cause you some big problems if she opens her mouth."

"I know it, but we're going to have to go on the assumption she won't. If I can get both of them to the fence I'll take Margaret one way and send this one the other way."

"Shit, she'll want money too," Sam said angrily. "This could blow up in your face."

"Well, if she does screw it up I've still got this knife here I took off a dead Hun and that .45 I showed you," Harold said with a grin.

Sam shook his head and stood. "You do that and you'll be the one locked up."

The next day dragged on into an eternity for Harold as he waited for night to come. Neither he nor Sam had told his parents about their plans for the evening not wanting them to be involved if something went wrong. Harold walked the sidewalks around their home all day smoking cigarettes and going over the entire plan in his mind continually watching the sun and looking at his pocket watch.

Finally, after another tasty and filling supper with the McGowan's, both men donned their heavy army coats and caps telling Sam's parents that they were going out for a few hours. The couple wished them well and went off to bed.

After walking in the cold, the two finally reached the darkened school at eleven o'clock. Taking up their usual place in an alley across from the grounds Harold pulled out his pocket watch and checked the time. Sam reached inside his overcoat and pulled out the bottle of whiskey that he and Harold had stopped to buy on their way over to the school. He removed the lid and took a large drink. Shivering from the alcohol, he passed the bottle to Harold who also drank.

"Ready to go over the top?" Sam asked with a big smile on his face.

"Yeah. Let's get this done," Harold answered drinking again. He wiped his mouth and handed the bottle back to Sam who poured some of the whiskey into his left hand and then smeared it on his face and down the front of his coat before taking another enormous gulp.

"I'll give you fifteen minutes to get back there and on that fire escape. Light your match when you're in place and I'll let all hell loose," Sam said. "You get that shoulder patch taken off?"

Harold reached to his shoulder feeling where his 65th patch had once been. "Done. Remember, there are two old spinsters who sleep in the house and that smaller woman. The other old lady sleeps on the ground floor of the barracks building. Make sure you keep them distracted at the front of the house because we're going out behind to the fence."

"I got it, I got it." Sam replied with a smile. "That was my idea, remember?"

"Okay. Ready?"

"As ready as I'll ever be."

"Thanks Sam for everything. I couldn't have done any of this without you."

The two shook hands and smiled at each other. Harold turned and casually crossed the street before ducking into the brush behind the school grounds. Within minutes he was through the fence and on the fire escape. With shaking hands, he checked his pocket watch in the moonlight, slipped it back into his pocket and pulled out a book a matches and lit one. He waited a moment and peered in the window tapping gently. In the front of the house he could hear Sam yelling profanities as a drunken man would. Peering in the dark window again, Harold tapped much harder. In the pale light he could see two figures emerge from a room down the hallway and scurry to the window. Harold turned and looked around below him and around the yard. Sam was now beating on the front door of the main house yelling and cursing in earnest.

The window slid open and Margaret began climbing out onto the fire escape. Harold grabbed her around the waist and pulled her completely out. She grabbed Harold's face and kissed him deeply.

"Harold," she said breathlessly with tears streaming down her face. "I knew you'd find me."

"And here I am."

The other girl threw Margaret's small bag of possessions out onto the fire escape and then began crawling out of the window.

"Come on you two," she whispered loudly. "You can play kissy kissy later. Let's get the hell out of here!"

Harold helped her out and dropped the two bags to the ground below wincing when they thudded into the cold, hard ground. Luckily, both girls wore dark shawls over their dresses which he hoped would camouflage them as they made their way to the hole in the fence.

"Let's move it!" Harold said starting down the fire escape.

By now Sam's yelling and pounding on the front door had caused a great deal of commotion in the main house. All of the lights were on and as he slid down the ladder he could see a flurry of movement downstairs.

"Get down and don't make a sound," he whispered to the girls who squatted down and pressed themselves close to the wall. Around the side of the barracks from where they were hidden Harold saw the old spinster who was the house mother in the barracks walking briskly to the main house to see what was going on. He heard Sam clearly now and suppressed his laughter.

"Open the door! I know you're in there! Let me in!" his friend slurred drunkenly while pounding on the door. "You can't lock me out of my own house damn you!"

Just as Sam shouted this Harold and the girls could hear glass breaking. The old spinster quickened her pace and disappeared inside the house. Harold turned and snatched up the girls' bags.

"Come on! Follow me and stay in the shadows. Don't make a sound!"

The three bounded through the dark grounds moving from tree to tree occasionally stopping to make sure no one was following them. Upon reaching the woods and scrub Harold took Margaret's hand while she took the other girls hand. He ducked low and led them along the small path he'd used the past few days until they reached the hole in the fence. Leading them through, they continued down into the heavier timber into the ravine. After ten minutes of hard walking and running they stopped, breathless and glistening with sweat. Margaret reached forward and squeezed Harold with all her might crying in between her heavy breaths.

The other girl stood and grabbed her small bag. "Got my cigarettes?" she asked.

"Yeah, right here. And here's twenty dollars to help you get to where you need to go," Harold said handing her the items.

"Aren't you a sweetie," she said smiling. "My name's Ginny. If Margaret ever gets tired of you, come look me up sometime."

Margaret turned and hugged her. "Goodbye Ginny. Be safe."

Ginny returned the hug and turned to leave. "You too, Margaret. You've got a good man there. Don't let him go."

"I won't."

Ginny slipped away into the dark timber leaving Harold and Margaret alone. They kissed and held one another. It all seemed too strange to be real.

After several minutes Harold stood and helped Margaret up. "Come on. We've got to keep moving."

"Where are we going?" she asked.

"As long as we're together, somewhere wonderful."

EARLY, IOWA

August 16, 1919

Harold climbed down the ladder and wiped his heavily perspiring face off on his shirtsleeve.

"Damn, it's hot," he muttered to himself. Taking two steps back, he looked at the side of the house he'd just finished painting. The comfortable two-bedroom house he and Margaret had recently bought and moved into in Early was coming along and was starting to feel like home. After their marriage, Harold and Margaret had stayed in Sioux City for several weeks while he worked at the packing plant where Sam's father had gotten him a job. He hated the work, gutting and skinning cows twelve hours a day and after a heated argument with his supervisor, stormed out. From Sioux City, the couple spent time in Omaha, Nebraska where there was work as a laborer on the river docks. Next, they found themselves in Moville, Iowa where Harold worked for a time as a clerk in a grocery store. He liked the job and the town which reminded him of Sac City but his increasing troubles with drink doomed him. Nothing seemed to suit him and for reasons he couldn't explain, he was often angry and resented being told what to do, especially by men who had never served in the military. As Harold often remarked, those men had no idea what he was going through and how he felt. *Fuck them* was now his most commonly used expression. Frank had even written several times promising to make him a full partner in the lumber yard but Harold adamantly refused.

Finally, while staying with his Uncle Theodore's family in Early, Iowa, he visited the farm implement business his uncle owned. Harold was intrigued by the farm machinery and soon found himself helping around the business as a mechanic. To his surprise, Harold discovered he had genuine knack for fixing and maintaining the machinery and within days of he and Margaret's arrival, Harold was again working full-time. He enjoyed the job and especially liked that everyone left him alone while he worked in an old stone building well separate from the main building. Theodore was the polar opposite of his brother Frank and was a kind, mild-tempered man who Harold respected. And better yet, he'd served in the army in Cuba during the Spanish-American War in an artillery unit no less. Everything seemed to be finally falling into place.

Wiping his face on his shirtsleeve again Harold walked around to the front of the house to get a drink of the cold lemonade Margaret had brought out. He saw Bobby crouched down throwing grass and dirt on a section of the yard with the stick he'd been playing with.

"What are you doing there, Bobby?" Harold asked.

"Um, nothing."

Harold walked over to the boy who quickly stood and took several steps backwards. Looking down at the ground where Bobby had been, he could see what his brother had been doing. He'd accidently knocked over a pail of paint and was trying to hide it.

"Dammit Bobby!" Harold growled. "That's a dollar's worth of paint right there. I can't get any more today either since the store's closed. I hope we have enough to finish."

"I'm sorry. I didn't mean to."

Harold scowled for a moment trying not to let his temper get away from him. "Well, don't worry about it. It's just a little paint."

Bobby had been staying with Harold and Margaret for the past few weeks to help out and to simply spend time with them before he had to go back to Sac City when school started. Though he would never admit it to anyone, Harold was beginning to look forward to Bobby's trip home. The boy chattered non-stop, was always getting into things he shouldn't and did other little things that infuriated Harold now. Margaret however, loved having the boy around and spent many hours reading to him or losing to him in endless games of checkers and chess. The two laughed and talked while Harold sat stewing in his chair in the hot evenings.

"Come on. Let's get a drink," Harold said walking to the small table in the shade.He poured a glass for Bobby and one for him. He drank deeply, relishing the cold, sweet sour wetness.

"So, did you kill a lot of Germans in the War?" Bobby asked.

Harold stopped drinking and glared at the boy. "What did you say?"

"Did you kill any Germans? Did you shoot them? I bet that would have been fun. Pow! Pow!" Bobby threw himself to the ground and held his stick as though it were a gun. "Pow! Pow! Another dead Hun for Private Brooks!"

Harold reached down and grabbed Bobby's arms jerking him upright. "Don't you ever ask me that again!" he shouted. "You don't know what you're talking about. It's not a game!" Harold brutally shook the boy while he continued to yell. "Never, ever ask me that again! And, I don't ever want to see you playing like that. Do you understand me? Do you?"

Harold felt the all-too-familiar rage overwhelming him as he continued to shake Bobby. No matter what he did now he knew he wouldn't be able to stop.

"Never, ever ask me that again Bobby!" Afraid of what he might do next, Harold pushed him harder than he expected causing the boy to trip and hit the ground heavily.

"Oh, my God..." Harold thought as he stood over his little brother shaking with fury.

Bobby looked up at Harold with huge wet eyes before a blood-curdling wail escaped his mouth. Harold's rage suddenly evaporated as quickly as it had come on. He opened his mouth to apologize but no words would come out. Reaching down to help Bobby up, the boy instead cringed and drew back while he continued to cry. Suddenly, Margaret appeared in a blur, knelt down and gathered Bobby in her arms. She looked up at Harold with a look on her face he'd never seen before.

"Harold!" she screamed. "What are you doing?"

Harold looked down at her with a mournful look on his face. "I don't...Bobby. I'm sorry!" He took a step towards them but Margaret stood and turned her back to him, shielding the child.

"Get away from him! You've done enough!" Margaret cried walking Bobby to the front door of the house and slamming it shut. Harold stood, still shaking, beside himself with grief. What had he done? He'd never yelled at the boy before and he certainly hadn't ever touched him as their father had always done.

He slowly walked to the front door and tried the knob but found it locked.

"Locking me out of my own fucking house are you?" he yelled. "You damn woman!" Harold beat his fists on the door but stopped not understanding what was happening to him. Suddenly, inexplicably, felt the urge to cry. Sitting exhaustedly on the front steps, he sat for a time sobbing and talking to himself, something else he did now but couldn't control. It was as though his mind was slowly unraveling and for months he'd found it hard to concentrate on anything. He was always tired and depressed and his anger had become worse and worse even with the smallest things. There was a change Margaret too, as though she were afraid of him. She always went out of her way to please him but Harold would often find himself angry with her for no reason. And Bobby, the boy continued to be the little brother Harold had loved his entire life but Harold had little patience for the childish behavior and carefree attitude he displayed. The damn paint too…

As the sun began to set leaving the yard awash in an orange brilliance, Harold shuffled to the small shed in the backyard, his refuge. Looking back at the house, he noticed Margaret had turned on the kitchen light. The smells of cooking wafted from the open window but he didn't care. Entering the shed, he closed the door and reached down behind a shelf into a hidden cubby hole to remove a half-full bottle of French Brandy. Removing the cork, he tipped it back and drank deeply. The Brandy burned and caused him to shiver and cough but he tipped it up and drank again forcing it down his throat. After two more gulps of the fiery liquid he reached further back into the hiding place and pulled out the leather-holstered .45 that had been his constant companion since France. Removing the pistol, he pushed the magazine release with his thumb dropping the mag into his hand. Seeing that is was fully loaded, he quickly snapped it into back into the mag well and pulled the slide back. For several minutes he stared at the muzzle of the pistol wondering if he had the courage to do what he'd thought about every day since coming home. Shaking himself back to reality, Harold looked around the tiny shed. It was a perfect place; it was quiet and he could drink and mull over the overwhelming depression and fear which had taken over his mind.

Nearly two hours later, the door of the shed creaked opened slightly. Margaret peeked in to see that Harold had fallen to the floor and lay crying and beating his fists on the hard packed dirt floor. He continued to talk and mumble to himself.

"What have I done?" he moaned. "I don't know what's wrong with me! I hurt Bobby! Margaret, what's wrong with me?"

Margaret knelt down and put his head in her lap. "It's okay," she said softly, stroking his hair. "It's the war. You just need some time to get it out of your head. All we have to do is pray."

"No! If you'd seen the things I saw and if you knew the things I'd done then you would know that there isn't a God. Anymore, I wish I'd have died over there like Mike and George did. Then I wouldn't feel the way I do."

"Come," Margaret said softly. "Let's go in and I'll run you a nice hot bath and you can eat. You just need to rest and not drink."

"What about Bobby?" Harold sniffled. "I can't face him."

"Bobby is fine. I talked to him," Margaret said reassuringly. "But, you just have to remember that he's a child and he still looks up to you. If you continue to abuse him he'll turn his back on you. When you feel that anger coming on you need to walk away. You need to talk to him. Okay?"

"Yes, I will." Harold answered trying to stand. He lurched forward but Margaret caught his arm and steadied him.

"Good. Come then, let's get you cleaned up. Remember Harold, don't you dare treat Bobby like your father treated you and don't you ever treat me like that either. Do you understand me?"

Harold moved to hug Margaret but she held him back and stared into his eyes.

"Promise me."

"Yes. I will...I promise." He knew he would try but deep down, Harold knew he was losing control of himself and it frightened him.

THE LIGHT

November 9, 1919

He was dying. The pain in his back never seemed to get any better and the way Margaret and his parents shuffled in and out of his room with gray, ashen faces confirmed what he knew. Occasionally, through the fog of pain he would speak to the old doctor, now tired and suffering the bloody, coughing effects of tuberculosis. The man was in his fifties but looked twenty years older. He too, would die within the month. Harold could see the death hovering about him as he had seen the same spirit hovering over the fields in France. Once in a while, the door of his room would open and his sister Mary would read to him from a creaky old rocker in the hallway. Bobby sometimes helped but he was afraid of his brother and had been ever since Harold had come home. He'd tried to persuade the boy to come in and read to him, speak to him, or just even look at him but he wouldn't. The child was afraid of the death that had come with his strange, scarred brother back from Europe. Bobby spent most of his time fishing and hunting squirrels down at the river with the black dog as his sole companion and usually arrived home very late at night often missing the weekly family visits to Harold and Margaret's new home in Early.

His fever and nightmares simply got worse. He could hear the doctor tell Margaret, "Boy's lucky. He just has a touch of meningitis in his spine. He might make it." Harold knew it was a lie. He had seen men in the army hospitals dying of the same thing. Their backs would contort into hellish, circus-like positions while they would spend days and often weeks in tortuous agony. They all had fevers, nightmares, and sometimes, total insanity brought on by the pain. One man, Harold remembered, had tried to attack a nurse in the Army hospital in Brest because she'd stopped him from killing himself. His eyes were large, dark, and completely lifeless. He hadn't gotten out of his bed, he had crawled, clutching the soiled, stinking sheets screaming obscenities while tried to escape from the inevitable end. He died two hours later.

While he slept, Harold would have dreams about his dead friends from the 65th and the men he had killed. In them, everyone was healthy and alive, the war was over, and it was summertime. The fresh organic, green smells of Iowa, church socials, the crabapples in full bloom and the taste of cold beer and the smell of his sweaty leather ball glove heavy in his nostrils filled his dreaming mind. He knew it was someplace safe and far away from the things that had made his life what it was now. Harold had spent his entire life trying to escape boredom, conflict with his father, Sac City and everything else he had ever imagined wrong with the world including himself. He'd barely lived through a year of utter terror and despair in the nightmarish landscape of ruined France. These new dreams were different and completely peaceful. Everything he had ever wanted and dreamed about in his short life was suddenly his but was something that he couldn't seem to hang onto and cherish for a lifetime. Margaret was always there and everything in their lives together was as it should be.

When Harold would awaken in the middle of the night he thought he was back in France because of the screaming and the stench of the dead and the dying men not fully realizing it was the one who was doing the screaming. In the few moments during the long days when he was lucid he cried softly to himself believing he'd brought Margaret nothing but suffering. They had waited so long and suffered through tragedies of their own before they were married and they were happy. But were they happy? Was this the sort of life she deserved? Now it seemed, God was going to take Harold away while Margaret would sit alone on the back porch of the house in the shade of the old elms and weep until her father was done praying for Harold. And late at night after the family had gone back to Sac City she would watch him cry out and writhe with pain in his sleep as the awful dreams of France came back to him and the meningitis got worse. The life they had dreamed about for two long years through a war, though the separation and through the trauma of the baby that she'd been forced to give up for adoption had never really been given time to begin. Harold wondered now if his father had been correct when he'd told him he'd ruin her life if he got involved with her.

Finally, close to daybreak, Harold felt the pain go away. He hovered above his body without fear or remorse as a bright light began to consume him. He could see Margaret sleeping innocently on the day bed she had dragged into their bedroom so she could be close to Harold and take care of him when he needed her help. He looked longingly at the woman who had made his life so complete and so happy for so short a time who he would now have to leave again. He felt her heart beating along with that of the tiny baby she carried inside her who would never be able to know who her father was or why he had died so young. But, he had a feeling that this was all meant to be and that his life had meant something. The warmth he now felt whispered softly saying he was going someplace where they would never be torn apart again. Harold allowed himself one last look at Margaret and then felt himself being pulled slowly into the warm light.

EPILOGUE

I n the middle summer of 1991, an old man lay dying in a hospital
bed. He knew the end was near but he wasn't afraid. His entire
life had become what it had been and it had been a full, complete life and he was proud of what he had accomplished. He knew
somehow that everything he'd ever done was worthwhile. He faced
his death with the same confidence he'd used every day since 1919
when he unwillingly became the man of the family, the heir apparent, and the one man, who only a boy of eight at the time, was
counted upon to carry on the family name and to live a better life
than the one his father had lived. An enormous and seemingly
impossible responsibility given who his father had been.

His only brother Harold had come to see him in a dream just
the night before. He hadn't aged a bit in the seventy-two years since
he'd last seen him and the old man cried at the sight of his long-
dead brother. In his dream, he had been alone, fishing in the river
down from the house, and across the field, and by the old barn on
the lane, and just down so by the old black oak, and over there by
the Andersen's old abandoned place just outside of Sac City. One
of his favorite places and one he hadn't been to in an eternity. As
he sat in the brilliant morning sunshine he was stunned to see
Harold come trudging through the thick underbrush whistling an
old Army marching tune to himself in between puffs on a French

cigarette. With his shirt unbuttoned to the mid-chest and his favorite bamboo fishing pole slung over his shoulder, he approached his baby brother, now an old man on the verge of death.

"Hi ho, Bobby!" he cheerfully exclaimed as though they hadn't seen one another in only an hour or so.

Carefully baiting his hook with a fat, squirming nightcrawler from the garden behind the house, he tossed the line out into a shady spot in the cold, gurgling river.

The old man had stared at this apparition not believing his eyes at first.

"Havin' any luck?" Harold asked eying his brother in between generous puffs on his cigarette.

"Uh, no, not yet," The old man replied uneasily. He stared with disbelief at Harold who practically glowed with life and supreme health in the rapidly warming morning. The scar across his scalp that he'd received in some forgotten battle during the war was gone, his back was straight and uniform, not grossly contorted from the meningitis that had killed him. His flesh too, wasn't pallid and stretched tightly over his bones as it had been in the weeks before he'd died. The old man continued to stare. Harold looked happy and healthy like he remembered him from so long ago. *He looked real.*

"You know, Bobby, we've been waiting for you for a long time."

"What? Who has?" asked the old man uneasily.

"All of us," Harold replied. "Mom's here. So is Edith and Will and Irene. We're still waiting for Mary, but Margaret is here and even that old black dog of yours...they're all waiting to see you. That dog..." Harold laughed shaking his head. "Son of a bitch hated me after I came home from France and still does. He wagged his tail when they carried me out of the house in the box after I died. Remember?"

He laughed at the memory but quickly turned more serious. "Dad's here too. He wanted me to come find you first. He's proud Bobby, awfully proud of you."

The old man choked a bit and let the end of his fishing pole drop carelessly into the water, something he never, ever, would have allowed in his long life as a serious fisherman. He looked at the apparition that was his brother who had left him so many years before still not knowing if he were real. But, the old man had to know after spending a lifetime without him, the one person who had protected him and understood him better than anyone else ever had. The two men sat in silence while the river slid by.

Still staring fixedly at Harold, the old man asked, "Why'd you die Harold? Why'd you have to go? Don't you know how hard that was for me to lose you? All those years…!" He looked away from the ghost biting his lower lip, trying his best not to cry.

Harold exhaled a blue plume of smoke into the warm breeze and cast his half-finished cigarette into the shimmering water. Looking deeply into his brother's still bright green eyes, he shrugged, his face turning serious.

"Hell Bobby, I had too. For you."

"For me? What are you talking about?" demanded the old man.

Harold quickly bolted upright with his eyes staring intently at the water, his concentration completely focused on the tempting bite his line was getting from an unseen fish. "It was fate, or destiny, or whatever in the hell you want to call that stuff," he offered continuing to softly pull on his fishing pole while he waited for the fish to take the bait. "Made me angry at the time, you know, when I went west. But, everything happens for a reason as they all love to say back on the other side," he explained with a funny sideways grin. "Do you remember sitting in church with fat, sweaty old Reverend Nicholson, and how he always talked about how God had something in mind for everyone? It sounded like a bunch of bull to me when I was a kid but when I was gone during the war I discovered a bit of what he meant. And then, when I came here… well, it finally all came together. I knew that I had to leave you both times because my only purpose in life was to get you to be the man you would eventually become. And dammit, I had to die to do that! When I ran away I did it partly out of resentment at having to spend my life raising you. I wanted my own life to live and well, I had to leave. The other part was that I wanted you to learn to live on your own, to be responsible for yourself without me there to do it for you. I thought I could make it up to you when I came home but I died before it all came together. It didn't seem fair to me at the time but it does now. Everything makes sense here. You'll see."

He quickly jerked the line and pulled the most beautiful trout onto the bank the old man had ever seen. Definitely a keeper. And, a first for Harold in the faded memory of the old man. Harold had never been able to fish worth a tinker's damn as he could recall and usually ended up asleep on the bank with his line running slack while the fish stole his bait. Just like their father.

The old man sighed deeply and stared out beyond the creek into the stand of timber and out to the green, hazy fields beyond. It seemed surreal but it also felt as though he were meant to be here. Everything was warm, he could finally breath again without a struggle, without the rot that had consumed his lungs and slowly killed him for years. He felt like a young man again, in fact more alive than he ever had been before. Glancing back at the ghost, he studied him carefully. It was Harold, but why? There had to be more to it all.

Harold got up, adjusted his pants and half-heartedly brushed himself off. Un-hooking the squirming, fat fish carefully from his line, he held it up and examined it with a smile before gently putting it back into the water. He looked back at the old man with a barely concealed smirk on his well-tanned face. There was a gleam of life and mischievous humor in his eyes that the old man hadn't seen since before he had run away from home in 1917 and the one thing he had always shared with his brother.

"Well Bobby, gotta run. Things to do. You taught me well, I never could catch a damn fish before. But, things are much different here. I think you'll like it." With a wink to his baby brother he turned to leave up the grassy path he'd come down only moments before.

"Where are you going?" demanded the old man standing up to follow his brother. I have so much to ask and..."

Harold turned back and smiled. "We'll see you tomorrow Bobby. All of us. You have one more thing left to do then you can fish, shoot, take things apart and visit all you want. Dad's going to be here with me right there on the bank waiting for you when you're done...over there where we used to come on Sundays. Trust me, it won't be much longer. Mom's working on a big chocolate cake and you can have as much as you want now. We'll even have ice cream. Say goodbye to my nieces, nephew and your grandkids for me. You did well with all of them too. You have a grandson named Bobby huh? I'll bet he's a handful!"

He stopped part way up the path and added, "Dad got his wish you know. You carried on the family name and made a worthwhile, proud life for yourself and your family. Think about it, the newspaper business you founded and all of the employees you had over the years. You treated them like they were family. Those people loved you Bobby, every one of them. The scholarship fund you set up at the high school so poor kids could go to college. The foundation you started to fund the library in town. You were the president of the school board for thirty-two years. Hell, the nature preserve you donated the land for. My god little brother, you did so much with your life. It's astonishing what you did, it really is. The thing is, I knew I couldn't have ever done any of that and I never could please dad no matter what I did. That was why I died. You had to find a way to be a good man, and your own man, which you did, without me there to protect you and do it for you. You never would have done any of the things you did in your life otherwise. We've been watching."

He paused for a moment, his face breaking into a wide grin. "Well Bobby, so long!"

With that, he was gone rustling up the path and out of sight, whistling the same old Army song until it too faded away on the gentle breeze blowing through the trees. The old man lay back in the grass and felt himself slowly drift on into another dream.

Robert Denton Brownell (born March 2, 1968) is an American author who lives with his wife Braedi, in Iowa. He received his BA in history from the University of Iowa where he immersed himself in fiction writing classes taught by students in the world famous Iowa Writer's Workshop. By day, he works for his family's business, Brownells Inc. as a copy/content writer and writes fiction whenever he can. His second novel, *The Crow Man*, was published in 2016.